Chance Would Be a Fine Thing

The Chances
Book 10

Emily E K Murdoch

ARE YOU SIGNED UP FOR DRAGONBLADE'S BLOG?

You'll get the latest news and information on exclusive giveaways, exclusive excerpts, coming releases, sales, free books, cover reveals and more.

Check out our complete list of authors, too!

No spam, no junk. That's a promise!

Sign Up Here

www.dragonbladepublishing.com

Dearest Reader;

Thank you for your support of a small press. At Dragonblade Publishing, we strive to bring you the highest quality Historical Romance from some of the best authors in the business. Without your support, there is no 'us', so we sincerely hope you adore these stories and find some new favorite authors along the way.

Happy Reading!

CEO, Dragonblade Publishing

Additional Dragonblade books by
Author Emily E K Murdoch

The Chances Series
A Fighting Chance (Book 1)
A Second Chance (Book 2)
An Outside Chance (Book 3)
Half a Chance (Book 4)
A Chance in a Million (Book 5)
Not a Chance in Hell (Book 6)
An Eye for the Chance (Book 7)
A Sporting Chance (Book 8)
Any Chance You Can Take (Book 9)
Chance Would Be a Fine Thing (Book 10)

Dukes in Danger Series
Don't Judge a Duke by His Cover (Book 1)
Strike While the Duke is Hot (Book 2)
The Duke is Mightier than the Sword (Book 3)
A Duke in Time Saves Nine (Book 4)
Every Duke Has His Price (Book 5)
Put Your Best Duke Forward (Book 6)
Where There's a Duke, There's a Way (Book 7)
Curiosity Killed the Duke (Book 8)
Play With Dukes, Get Burned (Book 9)
The Best Things in Life are Dukes (Book 10)
A Duke a Day Keeps the Doctor Away (Book 11)
All Good Dukes Come to an End (Book 12)

Twelve Days of Christmas
Twelve Drummers Drumming
Eleven Pipers Piping
Ten Lords a Leaping
Nine Ladies Dancing

Eight Maids a Milking
Seven Swans a Swimming
Six Geese a Laying
Five Gold Rings
Four Calling Birds
Three French Hens
Two Turtle Doves
A Partridge in a Pear Tree

The De Petras Saga
The Misplaced Husband (Book 1)
The Impoverished Dowry (Book 2)
The Contrary Debutante (Book 3)
The Determined Mistress (Book 4)
The Convenient Engagement (Book 5)

The Governess Bureau Series
A Governess of Great Talents (Book 1)
A Governess of Discretion (Book 2)
A Governess of Many Languages (Book 3)
A Governess of Prodigious Skill (Book 4)
A Governess of Unusual Experience (Book 5)
A Governess of Wise Years (Book 6)
A Governess of No Fear (Novella)

Never The Bride Series
Always the Bridesmaid (Book 1)
Always the Chaperone (Book 2)
Always the Courtesan (Book 3)
Always the Best Friend (Book 4)
Always the Wallflower (Book 5)
Always the Bluestocking (Book 6)
Always the Rival (Book 7)
Always the Matchmaker (Book 8)
Always the Widow (Book 9)
Always the Rebel (Book 10)
Always the Mistress (Book 11)
Always the Second Choice (Book 12)

Always the Mistletoe (Novella)
Always the Reverend (Novella)

The Lyon's Den Series
Always the Lyon Tamer

Pirates of Britannia Series
Always the High Seas

De Wolfe Pack: The Series
Whirlwind with a Wolfe

Noble titles throughout English history have, at times, been more fluid than one might think. Women have inherited, men have been gifted titles by family or gained them through marriage, and royals frequently lavished titles or withdrew them as reward and punishment.

The elder Chance brothers in this series agreed to split the four titles in their family line during the Regency era, rather than the eldest holding all four. It is a decision that defines their brotherhood, and their very different personalities.

Now with the next generation, one Chance father has allowed his son to inherit his title before his own demise, echoing kings and queens who have abdicated their titles throughout history. Perhaps his brothers, the uncles of this next generation, will follow suit...

Get ready to meet a family that is more than happy to scandalize Society...

Chapter One

November 1, 1840

MISS IRENE CHANCE looked around carefully and nodded to herself. Yes, the wedding had gone to plan, thank goodness. All she had to worry about was—

Sudden darkness. Hands had covered her eyes, her senses utterly disrupted, the hands large, strong yet soft. There was a presence behind her, someone who had decided she should not be permitted light.

Irene was not concerned. "Wilfred Zouch, you stop that this minute."

The snort of laughter behind her was as familiar as her own. "You can't blame a man for trying!"

"Trying what? I thought we had given up on that foolishness a long time ago," said Irene as the hands disappeared. She turned and looked up into the familiar face of her best friend.

Wilfred Zouch, utterly incorrigible idiot and the Duke of Aynor, grinned back. "You know me. I haven't grown up yet."

"That, I can well believe." Irene grinned, nudging him in the side as a footman passed them with a series of delicious things on a silver tray. "You haven't changed a bit in the last decade!"

Well, other than the fact that you've shot up a few feet and are now taller than me, Irene had to admit in the privacy of her own mind. It had come as a shock at the time, from the boy who had always been a few inches shorter than her. But no matter. She had grown used to it, in time.

"Your family puts on a rather wonderful party," Wilfred said happily, easily taking two glasses of champagne from a passing footman and handing one to Irene.

"It's not a party. It's Jess's wedding reception," Irene pointed out, sipping the wine. It was incredibly good. Where had her father been keeping this? "And she looks happy, doesn't she?"

The pair of them looked across the light and airy drawing room at the happy couple, currently receiving the congratulations of half of London.

"She does," came Wilfred's quiet voice.

Irene did not reply, just looked at them with a smile dancing across her lips.

In a way, she could hardly believe it. Jessica Chance was the most incorrigible wallflower. No one had ever thought she would wed, not after she'd reached the age of four and twenty. But here she was, married to Baron Llyne, presumably happy. She certainly looked happy enough.

Something tugged at the corner of her mouth, and Irene's smile ceased. How her sister could marry someone she had met mere weeks ago, however, she would never understand. Even if she and Wilfred had played a sizeable role, if she did say so herself, in the couple's reunion after a misunderstanding—but that was only because Jessica had seemed so miserable without him.

"We should go over and congratulate them." Wilfred's words cut through Irene's markedly unpleasant thoughts. "Come on, Reeny."

Her best friend grabbed her by the hand.

"You know I don't like that nickname," muttered Irene, trying to keep her wineglass balanced as her overexuberant companion pulled her forward. "Besides, they might want peace and—well, who would have thought it!"

As expected, her sister flushed at the sudden approach of people, but there wasn't much Irene could do now, so she kissed her sister's cheek and beamed.

"I am delighted for you, my darling," Irene said sincerely.

"And so am I," added Wilfred, who had somehow managed to grasp Lord Llyne's hand and was pumping it enthusiastically. Irene attempted not to giggle. "It's hard to believe, isn't it! A Pernrith Chance, getting married!"

Irene tried not to snort, but it was difficult. "It is certainly not something that I think will happen again soon!"

Her mind flickered to her other siblings. Her only brother and the eldest child, Michael, his gaze always on the horizon, always looking for the next adventure. Theodora, so quiet that only that similarly quiet gentleman of their father's acquaintance, Mr. Kennedy, ever seemed to get anything out of her. Little Gwendoline, hardly out in Society yet but already following in her eldest sister's footsteps and acting the proper wallflower whenever anything was demanded of her.

Honestly! Was it truly her fate to be the only normal one among them?

At her pronouncement, however, Wilfred did not laugh, as Irene had expected. "You—You don't?"

Irene blinked. Don't what? Oh, yes. Don't expect her siblings to get married. It was a strange response from her friend who had known her siblings since forever.

He could surely see how unlikely it was, couldn't he?

"Well, Teddy and Gwen aren't out, not properly, and Michael is too much a rakehell to be tied down," Irene explained with a shrug, her attention distracted by Lady Romeril, an intimidating woman of great height and even greater bearing, who was berating someone in a corner.

Who had invited her?

"And... Well, and what about you?" came Wilfred's voice.

It sounded a little strange, now Irene came to think of it. Her attention snapped away from the doyenne of Society and over to her friend, whose expression looked...

Had the man eaten an unpleasant oyster?

"You don't see me surrounded by admirers, do you?" Irene snorted, sipping her wine and enjoying the joke. "I spend too much time with you!"

Wilfred opened his mouth hurriedly, as though what he wished to say was something of great import, but he was interrupted by her sister's new husband.

"And for that, I must thank you both," said Lord Llyne, looking at Irene with not so much a purposeful wink, but he may as well have done. "Thank you. Both of you. Your Grace."

Irene could have rolled her eyes with irritation. Did the man have to make it so obvious that she and Wilfred were the ones who had convinced the idiot—the baron, she should say—to apologize to her sister?

Honestly, the man was dense. Lord save her from men who didn't see what was plainly right before their eyes!

Wilfred, of course, was just as subtle. "You owe me one!" he said, slapping Irene's new brother-in-law on the shoulder. "And please, I hate being called 'Your Grace.' By friends, anyway. Aynor will do."

Irene sighed as her sister Jessica looked between the two gentlemen, an expression of confusion in her beautiful eyes.

Once again, it would be up to her to bring some levity to the occasion and distract her sister entirely from the truth. "Yes," she said jovially. "I expect jewels of my own as recompense, now we know you have a fortune. Come on, Wilfred," she added, deciding that it was about time to remove the idiot from the man's presence before he revealed everything. "I think the punch is about to be served."

It was a pretty poor excuse, even Irene had to admit it—at least, she might admit it if pressed, but only to a select few who could be trusted never to remember her admission of fault.

Wilfred stared as though she had pulled off her own head. "You hate punch!"

Irene did not roll her eyes this time, but it was a close call. Did he not understand that she was trying to extricate them? "And I have a duty to attempt to like it. Almost every Society affair has it and it would be remiss of me not to attempt it. Come on!"

The last syllable of her statement was accompanied by a mildly violent tug of Wilfred's arm, which seemed to do the trick, though Irene was sorry to see her wine splashed over the rim of her glass.

Well, it couldn't have been helped. The most important thing was that they walked away from Jessica, who was asking her new husband what appeared to be some pointed questions, and Irene was not there to be yelled at.

Not that she thought it would come to that. It was down to her, after all, that this wedding was happening at all.

"You would think she would be grateful," Wilfred said cheerfully as he was marched across the Pernrith drawing room and into the large, open music room that adjoined it. "Seeing as it is thanks to us that—"

"And she doesn't know that, remember?" Irene hissed, smiling at her parents, who were seated happily on a sofa, their hands intertwined.

The last thing she wanted was for the Viscount and Viscountess Pernrith to know that they had their second daughter to thank for their eldest girl's marriage.

Wilfred's expression cleared, and he gave Irene a lazy grin. "You know, I think it's remarkable that you don't want anyone to know. I mean, I'd want some credit, especially with my parents."

They had reached the punch table at the other end of the music room and Irene picked up the ladle as she tried not to sigh. Why on earth would he—

"If they were still with us, naturally," Wilfred added, his voice lowering and an edge curling around his tone.

Irene hesitated, then poured an extra-large glass of punch, which she offered her friend.

Sometimes it was easy to grow exasperated with her parents. They were so...so endearing, so happy to get involved in their children's lives. Michael was irritating beyond belief, and as for Teddy and Gwen, the less said, the more charitable Irene would be, perhaps.

And then she would look at her best friend and see the sadness he kept quiet, hidden deep within him, only emerging at times when he was unable to prevent it from seeping through, and she would remember.

Wilfred Zouch, Duke of Aynor. Only child and orphan.

Irene impulsively slipped her hand through the crook of Wilfred's arm as they stepped away from the punch table. "You'll always have us, you know. The Chances."

"What, all of you?" Wilfred's grin was a tad too forced. "That might be far too much family, if you ask me."

She could not help but laugh as they stood to the side of the room and looked around them. "I know what you mean."

Her father, as the youngest of four brothers, had invited all three of his siblings, and their wives, and their children—and now some of them had spouses—to Jessica's wedding, as he should. Still, it was a lot for her sister, who liked quiet and a complete lack of notice.

How many cousins did they have, after all? Eleven? Twelve? Eleven, definitely eleven.

"Besides, I have you," Wilfred said simply. "I don't need any more family."

A comforting rush soared through Irene at his words. Their friendship was one of long standing, and in a way, she could hardly imagine the world without Wilfred within it. He was a constant. A part of her life's background, part of the furniture. She would hardly know what to do without—

"Whoops, one of your curls has come loose," said Wilfred, placing his punch glass on the mantelpiece and reaching out. "Careful."

"Have you got it?" Irene said, closing her eyes as his fingers moved close.

"Almost—almost—"

"It's these damned pins. I swear they aren't as good as they used to be."

"It's your hair. It's too wild and rambunctious."

"And how long, precisely," came a booming voice that was most definitely not Wilfred's, "has this been going on?"

Irene opened her eyes. Standing before them, holding a punch glass of her own and looking impressive, was Lady Romeril.

Irene's knees bent into an automatic curtsey. It was Lady Romeril, after all. She had been a part of Society before Society had even known what it was, as Irene's mother had once explained, and was so greatly respected that she could merely *hint* at a disreputable action and a young lady's name would be ruined.

Here was a woman who could make or break a person in Society. It would not do to act poorly before her.

Which was why Irene tried not to groan aloud when Wilfred said, "Hallo there, Lady Romeril, and are you enjoying the festivities?"

The older woman's lined face was not quite icy, but it was hardly encouraging. "I am, young man. I will enjoy it far more when my question has been answered."

Eagerness to answer the question was in no short supply within Irene's mind—the only trouble was, she did not quite understand it and had no wish to look the fool by inquiring.

Blast.

"I say again," Lady Romeril said, pulling herself upright in a creak of whalebone, "how long, precisely, has this been going on?"

Irene swallowed as she caught her mother's eye over Lady Romeril's shoulder. *Oh, dear.* This was not good—why, exactly, she had no idea. But the Viscountess Pernrith never fidgeted like that if something was going well.

"Oh, I don't know, about two hours," Wilfred said happily, clearly unable to read the tone of the conversation at all.

Irene attempted to delicately press on her friend's foot, but all the idiot did was say, "Whoops, Reeny, careful of my toes!"

"I do not mean the wedding reception, idiot boy," Lady

Romeril said icily to the gentleman—the *duke*—of six and twenty who towered over her. "I meant *this*."

Irene looked at Wilfred, utterly at a loss. For some reason, the man's ears had turned pink. Quite abruptly, he dropped her arm and moved an imperceptible two inches from her.

What on earth was going on?

"I am inquiring," Lady Romeril said slowly but loudly, as though to ensure the whole music room would hear, "when the courtship between the two of you began."

Irene stared, her pulse throbbing in her ears as the room fell silent, heads turning around to look over at them. Then the woman's words sunk in properly, and Irene laughed.

It was not the most ladylike of laughs. She had never managed to giggle sweetly like Jessica, or chuckle merrily yet in a controlled manner like Gwen. No, her laughs were always from the belly, deep and rich and growing in volume the longer the hilarity went on.

And this was truly hilarious. Her? Her and Wilfred?

"Oh, Lady Romeril." Irene snorted, trying desperately to speak but finding it a challenge through her laughter. "You are most amusing!"

She tapped at Wilfred's arm as she laughed, sharing the jest with him. For some reason, his face looked wooden.

Perhaps he was offended by Lady Romeril's joke. It was not a pleasant thought, but then Irene could not blame him. The man was a duke, after all. He would hardly welcome the rumor that he was in love with the daughter of an illegitimate viscount.

"Amusing?" sneered Lady Romeril. "You deny it, then?"

Irene giggled. "I cannot think of two people about whom you could have made such a quip who were less likely to ever fall in love."

"But you two—you are unchaperoned—"

"He's practically part of the family, and we are here, at a party with all of the Chances. Why on earth would I need a chaperone in such circumstances with *Wilfred*?" Irene was rather tickled; this was the most laughter she'd had in ages. "Goodness, what a joke!"

"Irene," Wilfred said quietly.

The older woman was still looking between them. "But my dear, the scandal. Your mother may be present, true, but the two of you are over here in this corner alone, whispering, holding on to one another's arms. He is *not* your brother, after all, and—"

"Oh, Lady Romeril, you have put such a smile on my face! I thank you for your attentions, but we really must go and see about my brother. You will excuse us."

Irene grasped Wilfred's arm and prepared to, not for the first time, shepherd him away from someone at Jessica's wedding party.

Lady Romeril was unmoved. "My dear, you are a Chance. You are no longer children, free to scurry about with your little friends. He's a *duke*—an unwed one, at that. Your family may be eccentric, but this truly stretches the limits of propriety."

"Come on, *Your Grace*," Irene said, using Wilfred's more formal address as she tugged him away from the glaring Society doyenne. "We must find Michael."

Through the music room and out into the drawing room, and through that too and out into the hall, past the burly footman, Dempster, who was helping a gentleman Irene did not recognize into his greatcoat, and out through the open front door into the freezing air. She supposed their housekeeper, Mrs. Kinley, was too occupied with the party to see their guest off.

Only once safely in the hall did she take a huge lungful of air and release her best friend.

"Honestly!" Irene exclaimed, her breath blossoming on the air despite the late-afternoon sun. "Why would she think such a thing?"

It was only when there was no answer to her statement but silence that she turned to Wilfred.

He was... Well. There was a strange look on his face, one that she had never seen before.

And then it was gone, melting away like the frost in the morning, and Wilfred was laughing, his grin lopsided and his eyes sparkling.

"She's not the first to presume something like that," he pointed out, sitting on the low wall outside the Pernrith Chance London townhome. "You would think we'd be used to it by now."

"Used to people assuming that there has to be something…something romantic between us, just because we like each other?" Irene said with a snort. "Just because we're friends!"

"It's not typical, even you have to admit that," Wilfred said easily. "There cannot be many gentlemen and ladies with a friendship like ours."

She could not help but smile. "No, I suppose not."

Because their connection went back… Well, forever, as far as Irene was concerned. Exactly how they had first met, she could hardly remember. There had been a scruffy-haired boy with bright-blond hair gazing at her over a wall, she could remember that. A boy who had looked upon her and Michael and Jessica, who had been playing hopscotch across the terrace at the rear of their London home with plenty of whoops and yells and laughter.

And over there, a young boy, perhaps her own age or more likely a little older, staring over a redbrick wall.

"Jessy?" Irene had said.

Her sister had ignored her and so the younger sister had wandered over to the wall where the blond-haired boy had disappeared.

"Hullo?" Irene had called out.

The face had reappeared. It had been crying, but even at such a young age, Irene had decided not to mention it. She didn't know much about boys, but her own brother, Michael, was always so bad-tempered when he had been crying.

"I'm Reeny," she had said, the childhood nickname which she despised now she had grown. "What's your name?"

After a moment of silence, the scruffy boy had reappeared.

He'd looked…lost. "Wilf."

"That's a funny name," Irene had not been able to stop herself from saying.

"It's Wilfred, really," said the boy, biting his lip. "And Reeny is a funny name."

"It's Irene, really," she had admitted. "Do you want to play?"

Why she had offered such a thing, Irene could not remember, not now. She could not remember the following day, when Wilfred had turned up on the doorstep and Irene's mother had taken one look, presumed he'd been a beggar boy, brought him inside, fed him hot broth, and forced Dempster to wash him.

When the Pernrith family had discovered that the scruff of a boy they had helped was the Duke of Aynor, the viscountess had needed to lie down.

And that had been it. It had started on either side of a wall.

Irene sat down on the low brick wall beside Wilfred and nudged him with her shoulder. "I do not imagine there are many people in the world with a friendship like ours."

Wilfred grinned. "Poor, fool them."

"That's what I say." She smiled back. "And if that means that some silly, old woman—"

"*Reeny!*"

"Well, everyone ties themselves in knots over Lady Romeril and she's surely not that powerful," Irene said dismissively. "No one's ever even really been clear with me as to what her title *is*. But if she wants to go around presuming the opposite of what is happening, then that's her prerogative. We know the truth. We know that we are good friends—"

"Best friends," Wilfred said softly, interrupting.

Irene rolled her eyes. "You never really grew up, did you?"

"Don't see any reason to do so," he quipped, nudging her this time.

The warmth of his shoulder, the strong press of his muscles, was all utterly ignored by Irene, who shoved back just as hard. It had only been in the last few years that Wilfred had gained the advantage of her in strength. He had been a small, weedy boy. Now look at him. Taller than her, and broader, with strength she had never expected.

"I suppose we shall just have to get accustomed to people making that mistake," Irene said lightly.

Wilfred waggled his eyebrows. "Do you mean to tell me that you are not going to fall into my arms and fall madly in love with me?"

Her laughter echoed down the otherwise-quiet street. *The very idea!*

"No, I don't think so," Irene said in a light voice. "And you're not likely to throw yourself down on one knee and protest your ever-dying love, are you?"

She leaned in toward her best friend in the whole world.

Wilfred's eyes glittered. "No. No, I'm not likely to do that at all. Not until you ask me to!"

Irene could not help but laugh again, and a joy spread through her as Wilfred laughed with her. Why, they were both ages from getting married to *anyone*, surely. If they had to at all. Were spinsters still so reviled in this day and age? Distinguished, titled bachelors most certainly weren't. He was a duke, yes... But there was probably some distant cousin in the family tree if he needed an heir, wasn't there? Why worry about such things? The very idea of her, and him, getting married!

Chapter Two

November 7, 1840

*T*HE TROUBLE WITH *loving a woman all your life,* Wilfred ruminated as he stamped his feet in the freezing night air, *is that your whole life becomes centered on that woman.*

It was a mistake to do this. He had known it, the moment he and his valet had returned to his townhouse in Bath yesterday for the beginning of the winter season and he'd discovered a small card waiting for him in his all-too-knowing housekeeper's hand.

"I thought you might return before it arrived," Mrs. Ansley had said with a smile that had lit up her dark eyes. "But no, she managed it before you."

Wilfred had attempted not to pull his housekeeper's hand off and only just managed it. The card had been light in his hands but had been weighed with the promise of opportunity. The promise of something he had not thought possible.

They were here. Already.

The Viscount and Viscountess Pernrith, present their compliments to the Duke of Aynor and inform him of their presence in Bath.

Wilfred had clutched at the card as though it had been made of gold. "They're here?"

"That's what it says," tutted his housekeeper, straightening his cravat like a mother hen and smoothing back his wayward fringe. "And your steward is looking for a new lodgekeeper, if you had anyone in mind. You're an absolute state, Master

Wilfred. Did you not even bother to stop at an inn on the road?"

He'd permitted the closeness and the incorrect address to the Duke of Aynor. Mrs. Ansley was more than a housekeeper, after all. It had been she who had told him—

Wilfred had pushed the thought from his mind. He was not going to think about them; he was not going to dwell on the past. He was only going to think about the future.

His future. *With her.*

That had been yesterday. Today, he was stamping his feet outside the Chance townhouse and wondering if he had made a terrible mistake.

"Do you mean to tell me that you are not going to fall into my arms and fall madly in love with me?"

"No, I don't think so. And you're not likely to throw yourself down on one knee and protest your ever-dying love, are you?"

She had not meant it, Wilfred tried to console himself. Irene had not really known what she had been saying. If she had any idea of his feelings...

But of course she didn't. Wilfred had always kept them deep inside, never allowing even a hint of them to escape his closely guarded heart. Not a single person in the world knew he was completely in love with Miss Irene Chance.

Well. Except Mrs. Ansley. And she wasn't going to tell anyone.

Wilfred pulled his pocket watch out of his greatcoat pocket and hissed at the cold. It was twenty past seven. He had rung the doorbell twice, knocked at the large, heavy door, and started to wonder—along, surely, with his coachman—whether or not they were truly at home.

But she had agreed to his suggestion, hadn't she?

Hissing through his teeth at the cold, Wilfred pulled the note from his pocket.

Marvelous idea. I'll see you at a quarter past seven. Bring your carriage, will you? We had to send ours back.

He hadn't quite understood that last part, but the point was,

Irene had agreed to accompany him. Wilfred had invited Theodora, the next sister, to act as her companion to chaperone the exchange. No one would ever be able to suggest he hadn't done this properly.

His stomach lurched at the very thought.

Done this proposal properly.

Perhaps this was a mistake. Perhaps he'd gotten the wrong day. Perhaps even thinking about declaring his undying love to an unsuspecting Irene was not a good idea.

Wilfred turned on his heels and started back for the carriage—

"Don't blame me for being late. It was my mother," Irene declared to the night air, slamming the front door behind her.

Wilfred blinked. He hadn't even heard it open. "Your—Your mother?"

"She *would* insist on attempting to explain the entirety of the plot to me as I left the house, which, as I told her, was quite ridiculous," Irene said, by way of explanation as she slipped her hand through the crook of his arm without waiting for an invitation. "I told her, Mama, you're not supposed to know what is going on in an opera. That is the whole point!"

And Wilfred melted.

Well, not exactly. What he actually did was laugh, comment something he hoped desperately was amusing in turn, shiver with delight as Irene laughed, and walked her to his carriage.

But inside, he was melting.

How could he not? Irene Chance was beautiful, and charming, and clever, and good hearted. She had chestnut-gold hair and a laugh that could peel paint. She was a minx with her elbows if she wanted to get through a crowd, and she had never said a bad word about anyone.

How could he not love her?

It was only when Wilfred had helped Irene into his carriage, therefore, that he realized what was missing. Or rather, who. "Is Theodora getting an earful from your mother too?"

Irene blinked. "Teddy?"

"Yes," Wilfred said patiently, trying not to shiver as he was blasted with a gust of freezing November air. It was all very well for Irene; she was seated in the warmth of the carriage. "Yes, I invited the both of you. So she could act as—I mean, you could chaperone each other."

He had not intended to hedge at the end of that statement, but he could not help it. She was looking at him with those dark eyes and he… Well. He fell into them.

Irene snorted. "Don't be daft! Teddy hasn't the slightest interest in such things. No, I told Mama you were surely asking Mrs. Brown to join us this evening." She peered around the small carriage, as if searching for a widow who had hidden between the cushions. "She needn't know your elderly neighbor has apparently lost her invite. If anyone asks when we get there, she's in our seats at the opera house, fast asleep, as usual." Her eyes sparkled at the scheme.

Wilfred smiled weakly. "Yes. Daft. Right. Good… Good thinking, that. Mrs. Brown."

And it was a compliment, really, he tried to tell himself as he shut the carriage door smartly and walked around to the other side. It was a compliment, that Irene never concerned herself with chaperones when they were alone together.

Still. He was a gentleman. And a duke. Some of them were complete rogues!

He wasn't, obviously, but it would be nice if *someone* thought he was capable of being a cad. Why, the viscountess hadn't even checked to be sure his neighbor had actually accompanied him. She'd just trusted sweet, innocent Wilfred to do the proper thing.

"Now, this opera," Irene said as Wilfred shut the door behind him and tapped the roof. "You have seen it before?"

"Never," he said brightly as the carriage lurched forward. "I saw it advertised as I walked past yesterday and thought it was just the thing."

"Is it a laughing opera or a crying opera?" Irene, great cultural expert, asked.

Wilfred attempted not to smile, but it was impossible. "Are there only those two kinds?"

"Oh, as far as I am aware, yes," said his best friend, smoothing out her skirts and pulling her pelisse a little tighter around herself. "You know it is very cold. The least you could do was offer—"

Wilfred pulled a heavy and very soft blanket from underneath the seat.

"Ah," said Irene happily, allowing him to place it around her. "Excellent."

It was but the work of a moment. Wilfred held his breath as he tucked the edges of the blanket around Irene's hips on the seat of his carriage. Even so, it was impossible not to inhale the warm, sweet scent of her. Impossible not to feel the swelling curves of her hips. Impossible not to notice how she wriggled slightly with delight at his touch.

Or was he mistaking that last part?

"Wilfred?"

Wilfred cleared his throat as he sat back. "Y-Yes?"

"You said, in your note, that you had something important to tell me," Irene asked serenely with bright eyes. "What is it?"

Wilfred's pulse skipped a beat and his tongue decided to go on strike.

Something important to tell her. Something important.

Well, it *was* important. Life-changing. Life-fracturing, if she did not respond as he wished. Life-altering, if he could no longer see Irene and the rest of the Chances. Life-ending, if he had to live the rest of it knowing that Irene saw him not as a man, but as a boy.

As a friend.

"Is it a surprise?" Irene's eyes gleamed in the dark and Wilfred's stomach twisted. "Is it a gift?"

"It's... It's not a gift, no," Wilfred managed.

There was no disappointment in Irene's expression and his affection for her only stirred all the more. This was not a woman who was only interested in the material things in life. This was a woman who cared about more important things. Like friendship. Like connection. Like love.

"Whatever it is, I know it will be wonderful," Irene said, tugging at the ties of her pelisse. "Goodness, I'm too hot now!"

The blanket had evidently done its work, for Wilfred looked on—unable to tear his eyes away—as Irene undid her pelisse and pulled it back, stretching forward and arching her back as she pulled the ties loose.

Arched her back and pushed forward her incredibly curved breasts.

Wilfred's inhale was lost, thank God, in the rumble of the carriage, but he could not drag his eyes away from the perfect mounds that surely *ached* to be touched.

He knew Irene, knew all her secrets. He would have known, wouldn't he, if she had kissed a man? She had never mentioned such a thing. Unlike most men his age, Wilfred himself hadn't kissed a woman, had never followed his university chums down darkened alleyways to meet with women of the night. He would have, before he'd realized his feelings, told Irene if he had—and she never would have ceased with her teasing. No, she could not have kissed another, either. Oh, to be the first man to give her a taste of pleasure…

"Wilfred? You look a mite too warm too," Irene said conversationally.

It was a good thing he was seated, or Wilfred was certain he would have tripped over his own feet. "Yes—hot," he managed.

"I don't doubt it. That greatcoat of yours looks very stuffy," she replied. "Why don't you take it off?"

Quite against his desperate crying out soul, Wilfred tugged it closer around him. The day that he and Irene started taking their clothes off in his carriage was the day that he expired.

But what a way to go.

"We're almost there," he said hurriedly, glancing out of the window. "Yes, we're here."

He couldn't decide whether he was delighted or distraught that their time alone in the carriage had come to an end—but then, his plan for his great announcement to the woman he loved had to occur within Bath opera house, and he felt a lightness in his limbs as his carriage pulled up outside it.

Which reminded him of something.

"Tell me," Wilfred said as his coachman opened his door. "Why do your family not have a carriage at the moment—sent it back where?"

It was most unaccountable. A viscount and his family, in Bath for the winter season, and without a carriage?

Irene was unable to reply while Wilfred descended from the carriage and walked around to the pavement, where he opened her door and proffered his hand in lieu of the coachman about to do the same.

He tried not to let his sharp inhale become audible as Irene took the offered hand. One would have thought he would have been accustomed to their casual touch, but no. Every time she took his hand, it was a gift.

"We couldn't afford to keep a carriage here," Irene said, her cheeks pink, though he could not tell whether that was due to her statement or because of the whipping, cold night air. "So we borrowed the Cothrom carriage and sent it back. Father was not pleased."

Wilfred decided not to pursue the topic.

It was complicated, the Chance family. Why, he had essentially become a part of it all those years ago, and he still did not quite understand it.

"I'm sure your Uncle William did not mind," he said, squeezing Irene's hand without invitation and placing it in the crook of his arm.

Irene snorted. "I am sure he didn't. I am sure he did not even notice."

There was no malice in her words, but Wilfred could feel the tension.

Four brothers, each inheriting a title from the estate that would usually have been kept for the eldest sons only. The Duke of Cothrom, the Marquess of Aylesbury, the Earl of Lindow…and then their illegitimate half-brother, given the courtesy title Viscount Pernrith by the eldest in an attempt to heal the breach.

At least, that was what Wilfred had been told.

It was the reason why all of Irene's cousins were lords and ladies, but she and her siblings were plain Mr. and Misses.

And she had never complained. She had never seemed to mind. Wilfred considered himself to know Irene better than anyone, sometimes even better than herself, and she had never seemed to mind.

But then there were moments like this…

"The Cothrom Chances don't even realize how much money they have, and I suppose that is a nice problem to indulge in," Irene said with a raised eyebrow. "But we're not here to talk about them. We're here to watch some poor woman waste away for love—"

"Or find love at a masked ball," interjected Wilfred with a grin as they stepped into the resplendent opera house, all red velvet and gold. "To tell the truth, I cannot recall whether this is a laughing opera or a crying opera."

"We'll have to find out," Irene said with a wink. "I suppose the seats you managed to get were good enough?"

Wilfred swallowed. "Good enough."

What he did not say was, *I did not need to buy seats.* What he did not tell her was, *I already own a box.*

It was perhaps not the sort of thing one said to a friend when they had just been declaring their own family's relative poverty.

Not able to afford a carriage?

He would never have presumed it of old Pernrith…but now he thought of it, it was not just the purchase of a carriage. It was the storage of the carriage, and the salary and bed and board of a coachman, at least two horses, and their stabling, and at least a boy and a man to care for them, and their salaries and their beds and their board…

Now that Wilfred considered the problem, he rather wondered how *anyone* could afford a carriage.

"Wilfred?"

He blinked. Irene was looking up with bright eyes and a curious expression.

"Where, exactly, are our seats?" she prompted. "Mrs. Brown stepped out in front of us and is already there, remember? Fast asleep?" She nudged her elbow into his side.

Right. Yes. Opera. For a moment, he'd almost forgotten the joke about Mrs. Brown as well. He couldn't think of anything witty to say in return. "This way."

The Aynor name was well known enough, even if the current Aynor face was not. All Wilfred had to do was delicately murmur his title and doors opened, higher and higher up as Irene's eyes widened and they were taken to—

"Goodness," she breathed. "You bought a house box?"

Wilfred's breath hitched as she stepped into it, the luxurious sofa seat that his father had ordered thirty years ago looking a little worse for wear but still with plenty of life left in it. "My father did. For my mother. They loved opera."

At least, he thought they had. He could hardly remember them, really, but music had always been playing in the house whenever his mother had been at home.

Then the music had stopped.

"They did?" Irene's face was curious, her lips puckered deliciously so, as she settled herself on the sofa, spreading out her skirts. "I say, this is a marvelously good idea. Far nicer than chairs."

"That's what I thought!" Wilfred said cheerfully, seeing with delight that the bottle of champagne in its cooler and the three glasses that he had requested were waiting, as he had specified.

Excellent. Well, there was no going back from here. All he had to do was sit down, tell Irene Chance that he was madly in love with her and would do anything to be her husband, and start a very happy life together.

Assuming she accepted him, of course.

"Goodness, is that for us?" Irene asked, her eyes darting over the champagne.

"It most certainly is."

"Three glasses?" Irene's eyebrow arched. "The third for Mrs. Brown? Or are you too tired for some champagne, madam?" She spoke to the empty space beside her on the sofa, as if the phantom chaperone were seated there.

"F-For Theodora," Wilfred said weakly. He couldn't be distracted by Irene's farce, as amusing as she always made such things.

Wilfred swallowed. He had told her he would only propose if…if she asked him to.

It had been a jest, that was all, but the words lingered in his mind and worried at him.

Was it possible… She did not know of his affections, to be sure, but would she not return them once she knew?

Wilfred cleared his throat as he sat beside the woman he loved. All he had to do was tell her. A long speech was not required—if anything, that was to be dissuaded. Reeny was not one for long speeches.

His shoulders loosened as he looked at her. Irene Chance. She was beautiful, yes, but she was precious for so many other reasons. And if she would let him, he would spend all his days making sure she was as happy as could be.

That was all he wanted.

"You know, I think if I could afford to come often, I could truly love opera." Irene glanced at the bottle. "Well, will you pour us some? Just the two glasses, though. Mrs. Brown is out cold."

"Oh, yes, yes. Of course," Wilfred leaned forward and picked up the bottle to pour her a glass.

"You are treating me, and you know how much I like a treat." His best friend beamed. "Is there an occasion, or an excuse for the reason that you are being so ridiculously delightful?"

Wilfred's pulse skipped a beat. "Perhaps."

"Oh, good!" Irene declared as she accepted the champagne-filled glass. "Well, then, to what shall we toast?"

He almost spilled the champagne as he poured himself a glass. "'Toast'?"

"Yes, we must have a toast," she said firmly, her eyes bright as he met her gaze. "And this is your treat. What would you like to toast to?"

Wilfred hesitated.

Us, he wanted to say. *How happy we could make each other. How easy this is, being together. Like breathing. Like laughing. Like soaring through the skies and knowing that nothing can ever harm us.*

I want to toast to us.

"To us," Wilfred found himself saying before he could stop himself.

Irene's smile seemed genuine—and utterly ignorant of his true meaning. "To us," she said, raising her glass.

The ding that the glasses made was lost in the raucous applause that had burst out as the conductor had stepped onto the stage. Wilfred watched as Irene took a large gulp then put her glass down before applauding in turn.

"This is going to be wonderful," she said with shining eyes as she glanced back at Wilfred. "My love of music and your love of opera—they go so well together, don't they?"

Wilfred's throat tightened. *Yes.* "Yes."

"Thank you for this evening," Irene said happily, picking up her glass of champagne and leaning back in the sofa. "This is going to be wonderful."

And without even a moment's hesitation, without any sort of embarrassment at the intimacy whatsoever, she took his hand, brought his arm around her shoulders, and snuggled into him with a happy sigh.

Wilfred tried, as best he could, to control his body's response to Irene's closeness, but it was impossible. She was so...so intoxicating. So freeing of his own inhibitions, not that they'd ever had any real inhibitions around each other. They had never needed to, Society's expectations be damned.

But as they sat here, the music starting up at the curtain rising and the first notes beginning and Irene pressed up against him and champagne bubbling in his chest and the warmth of her and the need within him and the adoration that had been there for years but Wilfred had never risked speaking of—

He knew he had to say something. Say something, or regret it, for the rest of his life.

Wilfred cleared his throat. "Irene?"

"Hmmm?" was her reply, her attention fixed completely on the stage. "Isn't she marvelous?"

She was referring, he knew, to the soprano on the stage who was singing her heart out.

"Yes. Yes, you are." It was a slip of the tongue, but Wilfred knew that this was the moment. He could be honest now. He could tell her, tell Reeny just how much he cared for her. How he adored her.

How he loved her.

"Irene," Wilfred said quietly, hardly able to believe that he was about to say this. "Irene, I... I know we have been friends for years. For a long time."

"For forever," came her vague reply, the music swelling so loudly that Wilfred almost had to speak, not whisper, to be heard.

"And our friendship matters to me. It is one of the most important things in my life, but I wanted you to know that... I mean, I *need* you to know that..."

His damned throat was closing up again!

Desperate for Dutch courage, Wilfred tipped a large gulpful of champagne down his throat and felt the warmth of the bubbles soar down his chest.

He swallowed, and said the words that he had practiced in his looking glass all morning. "Irene, I need you to know that I love you."

And that was when he stopped breathing.

For a moment that seemed to continue on forever, Wilfred waited. The words had been said. They could not be unsaid. And she had heard him. He was almost certain she had. How could she not have? The music wasn't that loud.

And Irene smiled, a slow smile that surely spoke of promise and their future and her own matching devotion—

She turned into his shoulder and looked up at him, meeting his eyes, and something stirred in Wilfred's loins.

"And I love you," she said blithely before turning back to the opera.

Wilfred's eyes were wide. Had she said—she couldn't have said—was it possible he was having a stroke?

Yes, the pain in his chest, the dizzying spin of his head, the *thump, thump, thump* of his pulse in his ears. It wasn't a stroke. It was a heart attack. He was having a—

"You're like my brother," Irene said calmly, sipping at her champagne and staring still at the opera as though she had not just destroyed Wilfred's reason for living. "Michael is my oldest brother, and you're my other brother. Which is nice."

Nice. Nice?

Wilfred could hardly believe it. *Nice?*

Of all the awful, offensive, and downright seditious things he had heard said about traitors to the Crown, 'nice' was even worse.

Nice was…dull. Boring. Uninteresting and unappealing. A nice man was one unthreatening, with about as much masculine desire as a bootlace.

Nice?

"Right," Wilfred said aloud, bewildered, hardly sure what he was supposed to say next. "Nice."

Irene snuggled into him again and he tried not to laugh, but then he might just cry.

He loved her. And she loved him—like a brother.

Well, that was it. He would never declare his affection for Miss Irene Chance again.

Chapter Three

November 9, 1840

WILFRED ZOUCH, DUKE of Aynor, was acting oddly.

Now, Irene was not normally one to be suspicious, but the man had given her three clear signs that something was dreadfully wrong.

Firstly, he bowed to her.

Bowed!

"Are you feeling ill?" Irene asked promptly, staring at the man in horror as he straightened up outside the Pump Rooms.

"Ill?" Wilfred said lightly. "No, I feel quite well, thank you."

"But..." There did not appear to be a way to say, *"But you have never bowed to me in your life"* without it sounding like censure.

And she wasn't complaining. Not exactly. It was just so...odd. Wilfred did not bow to her, and she did not curtsey to him. Why would they?

"Shall we?" Wilfred asked, offering his arm.

Well, that was more likely it. Irene took his arm and they entered the Pump Room, which was surprisingly busy this early in the morning. She had gone so far as to lose Wharton, the lady's maid she shared with her mother and sisters, whom the viscountess sometimes feebly sent to chaperone Irene while in public. The poor, overworked woman was never hard to lose on the busy streets of Bath or any other place and would usually give up and meet Irene back at home sometime later. And Irene knew her mother would only be mildly irritated when she found out, reminding Irene that Society at large had different opinions than the Chance family. Opinions Irene cared little about. She had thought she and Wilfred could benefit from the exercise on this rainy, wintry day with relative peace and quiet, but as it was—

And that was when Wilfred had done the second clear sign that something was amiss. He paused at the book and started to look down the names.

Irene stared. At least, she stared after she had straightened up, for the sudden cessation of movement from her friend had made her jerk backward from her intended steps.

"What on earth are you doing?" she hissed.

"Perusing the book," Wilfred said calmly, as though this was something he did every time they came to the Pump Room.

And he never had. Neither had she. What use did they have for the book which told them who was in Bath at present? There was no one else, other than each other, that they wanted to see.

So whom was he looking for?

"Does this have anything to do with the secret you were going to tell me last night, at the opera house?" Irene asked, the idea suddenly striking her.

If she had not been examining the man's face closely, she would have said that for a moment, a shadow passed across Wilfred's face. A shadow that was dark, and pained, and disappeared almost as soon as it had arisen.

Still, it had definitely been there. Hadn't it?

"No," he said lightly, turning the page.

Irene stared. She knew Wilfred better than she knew herself. His face was as familiar to her as her own, as were his habits. She had seen the boy grow and become a man, and he had done nothing to surprise her for about seven years.

And now here he was, bowing to her, and looking for—whom?

The prickling heat that was creeping through her was most unaccountable, and for a moment, Irene could not precisely tell what it was. When she realized that it was jealousy, she could have laughed at the shock.

Jealous? About Wilfred looking for someone else?

Ridiculous!

"Come on. I want to stretch my legs," Irene said with a tug at his arm. "After all, we have much to discuss about the opera, do we not?"

That caught the man's attention. Wilfred looked up, gaze narrowed. "We do?"

"That soprano! I thought she was going to fall out of that gown, and yet her singing was truly quite incredible. Perhaps that was why her stays were so loose." Irene clamped her lips together, as if fighting back laughter. "And the baritone…Wilfred? Is everything… Are you quite well?"

The gleam had disappeared from the man's eyes and he was looking as though…as though he did not know her.

Which was ridiculous. But Irene could think of no other way to describe it.

"You go on," he said quietly, releasing her arm and stepping back to the book.

And that was the third sign that something had gone terribly wrong with Wilfred.

It wasn't so much the letting go of her arm that was the problem. Hold her arm, don't hold her arm, what did she care? But it was the fact that he had encouraged her to walk about the Pump Room on her own.

They always walked together. Now that Irene came to think of it, she could not recall a time when she had ever visited the Pump Room without Wilfred. She must have done at some point, with her sisters, perhaps, or her mother. But no memories came to mind. It was always her and Wilfred.

And now he thought she should just walk about…alone?

"You are behaving most oddly." Irene had not meant to thrust her accusation at the man quite so violently, but really, the circumstances demanded it.

Wilfred was leaning over the book nonchalantly and turned a

page without even looking at her. "I have not the faintest idea what you mean."

Irene's lips parted in astonishment.

But he was—he was Wilfred. Her Wilfred. He had been the same man, the same person, forever. Slightly slow on the uptake sometimes and not particularly good at reading social cues, but the man was…was brilliant. He was charming and clever, and he never looked at her as though she were a woman, but merely as a friend. It was one of the things she liked best about him.

Wilfred would never look at a woman merely to admire. He wanted to listen to what they said. It was most endearing.

And now he was acting aloof and strange and distant, and Irene did not like it.

Jess had gone off and gotten married, and she… Well, Irene had always taken care of her. Jessica may have been the eldest Chance sister, but it was Irene who looked after her and the others. And she was gone and Wilfred was changed and…

Only then did Irene notice the heat that had blossomed within her, prickling and tight and scalding hot.

Everything was changing, and she hated it.

"You are acting strangely," Irene said, grabbing Wilfred's arm and pulling him away from that damned book. *What could he hope to find in there?* "When I say you are acting strangely—"

"Reeny—"

"And don't call me that," she snapped, ignoring the curious glances of other ladies and gentlemen as they promenaded up and down the place. "You know I don't like that."

"Isn't teasing what brothers do?" came the cool reply.

Irene stared up at the profile of Wilfred as they walked sedately along. "What—what brothers do?"

"That's what I am to you, isn't it?" he said blithely, not bothering to look at her as he spoke. "A brother."

"Well, yes," Irene said, not sure what this had to do with why the man was being such a dunderbore this morning. "But—"

"So there we go," Wilfred said quietly, keeping his voice low so no one else could hear him. "And as I am like a brother to you, I shall act as a brother does."

Irene almost tripped over her own skirts as she tried to stare and walk forward at the same time, something she did not usually have trouble with.

She was having trouble now. There was something…different, about Wilfred. Now that she examined him, she could see small clues in the corners of his eyes. The lines there that were always present due to his almost-continuous smile…they were gone. There was a hardness around his jaw she had never seen before.

No, that wasn't quite right. Irene remembered the day they had been walking in London and taken an alley as a shortcut, and there had been a dog there tied to the wall, tied and starving. And the same hardness had come across Wilfred's expression as Irene had rushed to the dragon, as her family always called dogs, and the hardness had not left Wilfred's face until they had safely found a loving home for it with his housekeeper.

Yes, it was the same hardness. But why?

"I don't understand," Irene found herself saying, with no guile or teasing at all.

That somehow gained Wilfred's attention. He halted, turning to her and only then did Irene realize just how tall the man was.

Which was ridiculous. She had always known it, but somehow Wilfred towered over her in this moment.

"I—" he began fiercely, and then the fire died away, and the same hardness returned as before. "I know you don't."

Without another word, Wilfred continued walking down the Pump Room, not waiting for her to join his side.

Irene could hardly understand what on earth was going on. This was not the Wilfred she knew. *He was perfectly fine last night,* she thought as she strode forward and walked silently beside him, trying to untangle the knot of confusion in her mind. At the opera house, he had been himself entirely.

But had he? He had been when they had arrived, but when

they had left… Well, he had been quiet. It had been a long opera; Irene had merely presumed the man had been tired. She couldn't begrudge him tiredness.

But this?

"Wilfred—"

"A great number of people appear to be in Bath early this winter," he said over her, still not looking at her. "I suppose there are a number of them you will want to see."

Irene gaped, utterly lost at the direction that the conversation was taking. "I…I suppose so, but—"

"And there will be people that I will need to see. Or should see. Or want to see."

The man wasn't making any sense. Why would he want to see anyone in Bath? Any persons the Duke of Aynor needed to see could have been seen in London before he'd come here. And Wilfred, he didn't want to see anyone. They spent all their time together.

Unless—

And that was when she realized it. The thought was sharp, spearing through her mind as though she had never had a thought before, and Irene stumbled again at the sudden insight it brought.

A hand moved swiftly, steadying her. Irene looked down to find Wilfred's hands, both of them. One held her arm, the other was at her waist.

He released her almost as soon as he had grasped her.

"Careful there, old thing," he said without smiling.

Irene did not reply. She was too busy staring in horror at what she had just understood. "You have fallen in love with someone."

It was all too obvious. The strange demeanor. The odd mention of his friendship last night at the opera house, as though reassuring her that she was still important even though he had found affection with another. The way Wilfred had been determined to look in the book to see who was in Bath.

He wanted to see whether *she*, whoever she was, had arrived in Town.

And if all of those clues were insufficient, the truth was perfectly clear by the high-red cheeks her best friend now displayed.

"You have, haven't you?" Irene breathed, stepping close to him and keeping her voice low. "You've fallen madly in love with some woman you hardly know, haven't you?"

"No," said Wilfred hurriedly.

His manner of denial was so blatant, it was all she could do to keep herself from laughing.

Wilfred, in love!

Well, that was a turnup for the books. She had never heard of something so extraordinary—though she supposed it would have to happen at some point. Strange. She had just presumed he never would.

"So, who's the lucky lady?" Irene hissed, a grin lilting her lips as she looked out at the many ladies promenading before them. "Is she pretty?"

"I haven't—"

"Because if she is not pretty, then I suppose she is dreadfully charming in another manner," Irene continued, both delighted at the idea of her friend's happiness and also something bitter mingling in her stomach. "How did you meet her?"

"Irene, I—"

"And yes, before you ask, I am very offended that I have not yet been introduced," Irene scolded, tapping him on the arm. "Unless—goodness, do I already know her?"

The thought was rather startling. To know the future Duchess of Aynor and not even know that she knew her.

And only then did the consequences of what she had discovered wash over Irene, and her teasing smile faded.

The future Duchess of Aynor.

Of course she knew that Wilfred would have to marry eventually. He was a duke. He had his family name to think of, his lineage to preserve. She had thought perhaps a cousin could inherit, but deep down, she knew he wouldn't want that. He needed an heir, and for that, a man needed a wife.

It was just... Well. That had always been something that would happen in the future. She supposed that now they were past twenty years of age, it was time for Wilfred to find a wife.

The thought was unpleasant and roared through her mind like a curse.

Irene shook her head as though she had water in her ears. Precisely why the thought should disquiet her so much, she did not know.

"You do not know her—"

"Aha!"

"Because there is no one to know," Wilfred persevered, his expression wooden. "Honestly, Irene, just...just drop it, will you?"

But for some reason, which Irene could not explain, even to herself, she could not drop it. "I suppose you were won over by her charming beauty, then?"

Wilfred said nothing. He just looked away, stonily, as though...

Well. As though they had had an argument.

Irene bit her lip. They never argued. At least, not since the Great Falling Out of '37, when Wilfred had declared her gown to be cerise and she had declared it to be peony, and she had not spoken to him for...oh, the best part of half an hour.

Her *sulk*, as he had always called it, had been broken by him returning to the Pernrith London townhouse with a large bouquet of peonies, which Wilfred had declared was nothing like her gown, but that she deserved the flowers nonetheless.

It was one of her favorite memories.

And now Wilfred was all at odds with her, and acting strangely, and had fallen in love without her noticing to some woman who was not going to treat him well.

How could she? This woman, whoever she was, did not know that Wilfred did not like hugs but liked his arm squeezed.

She did not know how his hair frizzed when it grew too long, or how he had learned to swim at Stanphrey Lacey, or how his pears had to be peeled before he could be prevailed upon to eat them.

This woman didn't know him at all. Whoever she was.

Unless… And the voice that whispered this at the back of her mind was cruel in its laughter as it said, *Unless she does know those things, and you just don't know her.*

It was difficult not to panic. Like her brother, Michael, Wilfred had disappeared off for weeks at a time when up at Cambridge, and the pair of them had gone, along with a few other friends, to the Continent for a four-month tour. Had he met her then?

Irene gathered herself up and stood tall. *No.* "So who is she, then?"

Wilfred's throat bobbed. "No one."

"You will tell me eventually, so you may as well save time and tell me now," Irene pointed out. When he remained silent, she wiggled her eyebrows. "I'm up for a guessing game if you are."

"Reeny—"

"You know I don't like that, and if you say it again, I shall presume you are saying it to vex me," Irene said fiercely. "Now, I presume you have not fallen in love with any of my cousins or sisters. There'd be no need to search for *their* names in the book."

There was only silence in reply—at least, silence from Wilfred. The Pump Room was starting to fill up with more and more people as the rain drove those who wished for a touch more company into the building.

Goodness, if they remained there much longer, then they weren't going to be able to promenade at all.

"Shall we go?" Irene suggested, taking Wilfred's hand. "It's going to be rammed in here soon—unless you would wish to stay and see if your lady love will make an appearance?"

She had said the final few words as a jest, smirking and squeezing his arm in that way she always did.

But Wilfred most unaccountably pulled away.

Pulled away. From her.

"We can leave if you want to," he said quietly. "I am not waiting for anyone."

Wilfred had started forward before Irene could gather her thoughts adequately, and even when she managed to make her feet move and her legs catch up with her best friend, her mind was still left behind by the wall of the Pump Room.

This was completely unaccountable. Did he not wish to tell her whom he had fallen in love with? There was surely no other explanation for his most strange behavior, and yet if he did not wish to tell her…

Well, she could not think of a reason why he would not want to.

Unless Wilfred thought that she would disapprove of his choice…

The rain was thrashing down when they reached the Pump Room porch. Irene blinked up at the sky. It did not look as though the rain was going to cease anytime soon; the clouds were dark and completely covering up the blue of the sky.

"It might lessen in a moment," Wilfred said quietly.

Irene tried to smile, and she leaned against the doorframe as they looked out at the rain. "If you had plans to walk with your beloved later, you might find it a bit of a washout. But then she might not enjoy walks. She might—"

"There is no one else, Irene," Wilfred snapped, turning to her and moving so quickly that Irene could not understand how he did it.

Her back to the doorframe, she looked up at the fierce expression on her best friend's face and her voice inexplicably faltered.

He was breathing heavily, and the sudden movement had put him momentarily outside the cover of the porch and so raindrops were dripping through his fringe.

Irene swallowed and found her mouth was dry. *What is going on?*

"Don't you understand?" Wilfred said in a low growl.

"Un…Understand?" Irene whispered.

She had tried to speak, but her voice had not permitted her anything more confident than a whisper. He was… He was being so un-Wilfred like that she did not know what to do with herself.

Her best friend had disappeared and this…this rogue, or rake, or something, had replaced him. The Wilfred she knew would never be so coy about a woman he cared about. Unless she was not a woman he cared about, but a mistress?

A twisting pain in her stomach, and lower, and Irene grasped at the stone doorframe with her fingertips to steady herself as the thought physically rocked her.

The very idea of Wilfred taking a mistress… He wasn't like that. He wasn't like her cousin Alexander, or her brother, Michael, or all the other dolts in Society who thought that bedding a widow or a servant was acceptable.

Surely, he hadn't…had he?

"Don't you know?" Wilfred growled, lowering his head so he was looking directly into her eyes.

And all Irene could see in them was blazing passion, passion for this woman, whoever she was, and she was angry that she would have to share this man with another.

How dare she, this woman, take him away? How could Wilfred even *think* about giving his heart to someone without introducing her first?

"No, I don't know," Irene said, struggling to find a little strength in her voice but forcing herself to speak. She was not to be cowed, not by anyone. Not even by Wilfred. She pushed herself forward and he was obliged to take a step back. "And if you don't want to explain it, then I do not know how I am supposed to know. I am not a mind reader, Wilfred. I need you to tell me."

"Need me to—" Wilfred broke off and turned away as though infuriated, though Irene could not see what could have distressed him so.

He stepped away, into the rain, and Irene did not even think before following him.

The pouring rain drenched her pelisse swiftly, the dampness immediately seeping through into her gown beneath it, but Irene did not care. She was following in Wilfred's footsteps, trying to increase her pace to get alongside him.

"Wilfred!"

"I have an appointment. You must forgive me," Wilfred said without looking at her, holding his hand out and hailing a hansom cab that pulled up beside them on the pavement.

Irene bristled. *Well!* If he thought he was going to step into that cab and just leave her here without any answers—

"You have a good rest of your day, Miss Chance," said Wilfred coldly, opening the door, lifting her bodily at the waist, and half-throwing her into the carriage. "Queen's Square," he muttered to the driver before handing him what appeared to be several coins and slamming the door shut.

Irene stared at the door as the carriage rumbled forward, herself the only occupant.

What in the name of—

Miss Chance? He'd had the audacity to call her 'Miss Chance'?

Well, she fumed in her damp pelisse as the carriage rattled her home. She wasn't going to stand for that. This woman, whoever she was, had managed to get her claws into Wilfred's heart and was clearly tearing it apart.

She couldn't stand for that.

Something had to be done.

Chapter Four

November 12, 1840

WILFRED GLARED AT the doorknocker.

It wasn't going to knock itself, of course, but a part of him felt that it should have. That he shouldn't be expected to do it. That once he did, there was no going back.

His breath blossomed out before him as the rattle of carriages behind him filled his ears.

Perhaps this had been a mistake. He had certainly made enough of those recently.

"You have a good rest of your day, Miss Chance."

It had been days and not a word from Irene. Precisely what Wilfred had expected, he did not know, except that being estranged from his best friend, even over something as foolish as this—especially over a problem that he himself had caused—was destroying him from the inside out.

Wilfred inhaled deeply and clenched his hands into fists, just for a moment, within his gloves.

Come on, man. Time to sort this.

He rapped on the door with the knocker.

It did not take long for the Pernrith footman to answer, and when he did, Dempster looked mutinous. "Your Grace."

Ah. Well, Wilfred should have expected Irene to tell the servants that he was not welcome. He had, after all, acted rather badly. He had grown irritated. Called her 'Miss Chance.' Even lifted her bodily from the pavement and—

Wilfred's mind was assaulted with the memories of that

moment. The light weight of Irene in his arms. The press of her waist. The softness of her. The scent, lavender, filling his nostrils and almost making it impossible to see, let alone think. The warmth that had lingered on his fingers.

"Yes?" said the servant gruffly.

"Your Grace!" said the stout Mrs. Kinley, appearing out from behind the footman and sparing the manservant a quick, almost condemning glance. The footman *was* being rather brusque with a duke, Wilfred supposed. But the housekeeper, with her puckered lips and clasped hands, was not exactly greeting him warmly, either.

Try as he might, it did not seem possible for Wilfred to speak. Or swallow. Or breathe.

"Miss Chance is not at home," said Mrs. Kinley with a frown.

Well, of course she wasn't. She had recently gotten married, so she would be on her honey…and only then did Wilfred realize. *Of course.* With Jessica Chance now married, Irene had inherited her honorific. She was no longer Miss Irene. She was Miss Chance.

"Oh. I see. Miss Irene Chance?" Wilfred managed to hazard.

The servant's face was impassive. "Yes."

"And you are certain?" he asked desperately.

There was a glint in the woman's eye that Wilfred did not like. "Yes, I am quite certain that Miss Irene Chance told me to tell you that she is not at home."

Oh. Right. Well.

Wilfred cleared his throat loudly as he wondered what to do with his hands. "You have known me for a long time, Mrs. Kinley. And Dempster."

The woman's face did not exactly soften, but it lost some of its edge. "A very long time, Your Grace."

Dempster grunted.

"And you know I would never do anything to hurt or upset Miss Irene. Miss Chance. Any of the Chances." Wilfred was not sure where he was going with this line of statements, but it was a way to fill the silence. Mostly.

The housekeeper nodded. "You have always been a good lad, and a good man. But if Miss Chance says—"

"Tell him to go away, Mrs. Kinley!"

Wilfred's spirits rose, even as a furious face appeared in the doorway beside her servants. "Irene."

"That's *Miss Chance* to you, apparently." Irene sniffed. "You may go, Mrs. Kinley. Dempster."

The housekeeper swallowed. "But, Miss—"

"Don't you make me glare at you too." Irene spoke over the servants, but she placed a comforting hand on the footman's arm and Wilfred had to look away in envy. "Please, Dempster. You are only just recovering from a cold. And, Mrs. Kinley, I know the chilly air is terrible for your elbows. Go inside. I can deal with His Grace."

Something sharp cut through Wilfred and right into him.

His Grace.

Dear God, now he knew how she'd felt when he had called her 'Miss Chance.' Was there anything so distancing as one's proper title? They had never used them with one another. They had never had to. They had always been Irene and Wilfred.

Well, for a great number of years, they had been Reeny and Wilf, but the sentiment was the same.

"I am not at home to strangers," Irene said stiffly, glaring down at him as the servants shuffled back into the house.

Wilfred tried not to let the pain of her words show. She was hurt, and he knew Irene. She only kicked out when she felt she was down.

"I—"

"I have absolutely no interest in anything you want to say, I am sure," Irene said, her voice sharp and her tone direct. "Go away."

"I am sorry, Reeny."

Irene opened her mouth, glared, closed her mouth, and glared again, seemingly for good measure.

Taking advantage of her apparently stunned silence, Wilfred rose a step, still a few feet away from her, but at least slightly more on her level. "I am sorry for the way I spoke to you. I am sorry for my odious manner the other day. I am sorry I called you 'Miss Chance'—"

"And manhandled me into a carriage as if I were a parcel," interrupted Irene, her cheeks starting to pink.

Wilfred hesitated. Truth be told, he did not really feel he could apologize for that. Not when he had relished the moment so much and had enjoyed revisiting it in his mind so frequently.

"Womanhandled you, I suppose," he hazarded in a foolish attempt not to apologize.

The pink in Irene's cheeks darkened. "You know what I mean."

"Yes, and I am sorry for the way that day ended," Wilfred said, retreating back to what he knew was true. "And I wanted to come before and apologize, but…"

His voice trailed away as words that he could not say filled his mouth.

But I was afraid. I was afraid that I would lose you. That I had somehow lost our friendship, and it is the most precious thing in the world. I feared that in one afternoon, I had broken something between us and I was too much of a coward to come here and find out.

Irene blinked. "But?"

"But I am here now," Wilfred said hastily, hating himself for being such a weakling but knowing he could not admit to the truth again. Not yet. Perhaps not ever. "And I am sorry."

Staring down at him, the woman he loved most in the world bit her lip as she examined him. Eventually, she said, "You do sound very apologetic."

"That is because I am," Wilfred said simply. "And I miss you."

The last few words had not intended to be said, and he hastily retreated a step back toward the pavement in his confusion.

But he did miss her. Not seeing Irene every day was like losing a limb. Oh, one could go on without it, but it was difficult.

Unbalancing. It required additional thought in each moment to ensure that one did not fall over.

For a painful heartbeat, Wilfred watched Irene and saw absolutely no shift in her features whatsoever.

Then her expression softened. "I am sorry too."

Now *that*, he had not expected. "Sorry for what?"

"I should not have pushed you. If you did not wish to tell me whom you have fallen in love with, I should not have persisted so."

Wilfred groaned. *Dear God, not this again.* How she had managed to fall down this entirely inaccurate track, he had no idea!

Well. Perhaps not entirely inaccurate. He *had* fallen in love, after all, just not with some chit of a girl who wasn't half of what Irene Chance was. Not that he was going to tell her that.

"I should have respected your decision to keep your affections private," Irene finished, her cheeks now a blazing red. "It… It is strange, isn't it? We have never had to navigate such a thing before. Secrets."

No. No, Wilfred had never looked at another woman in the same way as he adored Irene, not that she had ever seemed to notice, and as far as he knew, Irene had barely paid a moment's notice to any gentleman who crossed her path.

Sometimes he felt comfort in that. Sometimes he despaired that she did not even see him as a gentleman at all.

"So, are we friends again?" Irene said quietly, her voice far more timid than he had expected.

A rush of heat soared through Wilfred as he grinned. "We were never not friends, you know. Best friends."

"Well, best friend," Irene said, grabbing a pelisse that was almost definitely not hers and tugging her arms through it, "shall we go on a walk?"

"A—A walk?"

"I have had at least eight thoughts I have wanted to share with you since I saw you," Irene said happily, stepping out of her home and slamming the door behind her. Before Wilfred knew what was happening, she had slipped her hand through his arm and was walking with him down the street. So they were not to bother with the pretense of alerting her parents and calling for a sister to act as companion or her lady's maid to chaperone. He was far too used to that with her. He certainly hoped she was never so careless with another gentleman. Then again, she hardly saw him as a gentleman, did she, whatever the opinions of the likes of Lady Romeril?

"For a start," Irene said, drawing him from his thoughts, "are you staying for Christmas? You know I have to stay in Bath for Christmas, but I realized I did not know your plans. What are your plans, Wilfred?"

Wilfred could hardly speak.

His plans? He planned one day to tell her just how much she meant to him, to make sure she understood his meaning this time. He planned to make her happy, happier than she ever would be with another. He planned to help her realize just how wonderful she was.

He planned to absolutely never do any of those things.

"Wilfred?" Irene prompted as they turned a corner and entered a bustling street. "The whole point of a conversation is that you're supposed to reply."

He couldn't help but laugh at that, and his joy only increased as Irene giggled with him and squeezed his arm just how he liked it.

It was always so precious, being this close to Irene. Half of Society might look at them askance, wondering why exactly her parents permitted her, an unmarried lady, to walk out with a gentleman. The other half of Society had long known that the Duke of Aynor had a strange but utterly platonic relationship with the Viscount Pernrith's second daughter. Not that it excused the two of them flouting the rules in their eyes.

And he…he just knew that one day she was going to fall in love with someone and go off and marry him, and his heart would break.

"Isn't this marvelous?" Irene said conversationally as they waited at a street corner to cross the road.

Wilfred's original reply was lost in the rumble of a carriage, so he repeated it. "What, walking about Bath?"

"No, silly," she said with a laugh. "That we're friends again!"

"We weren't ever not friends. And we didn't ignore each other for very long," he pointed out, his stomach twisting painfully every second that they had been at odds with each other.

Not that she had to know that.

"No, I suppose not," Irene said thoughtfully as they stepped off the pavement and across the street on their way to Sydney Gardens. It was where their footsteps always seemed to take them when they were in Bath. "And yet it felt like a long time."

She could never know how much statements of that sort meant to him. Wilfred tried not to smile, tried not to make it too obvious that he was swelling at the idea that she had missed him.

"I like that we are such good friends that we can easily forgive each other," continued Irene. "It would be terribly unfortunate if we were to truly fall out. Don't you think?"

Wilfred had never allowed himself to think of such things. It was painful, the idea, cutting into his gut and ripping out his innards. Not something that he wished to experience.

"I suppose now Jessica is married, my parents will be hoping to marry me off," said Irene lightly.

Wilfred almost tripped over his own feet. "Wh-What?"

"Honestly, where are your manners, Wilfred?" Irene teased with a laugh in her voice. "Who taught you to…"

Her voice trailed away as her mind caught up with her words. For the second time that day, her cheeks pinked.

Wilfred held open the gate into Sydney Gardens and tried his best to console her. After all, she clearly had not meant to blunder into such a topic. In fact, it was rare indeed that it even came up between them.

"You do not have to worry," he said gently, squeezing her

arm this time. "I can speak of my parents quite easily. You know that."

"Still, I should not have said it," Irene said awkwardly. "I mean...you were just a child when they died. That terrible carriage accident."

"It was a miracle indeed that I was not in it with them," Wilfred said breezily, desperate to put the woman he loved at ease. "You must not concern yourself. I can speak of them quite calmly."

He could now, at any rate.

Irene had been right. He had been just a child, just seven years old. The sudden jerk into loneliness had been so rapid, he could hardly understand it at the time. One moment, they had been there, and then the next...

Irene removed her hand from the crook of his arm and Wilfred would have protested—at least, he would have protested completely silently and without an iota of expression in his face—but she instead slipped her hand in his, entwining her fingers around his own.

"You miss them," she said lightly.

Wilfred swallowed. He did miss them, but... "How can you miss something you can barely remember?" he said, far more lightly than he felt. "How can you miss a memory that has faded and faded like a cushion in the sun?"

He need not have bothered. Irene glanced up with a severe expression. "You don't need to pretend to speak all light and jubilation when it hurts, you know, Wilfred. You can always be honest with me."

His shoulders slumped as they turned a corner along the garden path. "I know. And I miss them. But I hardly remember what to miss."

Perhaps it was a common experience for all children who'd lost their parents at such a young age. Perhaps it was not only he who struggled sometimes to recall his father's face.

Oh, there was a portrait of them in the hall in his London

townhouse. The thirteenth Duke of Aynor and his duchess. They stood there, regally, his father holding the lead of a dog and his mother holding a small scruff of a child in a blanket. Him.

But without the portrait, would he still know that he shared his jaw with his father and his eyes with his mother? Without the painting, would he have known they'd had a dog? He could recall no such animal. Or was the painting not wholly truthful, a vision of what their lives could have been but without the accuracy he'd presumed?

A squeeze of his hands. Wilfred looked at Irene, who smiled.

"I lost you for a moment there," she said quietly.

The idea was so repellent, he swiftly spoke against it. "You will never lose me."

"Good," she said briskly. "Because I am your family now, Wilfred. Me, and my parents and siblings. We are your family."

A swell of emotion threatened to overwhelm him.

Because she was right. The Chances, particularly the Pernrith Chances, were his family. What they did not perhaps realize was just how true he wanted that to be.

"Come, let's sit down and observe the passersby," Irene said, pulling him toward their favorite bench.

Wilfred hardly wished to argue with her. Besides, sitting on a bench like this was another wonderful opportunity to find himself pressed up against the beautiful woman without her suspecting just how much he was enjoying it.

He crossed his legs hurriedly. Damn and blast it, the potency of her presence was getting worse and worse. That, or he was starting to lose control more easily.

What sort of a gentleman couldn't control his—

"Ah, look," Irene said quietly. "Look, over there."

Wilfred obediently looked. He saw a lady in a navy pelisse and matching bonnet, arm in arm with a gentleman a few inches shorter than her but with a top hat that more than made up for it. He was speaking to her in a low, hurried tone, which did not carry along the path, and the lady's eyes were downcast—though there was pink in her cheeks and a smile hinted at on her lips.

"Courting lovers, I would say," Irene said cheerfully, leaning back against the bench, her hand still entwined in Wilfred's.

"Oh, really?" he said as calmly as he could, as though his pulse was not pulsing so loudly he wondered why she couldn't hear it. "Without a chaperone present? Wouldn't you be more likely to assume they're already husband and wife?"

"More and more women are thinking as I do," said Irene stiffly. "That we are perfectly trustworthy to maintain our own virtue. Whatever Society may say. I mean, why is a simple exchange of vows, a couple of signatures on a piece of paper, what a man and woman must go through to enjoy a walk on a beautiful day together?"

A simple exchange of vows. A couple of signatures on a piece of paper.

Marriage was so dispassionate a topic in her eyes.

"I suppose some old woman sitting on a bench somewhere could be the lady's chaperone regardless. Perhaps my neighbor, Mrs. Brown." He winked through the thundering of his heart and Irene softened. "And what about them?" He did not point, but rather gestured with a nod of his head at a pair of people walking along the path toward them.

Irene turned to look at them, and Wilfred took advantage of the moment to look at her. Long, dark lashes, and pink in her cheeks surely because of the cold, and the curve of her lips he knew so well. Had memorized. Knew by heart.

"Them?" Irene murmured as the lady and gentleman passed them. "Lovers, of course."

Wilfred tried to breathe, cough, and speak at the same time. It did not go well. "Y-You mean—"

"Oh, I don't mean they have—I mean, they are courting," Irene said with a laugh, though the pink in her cheeks might have been a tad darker. "Courting lovers, like the first pair. I can spot them a mile off. And you'll be pleased to note there's a maidservant following a few steps behind this time. Some intrepid mama has done her duty by making sure her girl is under another woman's eye at every waking moment of the day. You may rest easy."

Wilfred swallowed.

And what, he wanted to ask, *do you think people see when they look at us? Here we are, you and I, seated in a public garden on a bench, hand in hand. Do you not think that they presume we are courting? That we are in love?*

That you are ruined because your pretend chaperone is always just "out of sight"?

His soul wrenched. It was painful at times, to be so in love with a person when they had absolutely no idea that you were so besotted with them. Sometimes it was like an injury to his side, twisting with sharp agony. Sometimes it was like a dull headache that lasted days: always there, and though you managed to function almost the same as any other day, it was exhausting, draining your energy.

What was he supposed to do?

"You know," Irene said happily, snuggling up to Wilfred and placing her head on his shoulder, "I shouldn't wonder that some people look at us and presume the very same thing."

Wilfred's heart stopped.

"Ridiculous, isn't it?" Irene murmured.

Wilfred's heart started beating again, though in a way, he wondered why it bothered if she was just going to break it every time he saw her.

"Ridiculous," he managed.

What he should have said was *"No, it is not ridiculous. Why would it be ridiculous that I would fall in love with you? You, so beautiful and so charming. You, with that scrunch of your nose when you're about to laugh and you don't think you should. You, and that family of yours, who call dogs 'dragons' and who welcomed me in like a son, like I could be a brother to you."*

But he didn't want to be a brother to her. Wilfred tried not to do it, knew he would only be torturing himself, but apparently, he could not help it.

He turned his head and looked at Irene. She was so close, her eyelashes fluttering shut as she seemed to enjoy his shoulder. Her lips were right there, mere inches away. A small movement, just a few inches, and he would be kissing her. Finding out, finally, what she tasted like. Discovering for the first time whether the need in him was matched by the need in her.

Wilfred swallowed. It would be utter madness. He shouldn't do it. He *couldn't* do it.

And yet the temptation was excruciating, twisting his insides in knots as his manhood jerked with desire, and then *need* for her. The need for this agony of uncertainty to be over was so strong that for a mere pulse, he leaned forward—

Irene opened her eyes and Wilfred jerked back.

"Having a best friend like you is so wonderful," she said quietly. "I honestly don't know what I would do without you. I hope our friendship never changes."

It would have been less painful if she had just stabbed him directly with a blade.

Wilfred tried to smile, but it was not customary to smile after one had received a mortal wound. "'Never changes,' huh? Are you certain about that?"

"Completely certain," Irene said simply. "I never want this to change, Wilfred. Never."

Could she know—had she guessed? *Is this,* Wilfred's mind thought wildly, *a subtle way of her attempting to let me down gently, to remind me of my proper place by her side?*

A friend, a brother, and never a lover?

"I will never change," he promised her.

It wasn't what she had asked him, but it was all he could commit to her.

No, Wilfred knew he would never change. His affections for her were eternal and he would never be able to remove her from his heart, even if he had wanted to.

But if these were the terms to which he must agree so that

they could remain close—if it was true that she did not wish for him to be any more than that, though he would never stop loving her—then Wilfred thought this was probably the best compromise they could find.

"So," Irene said briskly, lifting her head from his shoulder and beaming as though they had not just shared one of the most important conversations of their lives. "Shall we go to the market and see if there are any trinkets for sale?"

Wilfred smiled weakly. "Anything for you."

Chapter Five

November 16, 1840

"THERE HE IS!" Irene said with a jolt as Wilfred stepped into the drawing room. "And about time!"

There was a lazy grin on the man's face as he bowed to her parents. "The invitation said eight o'clock."

"'Invitation'?" Michael, the only Pernrith Chance brother and the only blond, guffawed. "Don't be daft—I imagine Reeny shot off a quick note and demanded your presence, am I right?"

Irene attempted not to be irritated, but with brothers it was very difficult. "It was a handwritten card!"

"But it was more of a summons than an invitation, yes." Wilfred grinned as he clapped Irene's brother on the back. "Better safe than sorry, I thought."

The whole Pernrith family laughed—all of them, that was, except Jessica, who was still on her honeymoon, and Irene, who scowled.

"I don't see why I should have to write any sort of fancy invitation for drinks and cards," she said smartly, throwing down her hand as her sister Gwen sighed with disappointment. "It's only Wilfred."

She had meant it as a term of endearment. That was how Wilfred understood it, Irene was sure, as he bowed over the hand of her mother and complimented her on the new curtains over the bay windows.

Which was impressive. Irene herself had not noticed there were new curtains. There were new curtains?

It was just the drawing room. True, their London home was far more impressive—it was the primary residence of the Viscount Pernrith since they had to let out their country estate, Wickacre Hall, and so her mother's attentions when it came to decorating had been far more focused on their Mayfair home rather than their Queen's Square one.

But really—were the curtains new?

Irene fixed her gaze on them suspiciously and her attention was distracted, so she missed what Wilfred had said. Whatever it was, it had clearly been very funny, for the whole room roared with laughter and her father nodded happily.

"That is precisely what I thought," the viscount said, his tall frame and warm presence filling the room. "Come, Aynor. Let me pour you a drink. Whiskey?"

Strange, Irene thought to herself as she shuffled the deck of cards and her sister Gwen muttered something about an unfair advantage. She never thought of Wilfred as 'Aynor.' He did, on occasion—though he rarely was around other men for such occasions to occur—have other men call him that in lieu of 'Your Grace.' It was his title—he was a duke—but he never felt like a duke.

Not that she had much of an idea what being around a duke felt like. Her Uncle William was a duke, and he was just…Uncle William. A little stiff and pompous at times, but one of the best-hearted gentlemen she had ever encountered.

And that could not be a ducal trait, could it?

"I was delighted to receive your invitation for after-dinner cards," Wilfred was saying to Irene's mother. "Your charming company is sorely needed after a long day battling the paperwork with my steward."

"Oh, goodness, I can't imagine," said the viscountess with a pretty smile as her husband handed their guest his drink. "I am delighted to offer you some diversion after such a day."

Irene continued to shuffle the cards, her attention entirely focused on the conversation on the other side of the room, by the pianoforte.

"Irene," her sister Gwen said peevishly, brushing her curls ineffectively out of her green eyes. "Are you ever going to deal those cards?"

She blinked. At the card table opposite her was Gwen, and to her right, Teddy. Theodora. Michael had been seated on her left, but he had—

Irene sighed. He had disappeared.

It was starting to become a habit of her brother, and not one which was particularly endearing to the rest of his family. Whatever he was up to, and Irene had to presume it was illicit—otherwise, why bother sneaking out while they were distracted—Michael was eventually going to have to take a mite more responsibility.

He was the future Viscount Pernrith, after all.

"Come, join us, Wilfred," Irene called out, a tug of something strange at the corners of her heart as she watched him converse happily with her parents.

It was a strange emotion, whatever it was. It was bitter, not joyful, and slightly like...

Well, it couldn't have been jealousy. What was there to be jealous of?

"What are you playing?" Wilfred asked jovially as he stepped across the drawing room, whiskey in hand, and sat beside her.

Heat spread slowly across Irene's body. It was like sinking into a warm bath, utterly relaxing and somehow managing to loosen all the tension in her shoulders.

Precisely *why* there was tension in her shoulders, she was not sure.

"We were playing whist," said Gwen darkly, "but someone was cheating."

As predicted, a chorus of cries and outrage immediately followed.

"I was not cheating!" Irene said hotly.

Teddy grinned, her elegant wrist hanging with a pearl bracelet that matched her necklace. "Just because you always lose."

"Now, now," began Wilfred. "Cheating is a fairly serious accusation."

"If the four of you can't play nicely," called over Irene's mother, "do end the game."

Irene did the only sensible thing she could do and kicked Gwen hard under the table.

"Ouch! That hurt!"

"I am not a cheat, and it is rude of you to say so, and you know how Mama gets. She'll be coming over here and deciding that we aren't old enough to entertain ourselves," Irene hissed. "And here I am, three and twenty, and you already seventeen."

Gwen glowered. "I'm going to bed."

"It's only just past—"

"I don't care," said her sister with just as much ferocity as Irene. Sometimes she forgot how similar they were. "I'm tired of this. I'm tired of *you*."

She stormed out of the drawing room without a second glance, an awkward and rather stilted silence falling on them all.

Irene glanced at Wilfred, who winked. A smile crept across her face. No matter what, she could always rely on her best friend to support her.

"Well, I suppose whist is out since four players needed—unless you wish to join us, my lady? My lord?"

"Oh, no, we'll let you young things play cards. Pick a different game, that's all," called over Irene's mother, who had deposited herself in a snug armchair and had a book in her hands. "Your father gets too competitive—and," she added at a glance from her husband, "he's far too good at cards. It wouldn't be fair on the rest of you."

Irene grinned as Teddy laughed. "Yes, something like that."

"I am very good at cards!" protested their father.

"I didn't say you weren't, Papa," Irene shot back over to him, shuffling the cards again. "But in deference to Mama…"

"I'm going to cut out too, you know," Teddy said suddenly.

"Oh, are you sure, Theodora?" Wilfred asked politely.

Irene rolled her eyes. How long had he known Teddy—and still he refused to call her by the family nickname! It was ridiculous, really.

"Yes, I wish to play the pianoforte and I so rarely have an audience this kind," her sister said shyly. "If you'll excuse me."

Pushing her chair back, Teddy walked over to the pianoforte and, after spreading her fingers happily across the keys, started to play a delicate minuet. Irene had to admit, she was getting better.

"It's just you and I, then, Reeny," said Wilfred, a twinkle of mischief in his eye.

Irene frowned. "Irene."

"Yes, yes, whatever you say," said her best friend, laughing now. "So what is it to be?"

As he spoke, Wilfred reached out to take the cards from her hands, but she wasn't going to allow that.

"Excuse you, I'm dealing," she said smartly, her lips curling into a smile.

"And excuse you, you were the dealer last time and so it is my turn now," Wilfred threw back, taking the cards from her hands.

"Wilfred!"

"Let go, Irene. I'm the guest. *You* should offer this to *me*!"

"Wilfred!"

The pair of them collapsed into fits of giggles as the deck of cards exploded out of their hands, shooting cards all over them and across the drawing room carpet.

Their laughter was accompanied by a rueful smile from Irene's mother, a shake of her father's head, and absolutely no notice at all from her pianoforte-playing sister.

"You dolt, look at what you've done!" Irene giggled, pushing back her chair to start picking up the cards.

"Me? Look at what *I've* done? You're the one who wouldn't let go!" Wilfred rejoined, chuckling in turn and mirroring her.

Soon they were both on their hands and knees, grabbing for

the cards and laughing as one of them took a card from under the nose of the other.

"That's mine!"

"Too slow, that's what I say—"

"The two of you, honestly," muttered Irene's mother from the comfort of her armchair. "You haven't changed a bit in ten years, have you?"

"Coming up to twenty now, can you believe it?" said Wilfred with bright eyes as he straightened up and nodded at the older woman. "And yet you don't look any different at all."

Irene's father scoffed and she laughed. "You charmer."

"It's the truth!"

"And that is why you are my favorite child, Wilfred," the viscountess said fondly.

Irene grinned and expected her best friend to do likewise, but for some reason, there was a dark shadow across his face.

At least, she thought there had been. Now that she looked at him again, the shadow had gone. If it had ever been there in the first place.

"Come on, let's play poker," Wilfred said, rising to his feet and stepping back over to the table. "And I'll deal."

Two happy hours followed, filled with laughter, slight cheating on Irene's part—well, she couldn't let him win every time, could she?—and the elegant playing of Teddy on the pianoforte. When silence filled the room, however, and Irene looked away from Wilfred, it was to see to her great surprise that not only had her sister disappeared, but her mother had too.

"Where's Mama?" she asked her father, who was stoking the fire with tired eyes.

"It's near midnight, my dear. She went to bed half an hour ago," the viscount said cheerfully. "And I am going up too."

Irene smiled as Wilfred suddenly rose to his feet.

"I do apologize, my lord, I have greatly overstayed my welcome."

"I do not believe it possible for you to overstay your welcome even if you tried, my fine fellow," Irene's father said with a wry smile. "It is good, as ever, to see you. Irene, you can let the fire go out. Mrs. Kinley and the maids are in bed by now, but Dempster will see to it."

"Yes, Papa," Irene said as her father pressed a kiss onto her forehead. "I've just got to finish beating Wilfred in this game and I'll head up."

"Sleep tight, Reeny."

"'Irene'!" she called as the door closed behind her father.

"I'm not going to let you win, Reeny," Wilfred said with a wink. "And then it'll be bed for you!"

For some unknown reason, the statement made his cheeks pink. Irene did not pay much attention to him, however, as she sought to roundly beat him.

It did not quite work.

"The trouble with you," Wilfred said with a lazy grin as he rose from the chair and dropped onto the comfier seat of the sofa, "is that you want too much to win."

"And that is a problem?" retorted Irene, following him onto the sofa. It really wasn't much of a sofa, more a large chair, and though it had fitted the pair of them easily when they had been children, it was a little more of a squeeze now.

Wilfred snorted. "You want to win so much, you forget that you're actually not a bad player. But you get yourself tangled in knots."

"I suppose I do. Well…" She yawned, tiredness tugging at her eyes. "I suppose I should throw you out."

Wilfred's chuckle was not only heard, but felt, as they were pressed up against each other so tightly on the sofa. "I suppose you must."

"Poor Dempster will wish to retire soon, and he cannot do so until I do, and I cannot retire until you are gone," Irene said lazily, the exhaustion of the day loosening her tongue.

Or making her speak utter nonsense. She was not quite sure which.

When she turned to look at Wilfred, however, it was not to see tiredness in his eyes but something quite different. Something she had never seen before.

It was… It was heat. How a man was able to *look* with heat, Irene did not know. She had never encountered such a thing before, but it was undeniable. The way Wilfred was looking at her…as though he were burning, and she was the only thing that could put him out.

Irene swallowed, her mouth inexplicably dry. "Wilfred?"

"Irene, I have to tell you something," he said in a rush. "And you might not like it, but I have to tell you. I cannot hold it back any longer."

Irene stared, her pulse skipping a beat as a sense of foreboding overcame her. Suddenly, the fact that they were alone in the drawing room, that her parents did not care about chaperones for her with Wilfred when there were no judging eyes, pressed against her mind. She needed a witness to this, surely, for Wilfred was about to admit something dreadful.

What it could be, she could not guess—but no man about to admit something inconsequential looked like that.

Her lips parted as she desperately thought what to say and for some reason, Wilfred groaned.

"Irene…"

She waited for him to speak, but apparently, there were no further words coming. Examining him closely, Irene realized the man had paid particular attention to his dress for this evening.

She had not noticed before. But was that not his father's cravat pin, the one he only wore for special occasions? And the man was wearing matching cufflinks, a small miracle, considering his valet hardly ever managed to convince him to do such a thing. And had he—had Wilfred combed his hair?

Why on earth would he pay such close attention to his dress for a simple evening of cards with her and her family?

"Irene," Wilfred said quietly, twisting slightly to look more directly at her but maintaining the contact between them—

contact Irene was suddenly highly conscious of. "Irene, I love you."

Though she waited for the rest of his sentence, Irene suddenly realized there was not going to be anymore. "I know. I love you, too—this is hardly news, Wilfred."

"But it is because I don't love you like a brother," he said in a rush, his eyes fixed on hers in a blaze of heat. "I love you as a gentleman. As a man adores and desires a woman."

Irene stared, her eyes widening as her lips parted in astonishment.

Well, it was a pretty poor joke. Why on earth did he think that would be funny? True, Wilfred was not one known for his particularly swift wit, but—

And then he was kissing her.

Irene gasped in surprise, the suddenness and unexpectedness of it all causing her shock and somehow, Wilfred's tongue was in her mouth!

She struggled, squirming away, pressing her hands against Wilfred's chest...his broad chest...as his tongue teased a jolt of pleasure through her that Irene had never felt before.

And before she knew what was happening, she was kissing Wilfred.

All thoughts scattered from her mind. Irene could not think, not while she was doing so much feeling. His hands on her arms, her hands splayed against him, she could feel his pulse and it was rapid as his lips pressed against hers, his tongue teasing her and shooting bolts of sensual decadence through her body that awakened parts of Irene she had not even known she'd had.

Her whole body was on fire, on fire for him—*on fire for Wilfred?*

Irene pulled away, almost breathless, and stared into the eyes of the man she had considered for almost two decades as her second brother.

He was short of breath too, and his hair had become mussed and he looked... He looked...

Irene swallowed and tried desperately to pull herself together. She was not attracted to Wilfred. *The very idea!*

"Have… Have you had too much whiskey?" she managed to splutter. "Losing yourself like that, taking me for this woman you are in love with?"

The moment of silence between them eked out into awkwardness and so far through awkwardness that they seemed to come through the other side and reach a strange sort of equilibrium.

The longcase clock in the corner continued to tick. The fire, dying in the grate, crackled as a log shifted.

And sitting opposite her on the sofa, both their bodies twisted now to face each other, was Wilfred. Her best friend.

Her best friend who had just kissed her soundly.

"Wilfred?" Irene said softly, hardly knowing what she was saying. "What—What was that?"

And as she waited for his answer, she was filled with conflicting emotions that roared through her like a torrent. Panic, and intrigue, and something that tasted like desire but surely could not have been.

She had kissed Wilfred. *Wilfred.*

Or at last, he had kissed her. It was most unaccountable. She could never have dreamed of such a thing!

Wilfred! Kissing her!

It had to have been a joke. A bad one, to be sure, connected to that silly declaration of love that he had pretended, but precisely why Wilfred would make such a jest, Irene could not tell.

What did it mean? And why was her pulse thundering so rapidly? And how could she still taste him on her tongue, sharp and spiced, like the whiskey, but also utterly different?

For a moment, Irene's gaze slipped from Wilfred's eyes to his mouth. His mouth, which had kissed her, and so expertly too, as though he knew precisely what she wanted, how she wanted to be kissed. She had not even known herself.

Wilfred has been my first kiss.

Utter madness entered her mind and for a moment, Irene wondered if it would feel that good, that delicious, if she kissed him again. If that was what kissing was, she could see why so many people were enamored with it. Maybe she should just lean forward, ever so slowly, and capture Wilfred's lips in hers and—

"You are right! You are right, of course. Too much whiskey," Wilfred said suddenly, launching up from the sofa so rapidly that Irene was rocked by the sudden absence of him beside her. "That's the last time I permit your father to pour me a third glass!"

He was laughing, a laughter of genuine merriment, and Irene attempted to laugh with him as though nothing of import had happened.

And in a way, nothing had. Why, all that had happened was that Wilfred had gotten a tad tipsy—something Irene had never done, but she had seen her mother do it once and it had been rather funny. He had said some words that he did not quite mean—oh, he meant some of it, but not like that—and he had mistaken her for this mystery woman whom Irene had very carefully not inquired about again.

That was all. It was nothing.

"Yes, my…my father's measurements are generous," Irene said weakly, remaining on the sofa, as she was not quite sure that her legs would hold her yet. She could still feel the press of Wilfred's lips on hers. "You have seen the way he serves Christmas pudding."

Wilfred laughed again and Irene joined him, but there was something different, something strange about their laughter now.

Before, it had been natural, light, warming. It had filled the space between them and told Irene that there were no better friends in the world than the two of them.

Now it was sharp, harsh, and though it still filled the space between them, it seemed to push them apart rather than bring them together.

"I had better be off," Wilfred said suddenly, turning and marching toward the door.

Irene almost fell over her own feet in her hasty attempt to get up from the sofa and launch across the drawing room. "Wait!"

Her best friend had already reached the front door where the family footman was silently handing him his greatcoat and top hat. Both of them turned to her.

"Yes?" Wilfred said politely.

Irene stared at him, then at Dempster, then back to Wilfred. What had she wanted him to wait for? What had she wanted to say?

The thought had flittered into her mind so quickly that it had slipped through her fingers before she could adequately grasp it. Now she was standing before her friend like a fool, not quite sure what she wanted from him but knowing she wanted something.

"I'll see His Grace out, Dempster," Irene heard herself saying, her mouth clearly deciding that it could take it from here without her.

"As you wish, Miss Chance." Dempster bowed, walking to the drawing room and entering quietly.

When the door shut, Irene said in a rush, "You have not forgotten that we have agreed to go shopping together."

Wilfred smiled, and there was a sadness in his eyes despite the smile, and Irene did not know why it hurt her so much. "I will meet you on the corner of Milsom Street and George Street."

"Yes. Right. Good." Irene wanted to say something else but the words wouldn't come. And what could she say? *So, we are now best friends who have kissed? Please don't tell anyone else about this? Why did you kiss me, and why do I want you to do it again?*

"Perhaps you should bring Theodora this time."

"Teddy? Bring *Teddy*?" Irene was quite sure she wouldn't, no matter what he said, but words still failed her.

"It isn't proper. To be alone together. Particularly in public."

"Oh. Right." Pain lanced through Irene's chest. He had not meant that. He did not agree with the old biddies of Society.

Why, Wilfred would never so much as look at her in that way they were all so worried about. Well, no, he *had* looked at her in that way. He'd kissed her. Even if nobody knew that. She swallowed.

"Irene?"

"Yes?" she said eagerly.

Wilfred put a hand on the door handle. "I have to go. It's late."

"Yes. Yes, of course you do. Of course it is." Irene laughed awkwardly and hated the sound. Since when had she ever felt awkward around Wilfred? "I will see you soon."

"Yes, you will. Good night, Irene."

Something in her tightened. It was gone in a moment, but she could not pretend it had not happened, nor could she understand why it had. "Yes. Good night, Wilfred."

He had stepped through the door and closed it before Irene could say another word—not that it mattered. She could not think of another word that she could utter. Instead, she leaned against the door and sank slowly to the ground. With a shaking hand, she raised her fingers to her lips and touched them.

Just moments ago, Wilfred had been kissing her.

How on earth was she ever to see him in public again?

Chapter Six

November 24, 1840

WILFRED INHALED DEEPLY and screamed into the cushion for a third time.

"Arghhhhh!"

"Now, normally, I wouldn't interrupt something as important as this," came a voice from somewhere to his left. "But I think in this case, I'm going to."

Wilfred pushed himself up from where he had been lying on the sofa and gazed blearily at the outline of a gentleman in the doorframe of his library. When he blinked, the outline found a little detail.

It was Michael. Michael Chance. *Michael?*

"What are you doing here?" asked Wilfred, his voice hoarse after screaming into a cushion.

"The butler let me in. Told him I knew the way," said Michael Chance breezily as he helped himself to a seat in an armchair on the other side of the room. He stared at Wilfred, seemingly expecting something. "Yes, it's lovely to see you, too. Yes, I will have some tea."

Wilfred glared for a moment at his friend but then stood up in high dudgeon and tugged at the bell pull.

Mrs. Ansley had to have been waiting outside the door— *undoubtedly listening to me scream,* Wilfred thought darkly—for she appeared at an astonishing rate. "Yes, Master Wilfred? That is— Your Grace?"

"Tea, cake, and whiskey," Wilfred said heavily. "In that order."

Her eyes glittered. "We seem to be all out of whiskey."

"Nonsense!" he barked. "There's always—"

"It is eleven o'clock in the morning," his housekeeper said primly as Wilfred tried not to notice Michael smirking. "I will bring plenty of tea, and a cake. That is your lot."

She did not wait to be dismissed by him—*which is probably all to the good*, Wilfred could not help thinking darkly. He clearly could not be trusted at the moment. His decision-making was absolutely awful.

What had he been thinking?

"I love you as a gentleman. As a man adores and desires a woman."

The mere memory of what he had said caused Wilfred to groan and sink back down on the sofa, lowering his head to the cushion.

"So, I don't actually know what happened between you and my sister," Michael said conversationally, as though he frequently had such conversations with dukes, "but she's not been the same since and you clearly have a decent amount of regret."

Wilfred sat up and glared. "If you are suggesting I did anything a gentleman ought not to…"

"I'm just saying, if I need to call you out to defend my sister's honor, could we wait until Thursday? I've got a very nice dinner planned with a family friend tomorrow," said Michael, his smile twitching, "and I'd hate to be killed before it."

"There's no need for a duel," said Wilfred quietly.

Not entirely. It had been a kiss, that was all. A single kiss. Irene Chance was not ruined, not as such—and as long as no one ever knew about it, there was sufficient plausible deniability for her reputation to be kept safe.

Wilfred swallowed. Not that he wanted it kept safe. He wanted to ruin her, ruin her for all other men. He wanted to make it impossible for her to ever stand near another man, wanted her to feel so intoxicated by his kiss—

"No need at all?" asked Michael as Mrs. Ansley brought in a

tea tray.

It was the hesitation that did it. If Wilfred had not hesitated, he knew, then his best friend's brother would not have widened his eyes and shooed away his housekeeper.

"His Grace and I need to discuss something important and private," Michael said rapidly. "Thank you."

Mrs. Ansley arched a brow at Wilfred but said nothing as she strode out of the room, shutting the library door quietly.

Then again, if she was still standing by the door two seconds later, she probably still heard the outburst.

"Dear God, man, my *sister*? What did you do to—you know what, I don't want to know." Michael was panting heavily, tea and cake utterly ignored. "How could you do it—ruin your best friend? Ruin Reeny! I never thought—"

"I have not *ruined* her, you fool, but if you do not keep your voice down, then *you* will!" hissed Wilfred darkly.

There was silence, just for a moment. And then footfalls, departing from the library door.

Wilfred glared at his visitor. "See what you've done?"

"What I've done—what *I've* done!" Michael managed to keep his voice low, but that did not reduce the intensity of it. "Christ alive, man, we took you into our family when you were but a boy and this is how you repay us?"

It was difficult not to feel the physical weight of the reproach on his shoulders.

Because Michael was right. The Chances had been very good to him, the Pernrith Chances especially. There had never been a family like theirs for embracing a lonely child.

That was part of the problem, wasn't it? If he hadn't fallen in love with the family as a whole, perhaps he never would have fallen in love with Reeny...

"Look," Wilfred said heavily, tea ignored but cake swiftly divided onto two plates. "Look, I didn't... She and I, we... There was nothing..."

It appeared nothing was going to diminish Irene's brother's

steely eye, so eventually, Wilfred realized that the truth had to be told.

A version of it, anyway.

"I kissed her," he said dully.

Michael stared, fork full of cake halfway to his mouth. Then he took a large bite and chewed slowly, never looking away from Wilfred.

It was a disorientating expression, to tell the truth. Wilfred could feel his stomach twisting as the realization of what he had done hit him afresh.

He had kissed Irene. Kissed her, and declared his love, for a *second* time, and she had thought him...what, teasing? Jesting? Drunk?

It did not bode well that she did not even for a moment consider that he could have been serious.

Michael swallowed the cake. "You kissed her."

"Yes," Wilfred said testily.

"And she kissed you in return?"

"Of..." Of course. That was what he had been about to say.

But the memory was fading; it had been fading from the moment that he had left the Chance townhouse. Now it was twisting, getting caught up with his daydreams and the dreams at night that he could not control.

Had Irene kissed him back? Had she wanted the kiss, just for a moment? Oh, it had felt wonderful, the sweetness and the tartness of her mouth, the warmth of her, the ways he had leaned into him...

But had she? Was that just his mind filling in the gaps of what he had wished had been?

Michael's voice interrupted his thoughts. "Goddammit, man, I knew you were in love with her, but I never thought you'd actually act on it."

It took a moment for his friend's words to register. Then—

"You—You knew?" spluttered Wilfred, cake utterly forgotten. "How could you know?"

"Anyone with eyes knows," Michael said calmly, halfway through his cake now. "My parents have talked about it for the last two years, and though Teddy and Gwen are too young to notice these sorts of things, it won't be long. Honestly, man, did you think it was a secret?"

Wilfred tried not to laugh. "It's a secret from the only person who matters."

Not that he hadn't tried to explain. Just as it had been at the opera house, it hadn't been a planned speech, that night at the card party, and perhaps that had been the problem. The words had tumbled from his mouth with absolutely no control and perhaps no coherence. Irene had certainly looked at him as though he were speaking utter nonsense.

Perhaps he had been.

Perhaps there was nothing to be done but accept that if she had any desire to return his feelings, she would have responded better to the kiss. Wanted to kiss him again. At least listened to his words.

"What you need to do," Michael said, smacking his lips as he finished the cake and put down his plate, "is stop moping about and court someone else."

Wilfred blinked. "You are joking."

"Oh, Reeny is pretty to be sure, but there have to be countless—"

"You are trying to dissuade me from courting your sister?" Wilfred could hardly believe it. The pain of the rejection was, in a way, as sharp as that of Irene's herself.

A rejection from Michael was, in truth, a rejection from the whole of the Chance family. He would be the one who would speak for them, as the future Viscount Pernrith. Irene would be under her father's protection and then, one day, if she did not wed, her brother's.

For Michael to say such a thing—

"You know I like you, Aynor. I've liked you for years. And if Irene had returned your affection, then I'd be here celebrating your upcoming nuptials. But I'm not," said Michael quietly. "So why not look elsewhere?"

The fire Wilfred had not even known was within him flamed, hot and bright. Cake and plate and fork falling to the carpet with a crash that scattered crumbs, Wilfred tried not to clench his fists as he spat, "'*Look elsewhere*'? With Irene, the perfect woman, already by my side? Why on earth would I even *think* to look at another woman when the only one I care about is already in my life?"

"In that case…" Michael began.

Wilfred did not let him continue. Flames were scalding the insides of his veins and his whole body seemed to be vibrating. "No, you don't understand. Irene is—She is—She makes me—Without her, I-I can't…"

His voice trailed off when he saw Michael's smile. "You really love her," said the Chance before him.

It wasn't a question. It didn't need to be.

"If I never marry another but spend the rest of my life dedicated to making Irene happy, as her friend, that will be enough," said Wilfred finally, sinking back down on the sofa. "That will be enough."

He had expected Michael to nod slowly. He had expected the man to sigh and lean back, yes. But he had not expected him to say what he then said.

"And the duchy? There will be no more Dukes of Aynor. Unless there's some distant cousin I don't know about who'd qualify as your heir at the moment?"

No, there weren't any cousins on the male line—not as far back as three generations, and then, no one living. Wilfred's stomach tightened. He had not thought of that.

Why should he, when all his thoughts were filled with Irene?

"Look," Michael said quietly, "far be it for me to interfere with my sisters."

It took all of Wilfred's self-control not to smile. He couldn't imagine that ever going down well, if Michael were to try.

"But I think that you might be approaching Reeny all wrong," continued Michael. "I'm not saying you don't know her. But you know her as a friend, and you want to know her as… God, I can't believe I'm saying this about my sister, but as a lover. She only knows you as a brother."

Wilfred winced.

"So court someone else. Hell, fake an engagement with someone else," said Irene's brother with a lopsided grin. "Make Reeny jealous. Make her realize what she's missing."

It was the most ridiculous idea Wilfred had ever heard. "You're mad."

"Maybe. But I'm not the one screaming into a cushion," pointed out his friend fairly.

"And the other lady? Where am I to find a willing partner, one who will not mind our 'courtship' not ending in marriage?" Wilfred was not even sure he had ever even *spoken* to another eligible lady at length, unless one counted Irene's cousins and sisters, and somehow, they didn't count. Irene's mere presence at his side had done a fabulous job of keeping eager mamas and their daughters at bay.

"I might have a suggestion. Let me know if you have the stomach for the charade," Michael said, standing up and straightening his waistcoat. "Now, I've got an appointment to make and you need to decide just how far you are willing to go to marry my sister. Ugh, still odd. Good day to you, Aynor."

Wilfred almost certainly wished his friend a good day, but he could not recall doing so. He had just sat there, in the silence of the library, the broken plate and scattered cake by his feet, thinking.

Make Reeny jealous. Make her realize what she's missing.

It was a ridiculous idea. A foolish one, one that could surely not lead to anything good.

But it might just work.

By luncheon, Wilfred had sent a note to Michael at the Chance townhouse and within an hour, a note had returned to the Aynor residence with a name and an address.

Wilfred was outside the address fifteen minutes later.

It was not a pleasant street, and not one he typically frequented. Some of the windows were boarded up and though the area had clearly once been rather pleasant, poverty had dragged it down. A few faces peered curiously as he knocked heavily on the door and waited for what felt like an age while his pulse beat faster and faster.

A woman appeared at the door. "Yes?"

"Miss Fletcher? Miss Annie Fletcher?"

The woman was pretty, in a plain sort of way. Straw-colored hair, small eyes, a rather nondescript nose. Wilfred could not describe her any other way; every woman paled in comparison to Irene. "Who's asking?"

"Mr. Michael Chance recommended you to me," Wilfred began awkwardly. How precisely did one go about this? "I need a favor."

Her eyes glittered. "Sixteen shillings, not a penny less."

"No—no!" Dear God, he would have to have a word with young Michael Chance. "No, there has been a misunderstanding."

"If you don't have coin, then I can't help you," Miss Fletcher said, pulling a threadbare shawl around her shoulders. "It's cold out and you're letting the warmth get away. State your business or go away."

Compassion flooded through him. This was not a woman who had an easy life.

"It's simple," Wilfred said shortly. "I'm in love with a woman and I want to make her jealous. Make her think that you and I are…are engaged."

As he had expected, Miss Fletcher's eyes widened. "Engaged? To *you*?"

"And you won't be, let's make that very clear," Wilfred said hastily. Perhaps this had not been a good idea. The Duke of Aynor should not be seen in this part of Bath…yet he could hardly falsify an engagement with a lady of good standing.

Her good standing would be reasonably short-lived.

Then again, it wasn't proper for a duke to be engaged to a lady in her position, either. So they'd have to come up with a proper history.

"All I wish is for your company in public a few times, to ensure she sees us," he said hurriedly, conscious he was starting to gain more than a few stares the longer he stood speaking with Miss Fletcher. "We shall keep your identity mysterious, imply, perhaps if anyone asks, that you're a lady from a foreign nation. You won't even need to speak. I shall pay you a guinea a day, when I need you."

Perhaps a guinea had been too much, judging by the suddenly eager look on her face. "A guinea a *day?*"

"Do we have an agreement, Miss Fletcher?" Wilfred said urgently.

He was almost certain he would regret this. This was foolishness, that was what it was—but he could see no other alternative.

Michael was right. Irene saw him as naught but a brother and while that had been a great comfort to him as a child, he wanted more now.

Familial love simply wasn't enough.

Miss Fletcher lurched and grasped his hand, shaking it heavily. "A guinea a day to walk about an hour or two with a gent? You must think I'm mad."

"I must think that you will be the soul of discretion and say nothing of this to anyone," Wilfred said firmly, drawing himself up and hoping that he was giving her a stern yet fair look.

Whether or not she understood it, he was not sure. She did understand the flash of silver as he produced half a crown from his pocket.

It had disappeared into her own pocket in an instant. "So when shall I expect you, sir?"

"I'll send a note," Wilfred said, trying not to think too much about it. It was a good idea. And it would work. "I'm afraid you'll have to buy new clothing." He brought out another coin, and she snatched it as eagerly as the first. "A gown. And a proper bonnet.

Something a—a lady would wear for a walk."

"I can get the clothes. You said you'd send a note. A note from who?"

Ah, yes. Probably shouldn't give his title. "Wilfred," he said quietly.

Miss Fletcher grinned. "All right, Wilf. I'll see you when I see you!"

And that, it appeared, was that.

Wilfred still felt the cloying air of the rundown street by the time he'd reached the corner of Milsom Street and George Street, but he tried to put the place out of his mind. He may never end up actually using Miss Fletcher as a source of jealousy for Irene, after all. He might wake up tomorrow and think better of it. Irene could arrive at their appointment and fling her hands around his neck and profess her love.

Well. She might.

Sadly, it was not to be. When Irene appeared around the corner—without her sister or even her lady's maid in tow, he had to note—and waved as she approached, Wilfred was filled with a bubbling affection that made him smile and know that he could never find such happiness as this.

When Irene reached him, she punched him slightly on the arm.

"Ouch!"

"My brother says you offered him the most splendid chocolate cake, and I have never had such fare when I have visited," Irene said conversationally, as though cake were the most important thing in the world. "How dare you?"

Wilfred could not help but laugh as he rubbed at the spot where she had touched him. The contact had been brief. Too brief. "You know you can come to my townhouse any time and demand cake. Even if I'm not at home."

It could be your home one day, he thought desperately. *Hang it all. A man shouldn't be pining like this!*

The trouble was, he didn't know any other way to pine.

"Now, don't you dare chastise me for not bringing my sister." She pouted playfully. "You know she'd rather be at her pianoforte than dragged through the shops."

Darn it all. Her pouting only made the need for a companion or chaperone all the more urgent. How could she not realize, after all of this, the danger? "And Wharton?"

"I left the house before she or Mama noticed. The house was all quite a flurry. That's what comes of sharing a lady's maid between three sisters and a viscountess—four sisters, if you count Jessica before she left and got her own." Irene gestured for him to follow. "Come on. I need a new bonnet and I can't keep borrowing Jessica's anymore." She looped her hand in his arm without seemingly a second thought and paraded him toward a modiste. "You are going to tell me what looks good."

It was all Wilfred could do not to allow his spirits to sink. "Oh. Oh, good."

It was not good. There was absolutely nothing good about Madame Decartes, the best modiste in Bath, to be sure, but the place was absolutely stuffed full of... Well. Stuff.

Hats and bonnets and turbans. Silks and cottons and muslins. Bolts of fabric and boxes of buttons and parasols and dainty shoes and impressively hefty trunks—

"If you're not going to be helpful, I shall send you away, you know," said Irene with a teasing grin. "You haven't told me how lovely I look."

"You look lovely," said Wilfred obediently, though he could not help the mischievous twinkle he was sure shone in his eye.

Irene giggled as she removed the hideous gray-and-yellow-striped bonnet from her dark curls. "Well, you have to say that. You're my best friend."

The lump in his throat did not make it impossible to speak, but it certainly did not help. "And that is the only reason why I am saying it."

Wilfred watched Irene as she slowly moved around the modiste's shop, touching buttons and stroking fabrics, and he wondered how on earth he was going to live without her.

For all his fine words to Michael about never marrying another woman, Wilfred was not so foolish as to believe that Irene would remain unmarried. No, there were a few other gentlemen at Madame Descartes who were evidently with sisters, their handsome gazes following the beauty around the shop with eagle eyes.

No, Irene would be courted by someone and she would fall in giddy love and she would marry. And Wilfred would be right there to watch her.

And have his heart broken.

"What about this one?" Irene had picked up a dashing navy number with military-gold buttons along the side and gold frogging along the edges.

"Very impressive," Wilfred said with a laugh. "But aren't you afraid that you'll be press-ganged into service?"

"Oh, they don't do that anymore," Irene said dismissively, but her eyes sparkled with curiosity. "Do they?"

"I have heard tell that strange things indeed go on in places like Cornwall, or Devonshire," Wilfred admitted, "though I speak from an utter lack of experience."

"Well, I do not think I should be a very good sailor," said the woman he loved as she removed the bonnet and placed it back on its stand. "I was awfully seasick that one time we went on a boat in Brighton, and I'm not sure I should like to swat a deck."

Dear Lord, how could he ever think about marrying anyone else? *"Swab* a deck."

"I don't think I would like to do anything to a deck." Irene grinned from underneath the most fantastically feathered bonnet that Wilfred had ever seen. In fact, he could barely see Irene. "You never wanted to go to sea?"

"Dukes do not go to sea, as a general rule," he said genially.

Perhaps he should not have said so. Now a few of the sisters to the gentlemen who were eagerly watching Irene's progress around the modiste were now staring in a completely different light.

Oh, blast.

Wilfred was no fool. He knew he was a duke, and a duke with a significant income, and that always attracted a certain amount of attention from mamas and their darling daughters.

He managed to avoid most of it. Irene usually did that on her own.

If these women had not known him at a glance, however, they might have assumed her to be his sister and not a competitor for his affections. After all, what duke escorted a lady to whom he was unrelated away from the watchful eye of a chaperone?

This duke does, he reminded himself.

"No, I suppose dukes have better things to do," said Irene, now adorned by a turban of the most fantastic silk. "Look at this!"

Wilfred did look.

Another observer might have seen a very pretty girl wearing a turban made of a silk that seemed quite extraordinary and impossible. One moment it looked red, and Irene would tilt her head and the fabric would somehow become purple, then blue, then a dark, shimmering green.

"Don't I look marvelous?" Irene asked, fluttering her eyelashes.

Need burned in Wilfred's loins. "You look like a peacock."

"*Wilfred!*"

"You look marvelous," he said obediently with a sarcastic air, but as she continued to smile, he added, much against his better judgment, "You… You look perfect."

She looked perfect in all of them. She looked perfect in all of them because she was Irene in all of them.

His flattery, however, did not appear to be taken seriously.

Irene snorted and removed the turban. "Now you're just talking nonsense. Come on. There must be a bonnet here that would suit."

Wilfred had seen it the moment they had entered Madame Descartes's boutique. In just a few steps, he picked up the delicately stitched, light-green silk bonnet. It was not overly decorated; it did not need to be. The woman whom it would adorn had more than enough embellishments.

"This one," he said quietly, handing it to Irene. "It will go with your favorite gown, for a start, but green goes with everything. It's why God put it so much in nature. And it will match your eyes."

Those eyes sparkled, and then Irene's lovely face lit up with well-worn laugh lines. "I'll buy it immediately."

"You're not going to try it on?"

"I don't have to," said Irene, warming Wilfred's spirits in a way she could not understand. "You chose it. And I trust you."

Chapter Seven

November 26, 1840

I T WAS THE jerk to her arm that did it.

"What have you stopped for?" Irene asked her brother, looking in the same direction he was staring with a great deal of curiosity. "What is it?"

It was unlike Michael to make such a point of stopping to look at something. His attention always meandered past things like oil and water, never quite connecting. But now he had stopped dead in the middle of the path in Sydney Gardens and was causing a small stir as other pedestrians enjoying the brisk midafternoon air had to walk around him.

"Michael!"

"By Jove," Michael said, his voice incredulous. "Is that— Aynor?"

"Wilfred?" Irene turned her back to her brother with a snort of laughter. "Do not be ridiculous. Wilfred told me he had a matter of urgent business to attend to this afternoon. Do you think that I would be walking with you if he were free?"

"No, it's definitely Aynor," said her brother. Much to Irene's surprise, there was a strange sort of delight in his voice. "Look."

Rolling her eyes and wondering why on earth she bothered to put up with him, Irene looked.

And her lips parted.

It was Wilfred. At least, it looked like a kind of Wilfred.

The Wilfred she knew, her Wilfred, did not wear a top hat like that. He did not choose a silk scarf to wear along with his greatcoat—her Wilfred always wore a woolen scarf. All the better to keep warm with.

But *this* Wilfred was wearing a silk scarf. The ends fluttered most pleasingly in the breeze, and the woman who was walking arm in arm with him smiled as he said something Irene could not hear.

Her pulse skipped a beat. The woman who was walking arm in arm with him?

No. No, she had to be seeing things. This wasn't possible. Oh, she had teased the man about a lady love and she had believed it at the time, but she hadn't *believed* it. She hadn't actually thought Wilfred had given his heart away to some woman she did not know.

And yet there she was. Tall, almost as tall as Wilfred, stunningly beautiful with radiant blonde hair that seemed to glow from the meager sunlight Sydney Gardens was enjoying this day. And she was smiling. Smiling at Wilfred. As though he had said something charming.

The twist in Irene's stomach was most discomforting. *The man has never said anything charming in his life.* What on earth could he have said to that woman to make her smile like that?

"Ah, I thought it was him," came a voice from a long way off.

Irene blinked. She and her brother were still standing in the middle of the path, still staring at the figure of a gentleman thirty or so yards away.

And it was Wilfred...but it did not make sense. Everything she knew about him railed against the sight before her eyes.

It was not possible. Wilfred, with another woman?

With a woman, Irene corrected hastily in the privacy of her own mind. It was not as though she had any claim on him. Not at all. He was Wilfred. She did not own the man.

Not really.

But where would he have even *met* her? How could he keep this secret from the person he insisted was his best friend all this time? Irene did not recognize the woman, and she thought the

Chances were acquainted with just about everyone in Society who came to Bath this time of year.

"How delightful to see him so happy," said Michael cheerfully.

Irene swallowed. Why did these words stick in her throat? "Yes. Yes, how delightful."

"I always think that when a man is happily in love, he is happy in all things," her brother said, his tone conversational. "Don't you?"

Happily in love. *Happily in love? With that woman?* "Yes. Yes, I am sure you are right." Irene blinked, her gaze sharpening. "Not that you would know about such things, Michael. What on earth are you talking about? You're—You're not in love, are you?"

She would have been suspicious, if her brother had not guffawed so loudly that he dropped her hand from his arm.

"You truly are ridiculous sometimes, you know," said Michael easily, shaking his head. "In love, honestly! No, it's Aynor who's utterly lost in love. Look at him."

Much against her better judgment, Irene did just that—and the unpleasant tug of pain in her stomach returned as she saw the way Wilfred looked at his companion.

As if... As if she were everything. Everything in the world.

It is not jealousy, Irene told herself firmly as she stared at Wilfred and the woman, whatever her name was. It could not have been jealousy because she had no claim to—there was no possibility of... He was not *hers*, after all.

Wilfred was not hers. He was, but he wasn't.

And yet seeing him there with that harlot—

Irene immediately stopped herself there. She was not like that; she did not drag other women down merely to pull herself up. It was not this woman's fault that she had not been introduced to the people who really mattered in Wilfred's life, was it? No. It was Wilfred's.

And with that in mind...

"Reeny—Reeny, where are you going?"

Irene ignored Michael's question entirely. "Do not call me 'Reeny,'" she said as she marched forward, leaving the path and making straight for Wilfred and his…his lady friend.

"But—"

"No *buts*," Irene said, shrugging off Michael's clasping hand and barreling forward. "I want to meet this person who has such a hold on my—on our Wilfred's heart."

"But if he hasn't already introduced you, perhaps you best leave them be."

"Wilfred!" Irene called out, ignoring the stares of others and flushing slightly at the outrageous thing she was doing. Shouting a man's given name in public, across a park? Her mother would be furious if she found out. She would just have to hope she wouldn't. "Wilfred!"

Wilfred had stopped. There was pink in his cheeks too, though Irene could not possibly think why, and the woman beside him—

The woman beside him had leaned close to him, whispered something in his ear, and Wilfred nodded.

The woman smiled.

Irene almost stopped up short altogether. It was so disorienting, the ground spinning like this and the sky shaking, that she almost did not know how she was still standing.

The intimacy between them…the way the woman was looking at her. What had she asked? What question had Wilfred nodded to?

It did not matter that she could no longer take any steps forward; Michael had reached her and silently offered a steadying arm, and Wilfred and his lady were now approaching them.

But no—the lady had unlinked her arm and was now walking in the opposite direction.

Irene's eyes watched her go. So, she was not even going to be given the honor of meeting the woman who had captured Wilfred's heart, was she? *Why not?* Was he ashamed of her? Was he ashamed of his own foolish behavior, that kiss that Irene had most certainly not thought of every hour of the day since, and far too much at night?

"Chance. Reeny," said Wilfred as he reached them.

"Irene," Irene said automatically. "Who was that?"

Her eyes were still following the woman out of Sydney Gardens. She received a few curious glances from others, too—but then she would, being so handsome.

And where was *her* chaperone? Wilfred was—at times—so concerned about Irene being seen without one, but there was this beauty, parading through the park first with a man, and now alone.

Unless she was one of those gorgeous, rich widows some men seemed to fancy. She'd put up with one presumably ancient man and now Society deemed her free to parade through parks with a much younger, higher-ranking, and good-looking specimen.

Wilfred *was* good-looking, Irene had to admit to herself. But the sudden focus on his fine features, the breadth of his chest…

Irene thought she was going to be sick. *This is ridiculous!* She had never felt like this before, never, and where these sensations had come from, she had not the faintest idea. It was madness. It was ludicrous. It was going to turn her insides out.

"Oh, no one," said Wilfred lightly.

Irene's attention snapped back to her best friend. "What do you mean, no one? Everyone is someone."

"She's just a…a friend," Wilfred said, now tangled in his words.

"And at this point, I leave you," said Michael cheerfully, letting go of Irene's hand and nodding to Wilfred. "I won't tell Mama I didn't escort you home, Reeny. Good afternoon, Aynor."

For a moment, just a breathless moment, Irene rather thought her brother did the most unaccountable thing and winked at Wilfred—as if they shared a secret.

But that could not have been right. For a start, Wilfred was not the sort of man to have a secret with anyone except her. And anyway, she must have dreamed it. She was so full of…of not quite fury and not quite jealousy that she had evidently supposed something that was not there.

The instant her brother was out of earshot, Irene said in a rush, "So who is she?"

"Who is who?" Wilfred said, clearly baffled.

She frowned. It was not very gallant of the man to forget the woman he had quite literally been walking arm in arm with not five minutes ago. "Her! That woman! The woman you were walking with!"

You know, Irene wanted to say. *The beautiful one. The elegant, tall one. The one who whispered in your ear as though she had known you for a thousand years.*

"What, her?" Wilfred's face was blank, as though he had forgotten the woman yet again as soon as the words had escaped his lips.

Resisting the urge to physically shake him, Irene attempted a laugh. It sounded very false. "Yes, her! The woman you were walking with."

"Oh, she is…she is…she is Miss Fletcher," said Wilfred lamely.

Irene tried not to think desperately about every single woman she had ever met, and whether any of them had ever mentioned a Miss Fletcher. The name was unfamiliar, though it had a sort of familiar ring to it. Perhaps her father knew Irene's father?

And "Miss," then? So not a widow? Where was the outcry when *she* appeared in public without a relative, a servant, or a nosy, old woman watching over her every move?

Irene fought back the urge to stomp her foot. "And she is?"

"Gone, for now," Wilfred said with a false cheerfulness that even she could see through. "Shall we walk?"

'Shall we walk'?

What, was she merely to be a temporary replacement for this Miss Fletcher while he could not walk with her? Was she, Irene, second choice to Miss Fletcher, but Wilfred would make do with her while his true love was absent?

The nausea rolled in her stomach. *Wilfred's true love.*

It should not have upset her like this, of that, Irene was certain. It should not have upset her at all. It was not *upsetting*. It was just that Wilfred had found a woman whose company he enjoyed more than hers and she was never going to recover from it.

"Irene?"

Irene blinked. Wilfred was offering his arm.

Well, she took it, of course. She could hardly not. Besides, she wanted to discover everything about this Miss Fletcher immediately.

"Where did you meet her?" Irene asked as they started to walk slowly across the park.

Wilfred glanced at her curiously. "Who?"

"Miss Fletcher, you dolt!" It was all she could do not to laugh. For some strange reason, if she did not laugh, she was liable to cry. "Honestly, one would think that you hardly knew her, the way you talk about her! Or..."

Her voice trailed away. *Or,* she had been going to say, *or that you know her so well that you want to keep her to yourself. That you don't want to share her, not even with me.*

It was a most disorienting thought.

"Miss Fletcher is a lady of my acquaintance whom I...I respect and admire greatly," Wilfred said stiffly, as though he were being forced to reveal his pocketbook spending to a stranger. "And that is all."

He does not need to say the last part, Irene could not help but think, *unless that is not, in actuality, all.*

Was he engaged to her? Was that why the lady's chaperones seemed to be more lax than some? Surely, the whole of Society would have known if the Duke of Aynor were engaged! But then, Wilfred had never been one for pomp and ceremony. Perhaps, then, the lady's family would have complied with his wishes. He was not the sort of man to send notices to newspapers and demand recognition.

A smile, small yet cordial, crossed her lips. He was not that sort of man at all.

Still, where—when—would he have even met her? He spent far more time with Irene, of that, she was certain.

"She asked about you."

If Irene had not had her arm linked through Wilfred's, she would certainly have ended up on the ground, her nose in the soil. "Wh-What?"

Wilfred nodded calmly, as though this were a perfectly normal thing to say. "Yes, she asked if you were my best friend."

Irene's smile was weak. "Oh. Oh, good."

He had nodded at the lady's whisper, she remembered, and Irene supposed it was good that Wilfred had owned her to the woman he loved. It would have been mortifying if he had denied her.

But still, Irene could not help but think as the icy wind rustled through the mostly bare trees and a few passersby pulled their greatcoats and pelisses tighter to them... *Best friend.* She had always loved that title—when she had thought about it at all.

But now...

"And we are best friends, aren't we? We have been for years," Wilfred said with a wry smile. "Do you recall the time I had to rescue you from that bull?"

The nerve! "It was not a rescue. It was a...a tactical retreat," Irene retorted, all thoughts of Miss Fletcher nearly forgotten as she nudged her best friend. "I had the situation perfectly under control."

"That bull was about to charge at you, and I picked you up bodily and lifted you over the gate," Wilfred said, chuckling under his breath. "And you still went back the next day!"

"I wanted to look at him," she said, trying not to smile but finding it difficult. "He was the new bull at Stanphrey Lacey and Uncle William had said—"

"Your Uncle William threatened to whip me within an inch of my life if I let you go back there again."

Irene glanced up, curious. "I did not know that."

"I did not tell you," said Wilfred with a shrug. "And yet he did not whip me when you did just that the following day. He knew no one could tame you."

There was nothing intrinsically provocative in what the man had said, but for some reason, heat was billowing through Irene, and she found that she was quite warm enough even in the chilly air.

'Tame' me?

"I do suppose I owed you one for that assistance," she admitted as they rejoined the path in the park and started to meander slowly along it. "But then, I *have* rescued you, in my own way."

"Rescued me?" Wilfred's laugh poured molten honey into Irene's spirits. "When have you ever done that?"

"Do you remember that first ball we both attended?" Irene said. "Lady Romeril's, I think, though goodness knows she does not host many. You asked my cousin Maude to dance, though you insisted later you were only attempting to be gentlemanly."

She had expected the groan but could not have predicted the look of genuine anguish—the wide grimace, the squinting eyes— that splattered across her friend's face.

"Oh, God."

"And she said—"

"'Not in a month of Sundays,'" Wilfred finished for her, wincing at the memory. "I had completely forgotten that. Thank you for reminding me."

"Well, I rescued you," Irene said primly, squeezing his hand.

This time, it was Wilfred's turn to roll his eyes, not something he did often, as they passed by a couple who were clearly trying their best not to kiss in public. The older woman keeping an eye on them by trailing a few feet behind probably helped with that. "You did not rescue me!"

"I danced with you!" Irene shot back, remembering the moment. The haze of the candles, the chatter in the ballroom, the way her heart had thudded… "And then in the ladies' powdering room, I waited until the Miss Quintrells were there and spoke very loudly of your elegance and charm at dancing, and your great wit and conversation, and how anyone who had the opportunity to dance with you was fortunate, indeed—ouch!"

For the second time that day in Sydney Gardens, Irene's walking companion had halted suddenly, causing her arm to be jerked back.

She withdrew it from Wilfred, rubbing her elbow. "What was that for?"

"You really did that?" he said urgently, as though the matter were of great import. "At Lady Romeril's ball, you did that?"

"Well, of course I did," Irene said, looking at her arm as though she could see through the layers. "That might leave a bruise, you know."

"You did not have to do that."

The statement was so matter-of-fact, Irene found herself saying just as bluntly, "And I did. Because I care about you."

They stood there for a moment, two people trapped in amber, and Irene looked into Wilfred's eyes and thought that in the right light, the man was more than merely *good-looking*. He was passably *handsome*.

The thought disappeared as soon as it had come.

"Besides, you'd saved me from bulls!" Irene teased, taking his hand and entwining his fingers with hers as though it were the most natural thing in the world. Because it was. "Bulls are far more frightening than balls."

"Perhaps for you," Wilfred said, pulling her along with him as he started to walk, taking another circuit of the park. "But I was truly humiliated that day. I thought I would never live it down, yet I have never had another woman decline my hand. To dance, I mean."

Irene saw a flash of understanding in his eyes and wondered why she had never mentioned this before. Why, because it had been nothing. A few minutes of thought, a few sentences spoken aloud. It had been the least she could do for her best friend.

"I have never thanked you for such a service," Wilfred said softly.

There was such heart in his voice, Irene hardly knew what to do with herself. "I... You would have done the same for me."

"I suppose I have, in my own way."

That was sufficient to catch her attention. "What do you mean?"

"Oh, I—nothing," said Wilfred hastily.

Far too hastily.

Irene frowned. "Wilfred Matthew Kirk Chesterham Zouch, Duke of Aynor—"

Her best friend winced. "Are you truly going to *full name* me?"

"Well! It is not 'nothing.' I want to know," Irene said fiercely, though she was almost certain she already knew. "Come on, tell me."

Wilfred looked hunted as they halted underneath a wide oak tree, its branches bare, but its structure still magnificent. "I would rather not."

And that answered all her questions. "It was about my father, wasn't it?"

It was not an enquiry, and Wilfred did not treat it as one. "Yes."

Irene inhaled deeply.

Her father. He was the man she admired the most in the world, yet so much of the world looked down on him due to a mere circumstance of birth. He was illegitimate. The old Duke of Cothrom, her grandfather, had fathered a by-blow then scandalously brought the child to live with his three lawfully born sons.

Her father and his three 'better' half-brothers. Oh, Irene knew the world looked at the Viscount Pernrith and sneered sometimes, but that hardly ever happened! Why would Wilfred have had to...

It hardly ever happened *now*. Up until three years ago, it had all the time.

Irene narrowed her eyes. "Wilfred Matthew Kirk—"

"Look, I did not like the way some of the gentlemen at White's were speaking of your father. Of your father, your brother, your whole family," said Wilfred shortly, his ears turning pink, as they always did when he did not like what he was saying but felt he had to say it. "Eventually, I... I snapped."

Oh. Well. That was understandable. There was only so long a man's temper could—

Wait a moment. Irene's lips parted. "When you say snapped, you... You don't mean that you snapped at them, do you?"

Wilfred would not meet her eye. "Not exactly."

Oh, goodness. "What did you do?"

"It only happened once," Wilfred said hastily, as though that resolved the matter.

They were still holding hands. Irene tugged his arm as she said fiercely, "You have to tell me, Wilfred. You're... You're my best friend. The person I trust most in the world. You shouldn't have to defend our family, but you did, and I want to know just how significantly we are indebted to you."

The fact that he would still not meet her gaze spoke volumes. "I called out Mr. Lister."

"You—You what?" Irene's voice broke as she pushed the man behind the oak tree so that the other people enjoying Sydney Gardens would not have to hear them. Lowering her voice to a hiss, she said, "You *called out* Mr. Lister?"

"He was speaking absolute rot. You should have heard him! Truly disgraceful things about you, about your father. I could not—"

"Wilfred!" Irene said in shock.

Calling someone out in this day and age...it was not just that the queen did not like it. Her uncles did not like it, either. Dueling had been forbidden for... Well, forever, as far as Irene was concerned.

And Wilfred had taken his own life into his hands for her and her family?

The man looked most uncomfortable. "I didn't hurt him. Not really."

Oh, dear God. "When was this?" Irene demanded.

Wilfred sighed. "About three years ago."

Yes, that would line up with the sudden decrease in insults from the bounder!

Irene reached out and placed a hand on Wilfred's chest to steady her. She would have grasped at the tree, naturally, but Wilfred was closer. "Did not Mr. Lister suffer a broken arm about three years ago?"

The guilt in his eyes told her enough, but Wilfred said quietly, "Not a break. A bullet. But that stays between you and I."

It was difficult to comprehend. Gentle, easygoing, sometimes a little slow on the uptake Wilfred had…shot a man?

"You did that for my father?" she whispered.

"I did that for you," Wilfred said quietly, his voice steady and his focus fixed on hers. "There is a great deal that I would do for you, Reeny."

Irene swallowed. She did not have the breath to correct him, and for some reason, in this moment, she had no desire to.

Wilfred had dueled a man, shot him, to defend her father's honor. To defend her own. He had risked not only his reputation, but his liberty, his very life, to ensure no one would speak ill of them.

"You must never fight a duel on my behalf again," she said, her voice shaking slightly at the very thought. "I can't—I mustn't lose you, Wilfred. Mere words, even foul words, are not worth the risk."

His hand had covered her own as it splayed against him. "Yes, Reeny. I promise."

Irene drew in a deep inhale and tried desperately not to think of that kiss as she shivered.

He was her friend. Her best friend. And he was clearly in love with this Miss Fletcher, whoever she was. His defense of her name was for her whole family, not just her.

"Come on. You're cold," came Wilfred's voice as he released her hand and started walking to the gate. "Time to head home."

Irene hesitated for a moment, then nodded as she followed him in silence.

Not that she needed conversation. She had a great deal to think about.

Chapter Eight

December 2, 1840

"Look," said Wilfred firmly, trying not to grin with delight, "you asked for my help and—"

"And so I expected to receive it!" shot back Irene, a dark look in her eyes as she tried to hold far too many parcels wrapped in brown string. "I suppose you helped Miss Fletcher with her Christmas shopping with far more alacrity!"

He should not have been so delighted. Wilfred knew it, but that did not change the shifting warmth in his stomach that made it impossible not to be elated.

She was annoyed. Annoyed! At him!

"Here," Irene snapped, shoving a handful of small brown parcels into his arms. "Hold these."

"You know, this would have been easier had you not insisted on losing Wharton, as usual. She would have carried some." Even so, Wilfred happily accepted the parcels, trying not to grin as his best friend and the woman he loved attempted to reorganize her handfuls of presents.

He could never have believed it would work so well.

Michael had been clear: just make sure Irene sees you with another woman, and that would do the trick. Wilfred had scoffed.

He was not scoffing now.

"I am tired of being watched by a poor, overworked servant who should not waste her time making sure I'm not dragged into dark corners and ravished." Irene froze for a moment and Wilfred wondered if she was thinking about the night he'd kissed her, but she quickly recovered. "I am certain Miss Fletcher doesn't struggle to hold all her parcels," Irene was muttering, almost as though she were not aware she was doing it. "Miss Fletcher, though apparently free to take walks in the park unsupervised, probably has a servant alongside her when she shops who's far more help than you!"

Wilfred knew he should not have been smiling. His best friend was annoyed at him, and he should not have been so ridiculously cheered by it.

But he was. If Irene had shown no interest in Miss Fletcher at all, well, then he would have given up the attempt and would have been out a guinea and a half crown, and that would have been the end of it.

She had shown far more interest in Miss Fletcher than he had, and ever since then, there had been an undertone of irritation with him that Wilfred had expected to grate him but was finding most exhilarating.

Irene was jealous.

"Right," Wilfred said happily. "Is that all?"

His best friend straightened with a glare that would have melted a lesser man. Wilfred was surprised it did not melt the frost that had not yet succumbed to the pale, wintry sun.

"It is not all," Irene snapped. "Why are you being so ridiculous today?"

"And why are you being so bad-tempered?" Wilfred asked mildly, secretly thrilled to ask the question. "I have not done anything to offend you, have I?"

Irene opened her mouth, closed it, opened it again and looked likely to speak, but then brought her lips together and said nothing.

The Christmas market around them buzzed with excitement. Wares were being offered and snapped up by eager customers seeking that perfect Christmas gift. There was a stand selling mulled wine, which spiced the air, and a bonfire at the end of the street had attracted a few street children, who were whooping and laughing as they leaped around it.

"You…"

Wilfred's eyes snapped back to his companion. "Yes?"

"You have not done anything wrong," Irene said lamely, with a weak smile. "Wait a moment. Give me those."

Most against his better judgment, Wilfred handed back the small parcels she had been finding so challenging to keep in her arms and watched as Irene stepped past a stall selling the most delightful pies—truly, he had never smelled better—and toward the street.

He watched with curiosity, trying not to notice the sway of her hips as she walked and the very direct way she moved through a crowd.

That was the trouble with Irene. You always knew she was going to get her own way.

She was currently getting her own way by barging past a gentleman who was about to get into a hansom cab and pouring the parcels she had purchased onto the seat. There was a rapid conversation with the gentleman, a conversation Wilfred could not hear, and then the man was bowing to her with a smile and Irene was talking to the driver.

Wilfred had to force a pleasant expression on his face and not glower at the man for having the audacity to talk to the woman he loved.

The poor man could not have known, after all.

The hansom cab lurched forward and Irene returned to Wilfred with a crisp nod. "There."

She sounded and looked most satisfied.

"Have you put all the gifts you have bought as Christmas presents…into a hansom cab?" Wilfred asked curiously.

"Yes," Irene said smartly, wriggling her gloved and now-unburdened fingers. "Goodness, that feels better."

"In a cab. On their own."

"Well, I don't wish to cease shopping. I haven't yet found anything for Dempster or Wharton," Irene said calmly, as though people decided to send presents away by hansom cab all the time. "I was most clear in my directions to the driver and told him that when all presents arrived safely at the Pernrith townhouse on Queen's Square, he could apply to the housekeeper and gain an additional shilling."

"You are very trusting," Wilfred observed, rather startled by her innocence.

Something mischievous glittered in Irene's expression. "Oh, Mrs. Kinley has a most excellent memory for faces. If the number of boxes that the driver gives her is not fourteen, I shall instruct Mrs. Kinley—or better yet—broad-shouldered Dempster to take a note around to the Peelers. No one steals from me."

No, you do the stealing, Wilfred could not help but think wistfully. She had stolen his heart five years ago and she had not even realized she had done it. It was truly a talented thief who stole without ever being the wiser themselves.

"And besides, you haven't purchased any Christmas presents at all!" pointed out Irene with a shake of her head. "You would have thought Christmas wasn't coming!"

"I don't have that many presents to buy!" Wilfred protested.

In truth, he had hardly any. When he had been a child, Mrs. Ansley had taken it upon herself to buy gifts for all his servants—making sure never to spend more than three shillings on a maid or ten shillings on the upstairs staff—and to his utter shame, he had never gotten into the habit himself.

Besides, his housekeeper liked doing that sort of thing. Didn't she?

"Who are you buying Christmas presents for, anyway?" asked Irene, casting him a look he could not translate.

It was an excellent question. Wilfred started counting on his hands. "You, of course—"

"Of course," Irene said with a giggle. "Something ridiculously expensive, of course."

He had wondered, when he had gone up to university and left the Chances behind, whether it had been truly appropriate for him to buy presents for young ladies to whom he was not engaged. He was, after all, a duke—and Wilfred knew that many in Society would talk if another gentleman of similar standing had bought presents for unbetrothed young ladies.

It was not done, after all.

But somehow he had kept doing it, every year, and Wilfred saw no reason to stop now.

"Of course something expensive," he said gravely as they started to meander through the stalls again, though Irene's laugh told him she had seen the sparkle in his eye. "Something each for your sisters—goodness, now your eldest is married, do you think I should buy her husband a gift?"

"Probably safer to get them a joint present," Irene said thoughtfully, picking up a handmade candle and sniffing it. "Too much tallow."

She put the candle down and they continued on.

"Something for Michael," Wilfred said, still counting on his fingers and wondering how he would ever repay Irene's brother for helping him make Irene actually notice him. "Something for your parents. And…that's it."

Irene stared, halting before a stall selling the most delicate china ornaments. "'That's it'?"

Wilfred shrugged. "I have no family. I only have you. Your family, I mean."

It was a slip of the tongue he had not intended, but it did not appear that Irene had noticed anything amiss.

"I suppose not. I just thought… Well. That you would have other friends. Gentlemen friends."

Most people presumed that, and time and time again Wilfred would attempt to explain that he had a best friend already. Her name was Irene.

"And what about Miss Fletcher?" Irene asked, staring at the china perhaps a bit too fixatedly.

He spoke before his mind could catch up with his tongue. "What about her?"

"Wilfred!" Irene tapped him sharply on the arm. "Do you not think you should be getting her a Christmas present? That is…if it is appropriate, naturally. Perhaps you should wait until you propose. If you have not already."

It was marvelous fishing. Wilfred had to give her the credit for it—not that he was going to answer her questions directly. He would rather keep her on the hook. "Perhaps I have."

"Well? Have you?"

Wilfred hesitated. This charade with Miss Fletcher could only last so long, and he did not wish to actually lie. Yes, he had thought to pretend she was a lady from France or somewhere else on the Continent if anyone asked, but he had managed to not have to actually explain that much thus far. He was not a liar by nature, and if there was one person in the world he did not wish to lie to, it was Irene.

"Oh, look!"

Wilfred did not need to ask what Irene was referencing. The snow had started suddenly, going from tranquil skies to clouds that gently divested themselves of their fluffy burdens. The flurries came down in twisting, twirling squalls, the light wind catching the snowflakes and lifting them up, just for a moment, before they fell down again.

Irene stared upward, eyes bright and exultation obvious. "I love snow!"

I know, Wilfred almost said. *I know everything about you. There is not a single thing that I do not know about you and I love every single part of you.*

He did not say this. Not aloud. "Do you wish to return home?"

"Home? When it's snowing?" Irene looked outraged. "And miss out on some excellent snowflakes?"

It was picturesque, even Wilfred had to admit. Bath was always beautiful: it did not require further adornment, with its yellow stone buildings and tall windows, the arching bridges and the delicate, little streets. But though it did not need adornment, it almost glowed under the yellow wintry sun and flutters of snow.

"Besides, we have not finished our Christmas shopping. You have not even started," Irene pointed out, gesturing for him to join her at another stall. "Here, it's Mepham and Sons, isn't it? From down on Milsom Street. I did not know they were a part of the Christmas Fair. Look, this might be good for Wharton. Or my sisters. What do you think?"

It was a jewelry stand. The planks of wood were covered with a sort of dark-blue velvet, though it was so worn, it was hard to tell if it could still be called velvet any longer. Upon the fabric was jewelry. Necklaces, and bracelets, and earbobs—

"And rings," Irene pointed out unnecessarily. "Do you think I should get Jessica one?"

"You already bought her that shawl," Wilfred managed.

He was standing in front of rings with Irene. True, none of them looked much like the sort of wedding band he would wish to select for her, but that did not signify.

Himself. And Irene. Jewelry—rings.

Breathe, man. Don't forget to breathe.

"What do you think?" Irene asked quietly, touching his arm.

Wilfred could feel the burn of her touch at his wrist; despite her gloves, his greatcoat, his jacket, his shirt, through all of that, he could feel Irene's touch. It was like honey and sunshine and a burning need to be even closer to her and—

"Or this one?" Irene picked up an earbob, a sapphire or something like it, and held it up against Wilfred's ear. "Stay still, will you?"

It was a statement, not a question, and Wilfred thought he would never move again. Irene was so close to him, leaning up to almost fall in his arms, her exhale warm on his face as she stared seriously at him.

She is attempting to ascertain whether she likes an earbob, he tried to tell himself. *This isn't about you.*

It was easy to forget that, to fool himself into thinking that

Irene was leaning this close to him because she was remembering that kiss. That moment when he had been certain she returned his affection. That they were going to be happy together, forever.

Wilfred swallowed. "I-Irene…"

"You're right. I'm not sure I like the silver with the blue," Irene said with a sigh, moving away and replacing the earbob onto the stand, much to the stall owner's evident disappointment. "How about this one, then? For Gwen?"

She had returned to him and was pressed even closer against him this time—or perhaps that was just Wilfred's wild imagination. This time, an emerald earbob, a pendant drop thing, Wilfred was not quite sure, was being held up to his ear.

Surely, she could hear his pulse this close. Wilfred was surprised Irene had not mentioned it, but perhaps that rosy glow in her cheeks was nothing to do with the snow and everything to do with their proximity.

No. No, he was being foolish.

Disappointment flowed through him as she moved away.

"Yes, I think I shall get a pair of these green ones, and that red pair too. Oh, and that silver bracelet is very pretty," Irene said lightly, as though she had not just been pressed up against a gentleman in public. "I'll have that too, for Wharton. She has triple the work now that Teddy and Gwen are more out in Society. Gwen will make her debut this upcoming Season."

"You are very generous," said Wilfred hoarsely. *Damn it, man!* He cleared his throat before adding, "To your servants, I mean."

"Wharton deserves it, with the runaround I give her so frequently." Irene grinned as the stallholder carefully wrapped up her purchases in boxes and brown paper. "And you are not generous yourself? Your Mrs. Ansley has a completely free rein, as far as I can tell."

"She's more a mother to me, really," said Wilfred with a laugh, looking at a few of the necklaces.

"And what are you getting her for Christmas?"

He hesitated, the truth somehow shameful now that he had

to say it aloud. "I'm not."

"You're not getting your housekeeper anything?"

"I mean, she gets her own present," Wilfred amended hastily, wondering why his additional statement actually made him feel worse, not better. "She has always done that. She knows what she likes and I trust her to figure it out."

Irene's eyes narrowed. "Wilfred Matthew—"

"Fine, fine, I'll get her something," he said hastily. *A man can only be full-named so many times in his life.* "How about…this?"

He picked up an elegant necklace, a string of pearls.

Irene examined him carefully. Then she smiled. "You have rather good taste in jewelry, you know."

Wilfred could not help but puff out his chest. "Well, I—"

"And I am sure Miss Fletcher appreciates that quality," continued Irene, her cheeks red.

That redness could surely have little to nothing to do with the snow continuing to fall around them, could it?

Wilfred could not tell. It was so strange, not being able to read Irene, and yet he could not help but feel gratified that his plan had worked.

Well. His and Michael's plan.

Because she *was* jealous, wasn't she? It was Irene who continued to bring up Miss Fletcher; he had not done so. She was the one who kept attempting to ask leading questions about the woman, questions he had carefully either not answered or answered, truthfully, that he did not know.

So why was this playing on Irene's mind to this extent? Why else, but that she was jealous?

And that has to mean, Wilfred thought wildly, *that she loves—*

"I think the pearls will do very well," Irene said with a nod, and the stallholder brightened up even further, starting to carefully place them in a blue velvet box that looked in far better shape than the stall.

A glow was sparking in Wilfred, and it took him a moment to realize why it had started.

He had done something nice for Mrs. Ansley.

It sounded awful when he thought about it like that, but he could not deny that it was gratifying, indeed, to think that he had done something pleasant for the woman who had been such a constant support and companion for him. And he *did* think of her as a mother, more so than even Lady Pernrith. She had been there for him during the most difficult time in his life, offering a shoulder to cry on when things had been too much, always there to welcome him home from school, holding his hand and guiding him into manhood…

And he had never told her. Well, he simply would have to. Maybe he could write it in a card, to go with the pearls.

The stallholder put the brown-papered parcel that contained the pearls into his hands. "Anything else?" asked the man eagerly.

Wilfred had opened his mouth to say that they had spent quite enough, thank you, before he realized…

Oh, bother.

"I don't have any money," he said blankly.

The smile disappeared from the jeweler's face.

"With me, I mean. With me. I'm a duke. I have a great deal of money."

"Don't you worry. You can pay me back when you get hold of some—or maybe Mrs. Ansley will do it, which will mean she'll pay for her own Christmas present, poor thing." Irene grinned, handing over a folded note to the clearly relieved stallholder.

"She gets the money from my accounts. I'll still be paying for it," Wilfred said awkwardly.

That was the trouble with being a duke. Being a gentleman at all. One simply didn't carry around money. Not more than a few coins.

Ladies did: mothers and daughters and sisters with their pin money, choosing what to spend it on.

But someone like himself? The very idea!

It would, however, have been easier to buy the jewelry from the man at his actual shop, Wilfred could not help but think. All he would have to do there is hand over his card and the whole problem would be put on his account, which Mrs. Ansley could sort out later.

Blast. She really did do a great deal for him.

"And what," Irene asked him as they meandered away from the jewelry market stall, grasping their most recent purchases, "are you going to buy for the most important person in your life?"

Wilfred's pulse skipped a beat. "I... I don't know. I'm not sure what would suit."

He was about to ask whether she would like to return to the jewelry stand, and pray to God that she did not select one of the pretty rings when he knew she wouldn't have marriage in mind when she looked at them like he did, when—

"I suppose you will have to ask Miss Fletcher what she likes, if you do not already know," Irene said primly. "I would have thought you'd know, though."

The reproof was light, but it fell like a weight upon Wilfred's shoulders.

The most important person in his life. Miss Fletcher.

Without wishing to give offense to the lady, he could not think of many people less important in his life than Miss Fletcher. No, it was Irene beside him whom he wished to shower with jewels, real jewels—there was a duchess's coronet in the safe and plenty of fantastic diamonds in his family's possession and he could pour them into her lap.

Irene giggled as she swung around, staring up at the sky. "Snow!"

Wilfred smiled. Not that Irene wanted diamonds. She was happy with a little wintry weather. She truly was the most wonderful woman he had ever met.

"The real question is," he teased, his pulse fluttering as he did so, "what are you going to get the most important person in your life?"

Irene tilted her head down to look at him. "Who?"

The pain was exquisite, but Wilfred did everything he could not to let it show. "Me, of course!"

He laughed as though it were the best joke he had ever told, and after a moment, Irene giggled and slipped her hand into his arm and muttered something that could have been, *"Of course it's you."*

Wilfred could not quite tell. His lungs were heaving so heavily with the pain of Irene not immediately choosing him as her most important person that he could barely hear anything. His ears stopped up with pain and his heart breaking.

Which is ridiculous, he tried to tell himself as Irene pulled him toward a stall that sold the most delightful bookmarks. She had a father, a mother, a brother, and three sisters. More cousins than you could shake a stick at. It was foolishness to the extreme to think that he outweighed all of them.

Still. He had hoped.

Perhaps it was the hope that was going to hurt him the most.

Chapter Nine

December 5, 1840

"**T**HE REAL QUESTION *is, what are you going to get the most important person in your life?*"
"*Who?*"
"*Me, of course!*"
"*Of course it's you.*"
"I'm just saying," came a teasing voice from the doorway, "is that enough ribbon?"

Irene did not immediately look around; she was using her thumb to hold down a complex piece of ribbon and her index fingers to hold some ribbon and her other hand—

The whole parcel fell apart, the ribbon slipping from her fingers and the brown paper opening up around the delicate china shepherdess that was, as it was turning out, almost impossible to wrap.

Irene sighed as her cousin Samuel, perennially lost looking with hair that swooped rather than laid flat, entered the room. "You are here to help, I trust?"

"Far be it from me to turn down a lady's request for assistance," said Samuel with a grin. "What are you doing here, anyway?"

It was a fair question, even Irene had to admit. It was, after all, his parents' home.

"Frank said that she would help me with the wrapping—something about a perfect engineering solution to calculating the precise amount of ribbon required," said Irene with a wry smile as her cousin dropped into the dining chair next to her. "She was helpful for about five minutes—"

"You mean, she lectured you for five minutes," interrupted Samuel with a snort.

Irene wanted to give him a stern reproof, but as that had been exactly what his sister had done, she was forced to say, "Then she suddenly stood bold upright, yelled something along the lines of 'It might just work,' and then ran out of here. Most incomprehensible."

"And yet very Frank," said Samuel blithely. "She's my sister, so I am allowed to say such things."

Well, she wasn't sure about that. Of all her cousins, Irene understood Frank the least. Two years between them, Frank was an intellectual who loved to work with her hands. Twice, she had heard her Uncle John scold her cousin Frank for getting engine oil on her gown, and the number of times her Aunt Florence had murmured to Irene's own mother that there was no possibility Frank would ever attract a suitor with ink stains on her fingertips… Well. Irene had lost count.

Frank's eldest brother, Samuel, peered at the gift Irene was attempting to wrap. "Who is that for?"

"My mother. She has started a collection, which makes me shudder to think how many we may end up with," Irene admitted, "but she likes them."

It had been the second-to-last present she'd had to buy, and it was proving a real bother to wrap.

Samuel leaned back in his chair, evidently not that interested in actually helping her. "Would it not be easier to wrap if it were in a box?"

Irene blinked. "'A box'?"

Why had I not thought of that? It was an excellent suggestion, and one she rather wished she had alighted upon herself. So why had the incredibly simple idea not occurred to her?

Because, a small voice whispered at the back of her mind, much to her surprise, *you've been too busy thinking about Wilfred.*

About his present, she corrected herself with a sudden rush of heat to her cheeks. The man was impossible to buy for. That was what came of being the second daughter to a relatively impoverished viscount, when your best friend was a duke.

"You look pensive."

Irene started. Her cousin was examining her closely, a strange sort of worry on his face.

Worry, about her? When there were people like Frank in the world?

"I'm just attempting to think of the perfect Christmas gift for Wilfred," she said with a wry smile, leaning back herself and giving up on wrapping the shepherdess until a suitable box could be procured. "The man is impossible!"

"'Impossible'? I always thought old Aynor was a considerably easygoing sort of chap," Samuel said mildly. "What's he done now?"

"Oh, nothing, except be completely inscrutable," Irene said vaguely, trying not to allow her mind to meander back to that walk in the park.

That walk he had not initially taken with her, but with that woman. Whoever she was. *Miss Fletcher.*

"It's just—he's a duke," she continued with a sigh. "The man has more than enough money to merely buy whatever he wants whenever he wants it. There's nothing he has ever denied himself and so thinking of a gift he needs—"

"Isn't the point of Christmas," her cousin interrupted, "that a gift is something you want, not something you need?"

There was absolutely no reason why her pulse would skip a beat at that precise moment. "But I don't know *what* he wants."

Oh, she knew his hopes and dreams. Wilfred wanted, Irene was fully aware, to found a school one day. He had been mightily impressed with her cousin Thomas's efforts with the St. Thomas's Orphanage and wondered if his own focus could be a school for the poor.

"I want the name Aynor to mean something," he had once said to

her earnestly. *"Not just in my lifetime, but beyond."*

But something small, something she could actually afford...and it had been his birthday but six weeks ago. It had been challenging enough to think of a birthday gift.

Irene's eyes sharpened. "Wait a minute. You're going to be the Marquess of Aylesbury one day."

It was perhaps not the most politic thing to say.

"What, you mean when my father..." Samuel started, a stiff terseness in his voice.

"No, no, I meant—well, Uncle William gave up his title of Duke of Cothrom for Cousin Thomas, did he not?" Irene said hastily, discomfort twisting her stomach. "It is perfectly possible that your father might do the same for you."

The look of horror on her cousin's face was quite unmatched. One would have thought his mouth had been pried open, his jaw unable to close. "You don't think so?"

"So you would be a nobleman with a fancy title. What do *you* want for Christmas?" Irene prompted, hoping to goodness he would give her a good idea.

Samuel wiggled his eyebrows. "Are you saying you haven't got me a present yet? Is this all a subterfuge? You've already purchased old Aynor a present, haven't you?"

"You know perfectly well that we outlawed cousin presents five years ago. It was getting ridiculous with so many of us," Irene said shortly, her temper rising. "No, it's—look, Wilfred is one of the kindest, most joyful people I know. He's patient, he's always on time—"

"Something my mother is still attempting to learn," interjected Samuel with a snort.

"He really is the most...the most impressive..." Irene swallowed.

She had never intended to begin a monologue of how amazing Wilfred was, and unfortunately, it appeared that her cousin was going to tease her about it.

Of course he was.

"You seem enamored of him," Samuel said lightly.

"I am not *enamored*."

"No shame if you are. He would be an excellent match for you," her cousin continued.

Irene almost laughed. An excellent match—for her? "You mean because I am a mere viscount's daughter with no title?"

"Because he is a good man," Samuel said steadily, a slight crease in his brow as he beheld her. "Can you think of one better?"

Certainly, she could. In a moment, the name would come to her and she could declaim it and that would show her cousin just how ridiculous he was being.

Excellent match, indeed!

The trouble was, now that Irene came to think about it, there was not a single name that came to mind. There were few people as tender as Wilfred, as charming as him, as kind as him. She could think of no one who was so utterly selfless in his manner of moving through the world, and he was... Well. He was not bad-looking.

Irene determinedly did not think about that kiss. *That mistake.* That error in judgment that both of them had somehow slipped into.

It would never be repeated, of course. Even if she—no, it was ridiculous.

"You do, don't you?"

Her cousin's words were more incredulous than teasing, and when Irene looked up, it was to see Samuel's wide-eyed face in slack shock.

"Do what?" Irene asked vaguely, still trying to get the memory of Wilfred's hands on her arms as he'd kissed her most thoroughly from her mind.

Samuel exhaled slowly, not taking his eyes away. "You love him."

"No, I—don't be ridiculous. I don't love—"

"Hallo there. Your mother said you'd be here," said Wilfred

happily as he stepped into the Aylesbury dining room.

Irene hastily rose to her feet in shock, her body propelling her in a direction that was utterly nonsensical. A pair of scissors, six feet of ribbon, and a flurry of brown paper cascaded from her skirts onto the floor.

"Careful, Reeny!"

Both Wilfred and her cousin shouted the two words as though that could change the fact that the scissors had stuck blade down into the carpet a good two inches away from her foot.

Irene exhaled shakily. "Whoops."

"Honestly, sometimes you're as bad as Frank," Samuel was muttering, but Wilfred had leaped forward and was already pulling the scissors out of the carpet.

"You're not injured?" Wilfred asked quietly, his gaze surveying her face.

"I-I… No, I am quite well," Irene managed.

That was, her pulse was thumping wildly and her nerves were taut from the shock of what could have been and Wilfred was holding on to her arms in the precise manner as when he had kissed her and the physical reminder was melting something strange in the pit of her stomach and her head was spinning—

"I think that's quite enough Christmas present wrapping for you," her cousin said firmly. "You can leave all that paraphernalia here, and I'll get the butler to find a suitable box for your shepherdess."

"I hope that's not my present." Wilfred offered a cordial smile, but his expression became serious again as he looked down at Irene. "You are quite certain you are unharmed?"

Irene barely knew what to say, what to think. The almost accident with the scissors was nothing compared to the frazzle she felt within her. There was something…something wrong, something off-balance about the way her heart was beating as she stood still held by Wilfred's warm fingers. Goodness, she could feel the heat of his palms through her gown as though he were touching her bare skin.

She swallowed. "I... I think it is time for me to go home."

"Excellent idea," Wilfred said determinedly. "I shall escort you."

"Oh, no, she's *my* cousin. The responsibility to chaperone belongs with family," said Samuel, though Irene could not help but notice it was weakly stated.

"Nonsense. I'm going in that direction, anyway, and you can trust her with me," Wilfred said confidently. "It isn't as if her parents haven't let her be alone with me many times before."

Something like a tingling thrill passed up Irene's spine, though she had absolutely no idea why. She had never heard Wilfred sound like that. So... So self-assured. So confident.

Samuel was shrugging as he started to leave the dining room. "I'll not tell anyone. I have a distant relative to visit. A great-aunt who has come to Bath for the waters."

Irene's curiosity picked up. "Great-aunt? Do we share her?"

"Yes, one of our fathers' distant relations, I'm told. I thought I'd look in on her. She's bound to a chair and hasn't been able to see much of Bath," Samuel said with a small smile. "I thought she would appreciate the visit."

"You're a good man," Irene said cheerfully, but she was halted from saying anymore by the soft murmur in her ear.

"Are you ready to go?"

There was absolutely no reason why her whole body should quiver as though warm air had been gently blown over her naked skin—and yet that was precisely what Irene experienced as Wilfred spoke.

It was ridiculous. Ridiculous!

"I... I... Yes," Irene managed, trying to smile. "Yes, I am ready."

It was with a rather vague sense of aloofness, like she were floating, that she walked out of the dining room and along the resplendent corridor—far more exquisitely decorated than her home, with luxurious wallpaper and gold-gilt frames around Old Master paintings—to the hallway.

And Wilfred was beside her.

Strange. He was not touching her, but Irene was somehow far more aware of his presence than usual. Was the man using a different cologne?

Irene inhaled deeply. No, it was the same scent as always. Something uniquely Wilfred, combined with sandalwood and a sharp hint of jasmine he had started wearing when he had gone up to university. It was so Wilfred that on the rare occasion that Irene walked past a jasmine plant, all she could think about was him.

That had not changed. So what had?

"Here, let me," Wilfred said with a clearing of his throat, taking her pelisse from a footman at the door as she finished putting on her hat and gloves.

It was ridiculous. The man had helped her into a pelisse countless times over the years. In truth, Irene wondered whether Wilfred had helped her on with a pelisse more than her own brother. More than Dempster.

So her body should not have responded the way it did as Wilfred helped guide her arm through a sleeve, slowly lifting up the heavy fabric to rest on her shoulders, his fingers smoothing down the fabric as though he were stroking her.

Irene found her eyelashes closing, just for a moment, as she enjoyed his touch.

Then her eyes snapped open. *Enjoyed his touch? Wilfred's?*

"You are fortunate the weather has held, though I think it may snow again before the day is out," Wilfred said conversationally, as though absolutely nothing had happened between them.

Irene blinked as they stepped out into the cold afternoon air. And of course, nothing had happened between them. Nothing at all.

"Yes. Snow," was all she managed.

Wilfred took her hand without asking and placed it on his arm as they started off down the street. "Are you certain you are quite well? You seem to have taken a bit of a turn there."

Irene swallowed and attempted to calibrate her body back to equilibrium.

Nothing happened. Oh, she had almost speared her own foot with a pair of scissors, but Dr. Walsingham was in Bath or there would be someone else that her family could call on, should the worst have happened.

The point was that it had not, and so there was absolutely no reason to feel slightly giddy, slightly breathless, somewhat as though her legs weren't working properly.

Irene glanced up at the gentleman beside her and the pit of her stomach did that strange melting thing again.

It couldn't have been Wilfred, could it?

How was he different?

"Oh—careful now!"

Irene almost cried out as the sudden lack of Wilfred twisted within her. He had dropped her hand without a second glance and rushed away, and for one horrible moment, she thought it was because he had seen his precious Miss Fletcher and realized he would far rather be with her.

But that was not what had happened at all.

"This street can be particularly troublesome," Wilfred was saying genially to a little, old lady who was standing on the edge of the pavement. "Here, please—allow me."

Irene watched, a small smile growing into a larger one as Wilfred carefully looked right, then left, then right again, waiting for a gap in the rumbling carriages and speedily moving horses. Only when there was a significant gap did he take the old woman's arm and slowly help her across the road.

He was just so…so good.

That was perhaps what Irene had been trying to explain to her cousin Samuel a few minutes ago. There were many words a person could use to describe Wilfred. Charming, jovial, rapturous. Perhaps even handsome, though Irene had certainly never dwelled on that fact.

But everyone who knew the man could agree that Wilfred was very, very good.

Wilfred said something to the old woman, both of them now on the other side of the road, and the woman beamed and patted his arm. She watched as he bowed to her most politely—far more politely than a duke really needed to—and waited patiently for there to be a big enough gap in the traffic for him to jog over the road back to her.

And she watched, knowing that something most strange was happening to her as she did so.

"Right, where were we?" Wilfred said cheerfully, offering his arm.

Irene took it and wondered how on earth she had not noticed his many qualities before. Oh, she *had*. She knew Wilfred better than she knew anyone. But she had never realized just how unusual he was. Charming yet respectful. Kind yet direct if needed. Just as polite to strangers as he would have been to the Queen of England.

"Irene?"

Irene started. They were walking again along the pavement. When had they started walking? "I beg your pardon?"

"I asked whether you had purchased all your Christmas presents yet," repeated Wilfred with a grin as they turned a corner. "Although I suppose you have time, if there are still a few you need to choose."

"I... Yes. No. Almost all of them," Irene heard herself saying.

Was she—was she blushing?

She was! And she was blushing because as they had turned a corner, the most outlandish thing had occurred.

Irene had looked up at him, his side profile as they walked along together, and realized—

Wilfred Matthew Kirk Chesterham Zouch, Duke of Aynor, is an incredibly attractive man.

Not just attractive: handsome. There were plenty of charismatic people—Irene knew a few—who were not traditionally good-looking but had sufficient charm to attract notice.

But Wilfred was not one of those gentlemen. He had the Grecian profile of a statue, all chiseled and fine eyes, a sparkle in his expression and a strength of character in his gaze that meant he was a physical specimen of intense beauty.

And his figure... Irene wondered how she had so rarely never noticed it before. Tall, broad, his physique would have been imposing in another man, but Wilfred was impressive in a different way. Impressively kind. And with very nice hands in his kid gloves.

Irene almost tripped over her own feet. *'Very nice hands'?* Where had that thought come from?

"You are very quiet," Wilfred said, dropping his voice so that only she could hear him. "Is everything quite well?"

"Yes, yes, all fine," Irene said hastily, trying not to look at his hands, gloved as they were.

How on earth had she not noticed, for years, that her best friend was one of the most handsome men in Society?

Why had no one told her?

"It's just, you look a tad hot—"

"Quite well, as I said," she said firmly, cheeks blazing.

"Good. It's important to me," Wilfred said quietly, his smile lilting in a way that made Irene's pulse skip a beat. "That you are well."

Because we are best friends, Irene reminded herself as she resisted the urge to fan herself or unbutton her pelisse. They had been best friends for... Well, forever.

The trouble was, she was starting to notice things these last few weeks that she had never noticed before. Things she would have expected to notice. Like how safe and warm she felt when her arm was entwined with his own. Like how her spirits always rose when Wilfred walked into a room. Like just how envious she was of that Miss Fletcher, standing in her place by Wilfred's side—

'Her' place?

"Here you are," came Wilfred's voice from a long way away. "Home. Your home, that is."

Irene blinked up at the townhouse as though it had somehow erupted from the ground. "Yes. Home."

And the thought of stepping inside, of stepping away from this man, was so suddenly repellent that Irene instinctively held tighter to Wilfred's arm.

"Reeny?"

"Don't call me that," Irene said vaguely. "Wilfred, what are you doing this afternoon?"

"This afternoon?" Her best friend frowned at the question. "Escorting you home, currently."

"I mean, what are your plans for after this?" she persisted.

This is a foolish idea. She did not even know why she was suggesting it. She did not know what to do with herself, her wild thoughts, her inappropriate appreciation of the man's physique.

Of Wilfred's body! It was ridiculous!

Wilfred took a deep breath, his broad chest expanding, and Irene's heart tightened. "I have no plans."

"Then… Then why don't we keep walking?" Irene suggested, her mouth inexplicably dry.

"Walking?"

"Walking."

Clearly, her suggestion was not a good one. "What, just…around Bath?"

"Around Bath," Irene said as strongly as she could manage.

Articulating why, precisely, this was important to her was rather a challenge, but she would try it. Because she wanted to. Because she wanted him. His company.

"Alone?"

"Well, we've already started a walk alone, haven't we? I'm not about to step inside and inform my mother of that fact to request a chaperone now."

Wilfred, still evidently muddled, didn't have a witty retort for that. "But walk some more? For what purpose?"

Irene swallowed. "For the purpose of walking around. To-gether."

His brow had unfurrowed at her last word and a smile beamed out from Wilfred's face that warmed Irene so directly, she could leave her pelisse at home and walk around in naught but her gown—or less. "Together. Yes, let's... Let's walk around."

And I am not going to examine this too closely, Irene thought privately as they turned from her front door and started a meandering walk along the Bath streets. Because if she did, she was not sure that she was going to like what she found.

As long as she was with him. Wilfred. Then nothing else mattered.

Chapter Ten

December 11, 1840

"TOO MANY CANDLES? Or not enough?" Wilfred asked, biting his lip.

He very carefully did not notice his housekeeper's eyeroll.

"It all looks magnificent, Master Wilfred," said Mrs. Ansley, once again refusing to use his formal address. "As you well know."

It did look marvelous, though Wilfred would only admit to as much in the privacy of his own mind. It sounded arrogant to even think such a thing—but then, he had put a great deal of work into making this evening perfect.

The ballroom in the Aynor Bath townhouse had not been used for... Well, now that Wilfred came to think about it, he could not recall the last time. His parents had been alive; it had been that long ago. He had crept down the stairs, holding his breath as though that would prevent anyone from spotting him, and had peered around the door into the splendid ballroom filled with swishing figures and laughter.

He had never seen the point of holding a ball himself.

Until now. The ballroom was lit with over a thousand candles, festoons of flowers hanging along the walls, and rose petals scattered on the edges of the room to add their perfume to the air. A great amount of polishing the gold-gilt panels on the walls had occurred over the last few days, and Wilfred had seen more than one footman looking a little harassed the last hour or so.

But somehow, it had all come together perfectly, and about

ten minutes before his invitations had summoned his guests.

Wilfred exhaled slowly as he took in the sight. "Yes, it looks good."

"'Good'! I don't think I'll be able to sleep without seeing polish in my dreams," muttered Mrs. Ansley as she ordered a gaggle of maids to hastily re-pin a festoon of flowers. "And the footmen have been ordered to bring up food at—"

"I am sure you have the entire thing under control, Mrs. Ansley," Wilfred said hastily as something caught his eye from the hallway, just visible from the other side of the room. "You will excuse me."

His housekeeper continued to mutter, but Wilfred could not hear her as he strode rapidly across the room. It wasn't possible— he had surely been allowing himself to think too much of Irene Chance, for he had thought he had seen her.

"Wilfred!" said Irene happily. "You don't mind that we are early, do you?"

"Reeny insisted—"

"Papa!"

"—insisted we were here first, in case there was any assistance we could render," said the Viscount Pernrith with a wry smile, clapping Wilfred on the back and shaking his hand. "You had better be careful, Aynor. She'll install herself as the mistress of your house if you're not keeping an eye on her!"

The Viscount Pernrith, the Viscountess Pernrith, the Right Honorable Mr. Michael Chance, and the Right Honorable Miss Theodora Chance all laughed.

Wilfred did not.

Neither did the Right Honorable Miss Irene Chance. In fact, now that Wilfred came to look at her more closely, he could see that she was…flushing?

Flushing? When did Irene ever get embarrassed?

"Don't be silly, Papa," Irene was muttering. "Wilfred's never hosted a ball before. I just thought…you know."

Precisely what Wilfred was supposed to know, he was not

sure. He had just noticed what Irene was wearing and breath itself was now no longer an option.

She looked…

There were no words. Wilfred's gaze raked over the most incredible silk gown, one that dipped lower than he had seen on her before—he had always paid careful attention to such things— yet it was still respectable, a hint of lace just barely covering the décolletage skimming above her gown. The hemline was long, giving her a fashionable train Wilfred would have paid more attention to if the gown weren't pinching in at Irene's waist in a way that made his fingers itch to hold her.

And that wasn't the only part of him springing to attention.

Irene had eschewed gaudy adornments, wearing a gold neck-lace with a single pendant, one perhaps of amethyst, accompanied not by matching earbobs or a matching bracelet but with amethysts dotted about her elegant updo, a small curl descending down the nape of her neck in a way that made Wilfred's mouth dry.

She was, in summary, the most beautiful version of herself that he had ever seen. And she looked impressive on a normal day.

"Aynor?"

Wilfred flinched as someone—Michael, he now saw—clicked his fingers right before his host's nose. "Wh-What?"

"I said, I hope you have some good claret in," Irene's brother repeated, his face a slight frown. "I do hope you're not sickening for anything."

For your sister, Wilfred could have said, but he was prevented from such madness by the viscountess.

"You should be delighted with your preparations, Your Grace," said Irene's mother with a smile. "I am duly impressed."

The fact that he wanted to impress her, he wanted to impress them all, was not lost on Wilfred, but it was the use of such a formal greeting that made his stomach twist. "Aynor, please. We are like family."

"We are not like family," the Viscountess Pernrith said, stepping toward him.

Wilfred could not help his stomach dropping as Michael wandered farther into the ballroom with his sister Theodora on his arm. Well, it had been very forward of him. Just because he thought of the Chances as his family, that did not mean—

"We *are* family," the Viscountess Pernrith said quietly, kissing him on the cheek. "My favorite son."

"*Mother!*"

"Well," said the older woman with a shrug, ignoring the call of Michael from across the ballroom. "That one is such a worry to us, you know, but you? Wilfred, you have never given me a hint of concern in all your days. Right. I had better find out where my husband has gone…"

She floated away, her gracefulness never changing with age, and Wilfred was left alone with Irene.

Well. As alone as one could be, in a ballroom.

"No Gwen?" he said aloud, trying not to think about just how beautiful the woman before him was.

"No, my parents said that until I—I mean, until I or Teddy…" She cleared her throat. "The plan is still for her to perhaps debut in the upcoming Season, but only if… If one more of her sisters…" Her words faded away into an embarrassed silence.

Which was odd. In fact, his best friend had been acting most oddly the last week or so, Wilfred realized. He had not put it all together until this moment, but…yes, most oddly. She had been looking at him…oddly. Lost her train of thought far more often. She had even started asking him for more walks, sans chaperones, as was Irene's wont, though she would say very little unless prompted on such excursions, and Wilfred could not understand for the life of him why she wished to talk with him along the dirty, busy Bath streets, where anyone might see them together unsupervised.

Most strange.

"If one more of her sisters marries. Until I marry. Or Teddy marries," Irene said in a rush. "It doesn't do to have too many daughters out in Society."

And suddenly, it was Wilfred's face that was flushed, Wilfred who found words difficult to grasp. "Oh…yes. Right. I see."

He did see. Or at least, he thought he did.

Was this Irene's delicate way of informing him that she would now be looking out for a suitor? Had her parents someone in mind? She *was* many years past her official debut. To be honest, he was sure only his frequent presence at her side had deterred other gentlemen from pursuing her until now. And because of that, because he had kept them all at bay—which he could only be glad for, really—she was nearing the age one might tentatively deem her a spinster. Not that he could ever think of her in a negative light.

To be honest, part of him had secretly hoped she'd embrace spinsterhood, if she were not to be his own bride. But with her beauty? Her charm? Her elegance? That was a fantasy. Wilfred had always known their friendship would outlast any husband who came to claim his best friend, but that the friendship itself would have to change. It would be forced to, unable to survive the shifting loyalties Irene would be faced with.

But the idea that it could happen soon—that she would be taken from him…

Which is ridiculous, Wilfred tried to tell himself. She had already spent far too many Seasons without a match. And he had no ownership over Irene. Even her future husband never would; Wilfred knew her well enough to be secure of that.

"It… It all looks wonderful," Irene said after she'd inhaled deeply.

Wilfred tried not to say, *It's all for you.* It was, but she didn't have to know that. "Thank you. I… I hope you enjoy it."

"I am sure I will," said his best friend quietly.

They stood there for a moment in silence, a strange sort of awkwardness overwhelming Wilfred mostly due to its novelty than the awkwardness itself, and then suddenly both of them spoke at the same time.

"I need to tell you—"

"I have to ask—"

"Master Wilfred!"

Wilfred blinked. *What?*

"Master Wilfred, your first guests are here!" called out Mrs. Ansley as she walked over to him, beckoning with her hand for him to come into the hallway. "Begging your presence, Miss Chance," she added with a faint blush to her cheeks.

He had never told his housekeeper how he felt about Irene. Perhaps, after his conversation with Michael, he had never needed to.

Wilfred turned to Irene. "You will have to excuse me."

"Oh, yes, of course, of course," said Irene hastily, waving him off in much the same way his housekeeper was doing. "You have your duty, as host. I suppose I shall see you—"

Precisely when he would see her, Wilfred never found out. Mrs. Ansley had grabbed his arm and was now bodily heaving him toward the front door.

"Master Wilfred, your guests!"

And there were quite a lot of them. Wilfred had not been sure just how many people one invited to a ball. One didn't want the place to look empty, after all, and there were bound to be several people who were unable to attend. Better to invite, say, fifty additional people on the assumption that they simply would not turn up.

Everyone, it appeared, had turned up.

"How lovely to see you, Your Graces. My lady—ah, my lord, you are not in London, I see," said Wilfred helplessly as scores of people poured past him through the hallway into the ballroom, each officially announced by his butler before they spoke to their host. "Lady Romeril—"

"You have never hosted a ball before," the older woman said accusingly, jabbing a finger so directly into Wilfred's chest that he rather thought it would leave a bruise.

He smiled weakly. "No! No, I have not, and may I say what an honor it is to have you gracing it with your presence."

"You may, indeed," said the woman curtly, eying him as though he were an interesting diamond she was considering purchasing. "No particular reason that you decided to host a ball all of a sudden, I suppose?"

It was with great fortitude of mind and strength of character that Wilfred only looked over at Irene, laughing hard at something her brother had just said, and did not declare his undying affection for the woman at the top of his lungs.

Wilfred cleared his throat. "No."

"Hmmmm." Lady Romeril did not appear convinced, though in fairness, he could not blame her. "Well. I expect I shall lead the dancing."

Well. No.

That was what Wilfred wanted to say. With no mother, no sister, no lady relative of any kind, he had hoped he could lead Irene out at the beginning of the dancing. Or at the very least, her mother. Though to be honest, he knew the honor would have to go to the lady who ranked highest in attendance, and that was unlikely to be the viscountess.

He wasn't sure *how* Lady Romeril ranked, exactly. If Irene's aunt or cousin-in-law attended—though the latter was unlikely, as she had recently given birth—there would be a dowager duchess and a duchess both, and they probably were higher in rank than the mysterious doyenne. Or was it the Duchess of Axwick who ought to have enjoyed this honor? He'd have to ask his housekeeper, as she was sure to have studied which estate was older.

Still, he was hardly going to say *no* to a woman whose power and influence over the entirety of Society meant that a young lady's prospects could be cast to the wind and a gentleman's honor could be irrevocably lost.

Wilfred smiled weakly. "It would be my honor, Lady Romeril."

She eyed him beadily for a moment as he attempted not to

show his disappointment. Then she cackled and poked him in the chest again.

"You think I would deprive you of one of these young snippets? You are very gracious, Aynor, if I may call you that. Just like your father."

The woman had swept into the ballroom before Wilfred could say anything, which was a great relief. What was one supposed to say to that?

"Got something in your eye, Wilfred?"

Wilfred blinked hastily. "No."

Irene peered at him. Precisely where she had come from, he had no idea. "I thought we could meander into the ballroom and look at people."

"Sorry, I have to stay here and welcome everyone," he declined with true regret. There was nothing he enjoyed more than observing people with Irene—though in fairness, he probably should not do such a thing at his own ball. "Being the host, you know. I have to ensure I welcome everyone."

And so he did: suit after suit, gown after gown, Wilfred welcomed people. And then he spoke with Mrs. Ansley to ensure that there was sufficient claret, considering that the entire Chance clan appeared to have arrived, even the new mother, the Duchess of Cothrom. And then he had to assist a footman who had been cornered by Lady Romeril, and then he had to greet the latecomers, and then he had to instruct the musicians, and then there was that opening dance with Lady Romeril, though that was the only dance he managed to undertake himself—

"Are you ever going to come and talk to me?" asked a voice that was more than a little piqued.

Wilfred would have smiled if he weren't feeling so harassed. *Balls!* Who would ever throw one once they'd experienced this chaos just once? "I'm sorry, Reeny."

To his utter astonishment, the expected refrain of *'Don't call me that'* did not appear.

Irene frowned. "I thought—well, I thought we would be able

to spend more time together."

Wilfred's stomach twisted as he attempted to take in this rather odd pronouncement.

Irene. Irene wanted to spend more time with him?

It was a foolish thing to find joy in. They were best friends, after all; they spent a great deal of time together.

But not like this. Not with her dressed up to the nines, looking so ready to be plucked...

Wilfred swallowed. "I just—it's my ball. I have to make sure everyone is having a good time."

"And are you having a good time?" Irene asked, eyebrow raised.

He smiled weakly. "Not especially, no."

The answering twinkle in his eye warmed him quicker than any amount of claret. "Well, then, we had better change that. Come on."

The way she grabbed his hand and pulled him forward was so familiar, Wilfred could not help but exhale with happiness, all tension in his shoulders melting away. Irene had done the same thing when he had first bumped his knee, dragging him to her mother to be comforted. She had done the same thing when they had accidentally bought a cow at Borough Market, pulling him toward the man and confidently saying that the Duke of Aynor's man would be around to pay for it later. She had done the same thing when they had last shared a picnic at Stanphrey Lacey, pulling him away from her family so they could ramble slowly through Stanphrey Lacey Forest, talking occasionally but otherwise just...just being together.

A lump formed in Wilfred's throat as she halted before the musicians and started whispering to them urgently.

And that would all end when Irene found a husband. When she went off to pull some other man forward into her next adventure.

"There," Irene said firmly. "Come on."

The musicians had started playing one of Wilfred's favorite

waltzes, and before he knew precisely what was happening, she had placed one of his hands on her waist and taken the other one in her hand.

Wilfred's throat bobbed. *Her waist.* The waist he had wanted to touch the instant she had arrived at the ball, his ball, and now he was doing so and it was glorious. She was soft and he wanted to put both hands on her waist and pull her tight against him.

Irene stepped into his embrace. "Dance with me, Wilfred."

What could he do but obey?

It was strange. From the instant that he moved and Irene moved with him, following his every step, almost anticipating his movement but waiting respectfully for him to act first, Wilfred could feel the stress of the evening melting away.

Sufficient claret? What does it matter?

"There," Irene murmured in a low voice.

Wilfred jerked his head around. "What—where?"

"No, I meant you," she said with a wry smile. "I can see you visibly relaxing. Is that better?"

It was on the tip of his tongue to say that he was better because he was with her, with her in a way he so rarely was. But he managed to stop himself as they swirled around the ballroom, her parents joining them as Michael flirted on the sidelines with a pretty woman Wilfred did not recognize.

"Much better," he conceded.

Irene's smile was kind, and knowing, and the only one he ever wanted to see. "You were so busy trying to ensure that everyone else was having a wonderful time that you had completely forgotten someone."

Wilfred's frame tightened. Dear Lord, he had? But Lady Romeril was quite happy, and the Duchess of Axwick—

"You, you dolt," Irene said conversationally, as though it were perfectly normal to insult a duke at his own ball in such a manner. "And you're relaxing now, aren't you?"

Yes, he wanted to say. *Except for a certain part of me that has only become more stiff the longer I hold you like this.*

"Yes," he said aloud.

Irene nodded with a satisfied expression. "There. I always know what's good for you."

Wilfred swallowed the instinct to say, *Yes, yes, you do, and it's you. It was always you.*

"Still, uh…" Irene's eyes glanced around the sea of faces. "You do seem to have forgotten someone else, haven't you?"

Forgotten? Him? He hadn't forgotten a thing.

"Miss Fletcher?" specified Irene with a raised eyebrow. "How could she possibly not have received an invitation?"

"Miss-Miss Fletcher?" For a moment, Wilfred almost choked as he led Irene through a turn. He wondered what his house-keeper would have thought if he had invited a woman of Miss Fletcher's standing. Still, he knew it was only right for Irene to expect her here, with how he had teased a relationship between them. "She was otherwise occupied this evening." At least, he assumed so.

"Hmm?" said Irene, her feet flowing naturally in the proper steps. "I find that rather odd, Wilfred. I would have thought perhaps you'd gone to all this trouble for her."

It was for you. Only ever for you.

He should tell her. This whole nonsense had gone on long enough, Wilfred knew. Yes, he had attempted to declare his love before—twice—and he had been a coward at the very last moment and held back the truth: that the kiss had meant everything to him and he did not wish for it to be their last.

Unfortunately, even if he had wished to say such an inflammatory thing to his best friend, whom he had kissed and from whom he had received nothing but a horrified expression in return, he would have been interrupted.

By Lady Romeril.

"Ah, Your Grace," she said stiffly as she was gently steered across by a flushing and most irritated Michael. "I see that you and the young Miss Irene are dancing together. A prelude to nuptials, I presume?"

"You presume incorrectly, madam!"

Irene's words had rung out across the ballroom so loudly that some of the dancers had actually ceased their waltz to look over at the scarlet-faced woman.

Wilfred dropped his best friend's hands.

"Quite incorrect, in fact, and I would ask you to keep such suppositions of inaccuracy to yourself!" hissed Irene, evidently trying to keep her voice down but not doing the best job.

"Irene," Wilfred murmured.

Precisely what he would have said after that, he was not sure. Once again, he was saved from his own stupidity by Lady Romeril's booming voice.

"Well, I declare, I meant no insult, Miss Irene. Though I suppose you are Miss Chance now, after your sister's impressive marriage," the older woman said with a faint smile. Michael, his steps rather stilted with an older lady for a partner, looked as if he wanted to disappear into the ground. "And you see no future for yourself in such a happy state with this gentleman?"

"I-I—preposterous," Irene spluttered, her face now a boiling red that Wilfred rather thought he could toast bread on, as they had done when they'd been children. "Utterly ridiculous!"

"Child, do you really think no one has spotted the two of you about town? With no chaperone in sight? It'd hardly be entirely proper for a betrothed couple, though it might be more forgivable, yet you tell me again and again, that is not the case between you."

Irene swallowed visibly. "Come on, Wilfred."

Perhaps undermining herself by grabbing his hand and pulling him away, Wilfred could do nothing but permit himself to be so dragged. Across the ballroom. *His* ballroom. Filled with people.

"Well!" Irene exhaled as she closed—or more accurately, slammed—the ballroom door behind her. "What do you think of that?!"

The hallway was empty, thank goodness, and Wilfred could

do nothing but stare at the beautiful woman before him who was still holding his hand. His pulse was pumping wildly and there was a frisson of heat pouring down his spine.

"'Think of that'?" he repeated, his mind attempting to catch up.

"That—that, what Lady Romeril said!" Irene exploded, thrusting her free hand toward the ballroom door in a wild gesticulation. "Can you believe what she said! That you and I—that we… And that we ought not to be seen in public together without a busybody watching over me. Can you think of anything more ridiculous?!"

Wilfred did not allow the pain searing through him to show on his face. At least, he did not think so. "'More ridiculous'?"

Irene looked up at him, her attention entirely fixed on him. "Do you think that there is anything more impossible?"

The moment hung in the air, a tinkling, sparkling moment that could direct Wilfred's path in one of two directions.

He knew he should tell the truth. Surely, this was the most important moment of his life. Surely, this was when he should spill out the honest thoughts in his mind; that it would be the greatest honor to have her by his side for the rest of their lives, not just as friends, but as lovers.

As my wife.

But as Wilfred looked down into Irene's clear-as-crystal eyes, he could see fear there. Fear, perhaps, that what they had would change. Fear that the rapport and comfort they enjoyed would be destroyed once he made it irrevocably clear that he wanted more. Fear that the friendship they had would be lost.

And he would not do that to her. Love her as he did, Wilfred would not allow those fears to become reality.

Much as it pained him, Wilfred cracked a smile and nodded. "Yes, yes, most ridiculous."

Chance would be a fine thing, indeed.

Chapter Eleven

December 14, 1840

*I*T IS MOST *inconvenient,* Irene could not help but think as she turned her fork over and over her salmon, to discover too late that one was devastatingly in love with one's best friend, and at the same time to discover that he did not reciprocate those feelings.

Dashed inconvenient.

"Reeny?"

"Don't call me that," she muttered, shooting her brother a glare.

He looked right back, evidently not bothered. "Then maybe you should answer to 'Irene.'"

Irene looked up. The entire dining table—her parents, Gwen and Michael, the Marquess and Marchioness of Dalton, who were their hosts for the evening; the Quintrells; the Duke and Duchess of Axwick; and Wilfred—were staring.

She smiled weakly. "I'm sorry, I was... I was lost in my thoughts. What was the question?"

Her mother sighed and her father shook her head, which in many circumstances would have made her feel most unpleasant. As it was, her stomach had been churning greatly already and Irene was not sure whether she could feel any more nauseous.

"Pass the lemonade, Michael," Gwen said in the silence.

"Get it yourself. You can reach," came the response.

The two siblings began to bicker, as they so often did, and Irene slumped back against her chair and smiled weakly at the gentleman seated opposite her.

Wilfred.

"Do you think that there is anything more impossible?"

That was what she had said. There, in his own hallway, when she had given him the perfect opportunity to tell her that he loved her. She had given him the best opening: ensured they were alone, tried to show with her eyes that she wanted to be wrong, that she wanted him to throw caution to the wind…

And he had made it most clear that he would never love her.

Which is unfortunate, Irene thought darkly as she poked at her salmon. Because in that moment she had come to a fairly calamitous realization.

That she was completely in love with him.

Wilfred. There he was, seated beside her mother and regaling her with a charming story making all around him laugh.

Wilfred, who, whenever he arrived unexpectedly at their house, was immediately welcomed in as family, his protests that he could not stay for luncheon always soundly ignored.

Wilfred, who smiled and winked across the table when her father tried to explain to Gwen, the youngest of the Pernrith Chances, that she could not attend Lady Dalton's card party next week because Irene and Teddy were going and it simply wasn't done to have so many daughters out in public.

Wilfred. Her Wilfred.

And she was in love with him.

"—such a pleasant ball," Lady Dalton was saying to Wilfred with a glance toward her daughter. "You simply must host another one."

"—heard from my man in the country that the frosts there are simply criminal—" the Duke of Axwick was saying in a gruff voice, his gray hair matched by the grayness of his beard. "Absolutely shocking for this year's crops—"

"—had to send her to that finishing school in France," one of the Quintrells was muttering to Lord Dalton. "A very impressive place, they tell me. I shall have to hope—"

"You are very quiet," came his low, warm voice from the other side of the table.

Irene started, hating how her body responded to him. She looked up into his handsome face, the handsome face she had somehow not noticed for years on end, and tried to smile.

How precisely did one smile at one's best friend whom one now realized one was in love with but in the very same instant that the person had realized it, they had been politely and kindly rejected?

"Yes," she said aloud, unable to say anything more.

Wilfred nodded slowly as the chatter around the dining table raged. "Yes."

Why, Irene thought furiously as she forced herself to spear a piece of salmon and shove it in her mouth, *did I have to fall in love with someone who is so utterly out of reach?*

Not just because he was Wilfred, although that did not help. Best friends did not become husband and wife. It simply was not done. Then again, best friends were not very often man and woman. Not in Society, at the very least.

But really, the cause had to be because he already had fallen in love with someone else. This Miss Fletcher, though he spoke of her infrequently, was clearly the woman he was in love with—a woman she had only met once and who clearly did not appreciate Wilfred like she did.

As he ought to be.

"—ladies should go through," came a voice from a long way away.

Irene blinked. *'Go through'?* But surely not. She had not even finished her...

She looked down. The salmon was gone, though when it had departed, she was not sure. There was a splendid slice of some sort of jelly in a bowl before her, entirely untouched.

Oh. Right.

In a sweeping rustle of silks and muslins, the ladies departed from the room. Irene was tempted to ask Wilfred to join her—

after all, the last thing she wanted to do was titter about tittle tattle with her mother and her friends, Teddy was playing on the pianoforte, and Gwen was looking so irate, she was hardly going to be in the mood to talk.

Wilfred's eyes followed her around the room. It was all Irene could do not to trip over her own feet.

It is most inconvenient, she could not help but think as she sat demurely with her hands folded in her lap as her mother chattered elegantly on. She had never noticed Wilfred like... Well, like *that.*

As a man.

And now that she had realized that his hand on her waist in the waltz had made her want to press her lips against his and take all her clothes off, she had to simultaneously discover that he had absolutely no interest in her whatsoever.

It was dashed irritating.

And painful. Irene did not like to admit it, even to herself, but she had cried herself to sleep the previous night. Wilfred was lost to her, lost when she had not even realized she wanted him so badly. She ached for his company, his touch in a way that she had never thought possible.

But the specter of Miss Fletcher hung over her hopes and dreams, destroying them entirely.

"I said, Reeny, are you quite well?"

Irene blinked. Wilfred was seated beside her on the sofa, which was impossible because the men hadn't yet joined the ladies.

"You do look a little pale, Reeny," her father said, kneeling before her and pressing a hand against her forehead.

Clearly, she had been lost in her own thoughts far longer than she had thought. Irene tried to smile. "I feel quite well, Papa."

"You do not need to be brave, little one," said the Viscount Pernrith in a low voice, the drawing room filled with chatter as others continued their conversations.

Irene started as someone took her hand, but as she looked,

she saw that it was Wilfred. He had done so without a second thought, clearly, and no one had thought anything of it because... Well. It was Wilfred.

It's Wilfred. Irene squeezed his hand and blinked away tears that rose unbidden. His warmth, his comfort—it meant so much to her and she was going to lose it because she was so foolish as to not notice how precious he was. How special.

"You do not feel quite yourself, do you?" Wilfred asked quietly.

Irene gave a shaky laugh as she spoke the truth. "N-No, not really."

"I can take her back to your house in my carriage, my lord," Wilfred said in a low murmur. "Your family undoubtedly would like to stay and enjoy the rest of the evening—it would be no trouble and I was thinking of departing, anyway."

Irene watched her father glance around the room. Her mother was having a clearly very pleasant conversation with Lady Dalton, and Gwen was now playing the pianoforte in the corner and singing a duet with a man Irene did not recognize while Teddy turned the music sheets. Evidently, her family would not wish to leave so early.

The Viscount Pernrith bit his lip. "If you are certain you do not mind the fuss, Aynor. But I will have to insist her brother accompanies her as well, whatever his wishes." He leaned forward. "There are too many ladies who love to gossip at this gathering."

"I understand. And it would nonetheless be an honor," said Wilfred calmly, rising to his feet and pulling Irene up with him. "Come on, Reeny."

Gazes fixed on them as they started to walk to the hallway door, and Irene caught a whisper from Lady Dalton.

"But, Lady Pernrith—your unmarried daughter, and a gentleman, all alone in a carriage? If my Marjorie were here instead of at her finishing school on the Continent, I would never let her go without a chaperone."

"Of course we shall not allow such a thing." The viscountess's laughter was a little strained, no doubt because she knew how often Irene and Wilfred truly were left alone. "My husband is just getting our son... Ah, here's Michael now."

Michael, who was never exactly one to enjoy a dinner at one of his parents' friends' homes, nevertheless wore a pinched expression as he allowed the footman to hand over his hat and coat, jamming them on as his eyes darted toward Irene on Wilfred's arm. Then the annoyance seemed to wash away and he smiled, though Irene could not tell what he was smiling *about*. She felt too ill to contemplate it all.

Her attention. as her brother stomped outdoors ahead of them, was still focused on her mother's conversation. And her heart broke as she heard her mother's continued shaky laughter. "Though I must remind you, Lady Dalton, that's just Wilfred! He's a brother to her, a brother to all of them. I don't have to worry about him! Were it not for proper rules of decorum, I'd consider him as proper a chaperone to my daughters as their own brother."

Lady Dalton tutted. Clearly, she did not agree.

But the viscountess was right. Much as Irene may now wish otherwise, Wilfred would never again attempt anything resembling the ravishing Society seemed to worry occurred between an unmarried woman and an unrelated man every moment they dared to be left alone: Wilfred was not in love with her, and had no designs on her person.

More's the pity.

In a sort of haze, Irene allowed Wilfred to take her things from the footman and help her into her pelisse. This time, when he slowly lifted the heavy, woolen garment up to her shoulders, his fingertips brushing the nape of her neck, his breath on her ear, a molten pool ached between her thighs and Irene had to prevent herself from turning around and throwing herself into his arms. When he tucked her hand into his arm and led her outside the Dalton townhouse and into the waiting carriage, Irene held back from clasping on to his hand and weaving her fingers between his own. And when Wilfred stepped around the carriage and entered by the other door, she tried not to show her delight when he sat beside her, and not opposite her.

The carriage was small and her hips were pressed against his, and it had happened a thousand times before and she had never felt like this.

Irene blinked, almost not noticing the obvious until she pointedly tore her eyes away from their touching thighs. Her brother was not seated across from them. No one was. "Where's Michael?"

A knock on the carriage window caused her to jump. Michael's face appeared through the window, his voice muffled as he spoke to the pair through the glass. "I have somewhere I'd rather be than attending my sick sister at home. I'll walk. You can thank me later!"

And then he was gone.

"Th-Thank him?" Irene wondered aloud.

Wilfred did not comment, nor did he go after her brother and insist he accompany them. The gossips were surely satisfied now by their display of propriety at the door. Instead, Wilfred simply tapped the roof of the carriage, took one look at her, and placed an arm around her. "You'll warm up soon."

Irene sagged into his embrace, her eyelashes fluttering shut and her heart twisting with simultaneous delight and grief.

How could I not have known? How could she have spent hour after hour with this man and not realized she was in love with him? That these sensations, this bliss she felt when she was with him, this knowledge that he was the absolute best part of her, had been there all along and she had just misread it all?

Her own heart was a closed book to her, it seemed, for she had possessed the pages but never perused the paragraphs.

And now…now he was lost to her.

"I am sorry you are not feeling well," Wilfred said quietly as the carriage rattled along the Bath streets. "I should have taken you home during the fish course."

Irene smiled weakly. "We could not have just walked out of the Dalton dinner."

"We could, and I would have made sure we did, if I had any sense," he said softly, glancing at her, his nose mere inches from hers. "Dragging your brother along to pretend to play chaperone and all. There is very little I would not do for you, Irene."

Irene swallowed. *I should not be thinking of kissing Wilfred.* She should not have been calculating just how far she would have to lean before her lips touched his own. She should not have been conscious of his arm around her, the safety and the heat he offered.

After all, he was not thinking of such things.

"You…" he said softly. "There is something different about you."

Irene stiffened. "No, there isn't."

"And how, precisely, can you deny it when you do not even know what I think is different?" her best friend teased.

How, indeed? "I am perfectly well," Irene mumbled, knowing full well it was not true but refusing to even countenance the thought of revealing the full depths of her misery.

It was a misery of her own making. She should have known she loved him—loved him as a man, not just as a brother. Then perhaps—

But no. Irene knew she was not brave enough to profess her undying love to a gentleman without knowing what response she would receive. The very idea of saying such a thing to Wilfred… Although of course she knew now his affections were engaged elsewhere.

She had lost him.

"You look well. I mean, you look as beautiful as you always do," said Wilfred lightly.

The boiling heat between her thighs twisted. "I do?"

"Yes. You are a very beautiful woman, Irene," said the man with whom she was completely in love. "You always have been, ever since we were children."

Irene tried to smile. It was a compliment of a brother, nothing more. She had to face facts: the gentleman she adored had no interest in her. Not in that way, at any rate. Not when he wasn't confused because his head was full of drink.

"But there is something…something off about you. Something different," Wilfred continued. "Something has changed between us. Since my ball."

It was a good thing the dark evening hid the details of her face, for Irene was certain she was a brilliant lobster red. Her cheeks certainly felt as though they were burning, heat pouring off them so rapidly that she was soon no longer in need of her pelisse.

"Nothing has changed," Irene said, regret seeping into her voice.

If only something had changed. If only, when she had given him the opportunity to change the dynamic between them, he had taken that chance.

As it was…

The carriage jolted suddenly and they were both jerked to the left. This pressed her up against the side of the carriage, but in turn it pressed Wilfred up against her.

"Whoops," said Wilfred quietly. "Forgive me."

And yet he did not move. His free hand was pressed against the side of the carriage, encircling her, pinning her to the corner and leaving her with nothing to do but breathe him in.

Irene swallowed. She looked up into Wilfred's eyes and knew she would never be brave enough to lean forward and take the kiss that she felt within her soul belonged to her.

He was panting slightly harder now. Perhaps the knock from the carriage had been more dramatic than she had realized?

But no, he was leaning, and Irene could not understand why he was doing this, why he was crowding her, but then he would not know her thoughts were crowded by his mere presence, her desire for him new but already intense, overwhelming her senses, overpowering her thoughts—

Wilfred moved away. "Sorry about that."

Irene tried to smile. "No… No apology necessary."

It was disheartening, indeed, to see just how little effect she had on him. As Wilfred crossed his legs and looked from her to the window, Irene could see that the moment they had just shared had meant far more to her than it did to him.

Which is to be expected, she told herself firmly as she in turn looked away and out of her window. He did not love her. Not like that. He loved Miss Fletcher, and a fumbling confession and one kiss on a sofa after the man had drunk a touch too much of her father's spirits was no real sign of love.

Would he propose matrimony to Miss Fletcher? Would she accept him? Would Irene be forced to sit in a church and hear Wilfred, *her* Wilfred, vow to love another woman for the rest of his life?

"Here we are," came Wilfred's gentle voice.

Irene started as the carriage drew to a halt. "'Here'?"

"Your house. You really are not very well," her best friend said with a wry smile as he descended from the carriage. When he reappeared again and opened her door, he held out a hand. "I've got you."

It was all she could do not to fall into his arms and weep. No, he didn't have her, and she so desperately wanted him to, it was ridiculous.

Was this what love was? A complete overpowering of all rational thought? A desperate need to be close to that person, even if you knew they could never admire you, love you, desire you in the same way? A total loss of one's head?

Chance would be a fine thing…

"Reeny?"

Irene blinked. Wilfred was still standing there with his hand out, ready to help her out of the carriage. Ready to help her through anything.

Until he married another, of course.

"Yes, right," she said quietly, taking his hand and trying to ignore the quake of heat that cascaded up her fingertips at the meager touch.

The night was young. They had left the Daltons' relatively early, for there were still many people meandering about the streets. Wilfred pulled her protectively to his side as he walked her up to her front door.

Or at least, Irene hoped he pulled her to his side protectively. She was sure there was another reason, perhaps one not nearly so romantic, but she would prefer to ignore that option for now.

They stopped before her door and Wilfred turned to face her. "Here you are."

"Yes. And here you are," Irene said without thinking.

He grinned. "I hope you feel better soon, Reeny."

He started to walk away before she could think of anything rational to say, and that was why when she opened her mouth, only the irrational emerged. "Wilfred—wait."

And he halted, turning immediately, obediently to return to her side. Well, to stand opposite her. Very close, now that Irene came to think about it.

"Yes?" he said softly. "What is it, Reeny?"

Irene looked up into those clear, blue eyes and wondered how she could ever have looked into them and not fallen in love with him. He was so...

So good. So kind. So handsome. So charming. There were a thousand and one traits of Wilfred Matthew Kirk Chesterham Zouch and she had known them for years and she had not fallen in love with him?

Or perhaps she always had been in love and she had just never known. It was a cruel trick of fate, to withhold this self-knowledge from her until it was fully useless.

Movement. Warmth. Scalding tingles up her arm.

Irene looked down. Wilfred had taken her hand in his. Even through their gloves, she felt it.

"You know, you don't correct me when I call you 'Reeny'

anymore," he said softly. "Why?"

Swallowing hard, Irene allowed the truth to slip from her lips. "I don't know. I hadn't noticed."

"It's strange. You know someone for forever, then they grow up and become something the same and yet so different," Wilfred said, his voice low. Irene shifted on her feet—*to hear him better,* she told herself firmly. "I've taken you back here, back home, perhaps a thousand times. It's the same home. You and I, we are the same. And yet..."

His voice trailed away.

Irene tried to inhale, but it was rather difficult when the air was being dragged from her lungs as her pulse pounded. "And yet...things are different."

How she possessed the bravery to speak those words, she did not know. What she did know was that she wanted to hold him, press her forehead against his own, breathe in his air, know they would never be parted.

Wilfred's expression changed, ever so slightly. "Yes. Things are different."

This was her moment. Irene knew she may never get a better one. This was the opening to reveal that in fact what Lady Romeril had said was her heart's one desire. That she wanted to be his wife, his lover, his best friend for the rest of her days and it would be her honor to grow to deserve him.

Fear fluttered along her pulse. Rejection was not something anyone craved, but Irene could not think of a worse rejection than that of her best friend.

So she had to say—

"Well, in you go," Wilfred said bracingly, stepping back and rapping on the door. "I suppose your footman will still be—ah, there you are, Dempster."

The burly man was blinking curiously. "Miss Irene? We did not expect you back for quite some time."

Irene managed a smile, but it probably looked like a grimace. So, she was being dismissed. Perhaps Wilfred had guessed what she had been about to say. He clearly did not wish to hear it.

"Good evening, Wilfred," she said as cheerfully as she could manage. "Thank you for seeing me home. It's quite all right, Dempster. I can manage the steps on my own."

Without a backward glance, for she knew it would only tear her apart, Irene strode inside and slammed the door behind her.

Her family's sole footman stared in evident marvel. "What was that all about?"

"I can't talk now, Dempster," Irene said miserably, leaning her back against the front door and slowly allowing herself to slide until she was seated on the floor. "I don't think I want to talk ever again."

Chapter Twelve

December 17, 1840

WILFRED STAMPED HIS feet, hoping the movement would force some warmth into his toes. All it actually did was throw up a flurry of melting snow over his boots, chilling his toes even more.

Where is she?

Irene was not usually one to be late. His invitation was very clear, and even if his note had not been, the concert was going to start with or without them.

He hoped it would start with them.

"There you are!"

Wilfred whirled around with a lilting smile on his face. "What do you mean, *here I am*? Where have *you* been?"

"You said to wait by the pillar where we saw that kestrel, two years ago," Irene said, her teeth chattering lightly, her hands lost in a muff. "Over there."

"This is the pillar where we—never mind," said Wilfred hastily as their teeth started to chatter. "Let me guess. Theodora could not make it?"

Irene cleared her throat, the pink on her cheeks from the cold quite vivid even in the dim streetlight. "She was going to come, but I told her and Mama that Mrs. Brown would be joining us, so there was no reason for her to."

"Mrs. Brown again? The elderly woman who can barely be compelled to leave her house once a fortnight?"

Irene winced. "And that's why she's already asleep in our seats?"

Wilfred shook his head. However Irene teased him, he was not fool enough to not realize he and Irene danced a very dangerous dance, with all these public appearances, her chaperone *just out of sight*. He'd become more and more aware of the fact in the past couple of months. Frankly, he had to admit a part of him—just a small part, an infinitesimally small part—may have hoped the gossip rags marked her as ruined by him. It'd practically force her to marry him, to save not just her reputation, but her sisters', maybe even her cousins', too.

But no. He would never be happy with that outcome, with her forced into his arms so unwillingly. With the Chance name dragged through the mud, after all they had done for him.

"Come on," he said quietly. "Let's get inside."

The Assembly Room was far more temperate, thank goodness, than the freezing night air. Wilfred could not help but feel sorry for the footman upon whom they were piling their outer clothes. His great coat, his top hat, his scarf, his gloves, Irene's pelisse, her bonnet, her gloves, her muffler, her scarf—

"Are you quite all right under all that?" Wilfred asked helpfully to the footman whose mouth and nose were now hidden by the piles of clothing.

The thin footman's eyes widened and he made a muffled noise. Then he nodded, and tottered away carrying what appeared to be a ton of clothing.

"Well, it was cold out," Irene said defensively as she watched the poor man stagger along the corridor. "This winter has really turned nasty—and I wouldn't have gotten so cold if you hadn't been waiting at the wrong pillar."

Wilfred smiled, despite the completely inaccurate accusation. "And I am sorry for that."

His best friend was instantly mollified. "Well. Good."

Trying not to notice that she was wearing a quite splendid silk gown of dark green with the most spectacular embroidery around the hem, neckline, and cuffs—*don't look at the neckline, man*—he offered his arm. "Shall we?"

Perhaps he was wrong, but Wilfred thought that Irene hesitated, just for a moment, before taking his arm. The reluctance, if it had existed, did not last long, however. It was over in a blink and then she was holding on to him, her warmth seeping through his jacket and shirt to his very skin, and he was trying to remember how to walk in a straight line.

"I had not realized there was a concert tonight. I am glad you sent over that note," Irene said breezily. "I thought before I opened it that it would be the announcement of... It doesn't matter. Do you know who is performing?"

An announcement of what?

The thought clouded Wilfred's mind as they stepped into the room filled with chairs and chattering people all waiting for the musicians, seated at the front of the room, who were tuning their instruments.

What could Irene have thought he would be announcing? Surely not his affections for her; that would hardly have been appropriate, to do such a thing in a note.

Wilfred pressed his hand against his trouser pocket. The box was still there. *Good.*

It had been Mrs. Ansley's idea to do it this way, though she had not known it. That very morning he had been seated at his study, ostensively reading through the reports from his steward but in truth not taking very much in.

And she had come in with that look on her face that he well knew, and at times feared, and she had sat without invitation on the other side of his desk, and she had looked at him.

And Wilfred had swallowed.

"Mrs. Ansley," he had said cheerfully. "How may I help—"

"Whatever it is that is eating away inside you, Master Wilfred," his housekeeper had said sternly, as though he had been caught scrumping apples from a neighbor's orchard, "I hope you are going to do something about it."

Wilfred had blinked. "Y-Yes, Mrs. Ansley."

"Because it does me no good at all to see you twisting y'self into knots," the older woman had said severely, as though it were a chief moral failing of his. "And though I don't know what on earth it is, I can see that you need an answer, one way or the other. Time to ask, if you ask me."

And his spirits had swelled and he had realized the deep truth of her words. *It is time to ask.* No more waiting around to see whether he could convince Irene to somehow realize that she was the only woman for him.

He would have to tell her so.

"Thank you, Mrs. Ansley," he had said to her with a broad smile.

"My pleasure, Master Wilfred," his housekeeper had said, rising from the seat with a creaking of bones that sounded most ominous. She did not speak again until she had walked across the study and opened the door. That was when she hesitated. "And Master Wilfred?"

Wilfred had looked up from his steward's reports. "Yes?"

And Mrs. Ansley had smiled. "I hope Miss Chance says *yes*."

That had been this morning. It had taken Wilfred no time at all to visit his bank in Bath which, serendipitously, was the location of the Aynor family jewels. His grandmother's fiftieth birthday present had been a large sapphire ring, a gift from his devoted grandfather, and Wilfred could think of no better symbol of his devotion to Irene than to give her a family heirloom as a welcome into his family. The family they would create together.

And now it was within his trouser pocket, pressing against his leg as he and Irene found seats near the back.

"I adore Christmas music," Irene was saying happily as she folded her hands in her lap. "It heralds the new year, one of my favorite times of year. Full of fresh beginnings, new opportunities. Don't you think? Wilfred?"

Wilfred swallowed, his mouth irritatingly dry and his tongue apparently unattached to his mind, for no words were forthcoming.

"I'm glad you sent that note. I was worried that...that my

behavior at Lord and Lady Dalton's home..." Irene's voice trailed away.

It had been a curious evening, indeed, and Wilfred had been forced to hide the tenting of his breeches when his carriage had thrust him toward Irene in that incredibly seductive manner. Her brother had given them that chance at privacy, and he had failed to make the most of it. It had been all he could do not to kiss her hard as they'd stood outside her home.

The Chance footman, however, had prevented that. Which was perhaps quite right.

"I wasn't quite myself," Irene said briskly, smiling then looking away toward the musicians. "I...I wasn't quite myself."

Wilfred permitted himself a small moment to glance over while her attention was so distracted.

God, she is beautiful. He could lose himself in the minutiae of her face for the rest of his life, and that was ignoring her figure, which he very much could not ignore most of the time.

But in addition to her beauty, there was a...a nervous twitching along her smile that he had never seen before. Irene was not afraid of anything, not really. Certainly not the gossip rags descending on them due to the risks they took spending time so often in public together without anyone else to watch over her— attested to by the fact that there was an empty seat beside her he'd reserved for Theodora, or "Mrs. Brown" in Irene's estimation. There was little that could make her nervous and Wilfred was certain he was not on that short list.

So what is wrong?

A falter crept into his thinking. He had been determined to do it: after waiting for so long for the right moment, Wilfred had decided to make his own right moment.

It was time that he made his stand.

Only now he saw that there was still something not...not quite right about Irene did he wonder whether this was the right, right moment.

Oh, Lord, my mind is wandering...

"How are you feeling, Irene?" Wilfred hazarded.

That was it; gain more information. Perhaps he was just seeing things. Perhaps he was spotting problems where there were none.

Irene glanced at him, just for a moment, then appeared to turn her head resolutely away. "Fine."

'Fine'?

Fine? What did that mean? No one ever actually said 'fine' in response to such a question, did they? It was…vague. Unhelpful. Imprecise.

Wilfred cleared his throat. "Well, I hope you feel better in a few moments."

After he had revealed his devotion to her. After he had told her that he loved her. After he had asked her the most important question Wilfred was certain he would ever ask her. Ever ask anyone.

After he had asked her, Irene Chance, to become his wife.

Irene smiled briefly but without turning her head to face him. "Yes, I…I am sure the music will make me feel much better."

Wilfred's jaw dropped, but he managed to close it in time to prevent her from noticing.

That was… Well, it was not the response he had wanted. *But then*, he reminded himself, shifting nervously in his seat and feeling the ring box press against his thigh, *she does not know what I'm intending, does she?* She could hardly be glad about such a surprise before it was sprung.

Clearing his throat and wishing to goodness he had thought to write some of this down, he said in a low voice, "Irene—"

"Ah, there's the conductor!" Irene craned her neck to peer at the man who had just stepped out to rapturous applause. "All the way from Vienna, I think I heard someone say."

Wilfred blinked. Was she listening to the chatter around them, rather than him?

The conductor bowed, then tapped the music stand before him and held out his batons with a flurry that made Wilfred think he had been buffeted about by a strong wind. Then the baton swept down and the music began.

And it was good. If Wilfred had had no other ulterior motives for attending tonight's concert, he was quite sure he would have enjoyed it immensely.

As it was...

"Irene," Wilfred whispered, under the loud melody now being played.

"Hmmm?" His best friend leaned closer to him and he was immediately distracted by her warmth. Her scent.

Clearing his throat did nothing to allay his nerves. Which was unfortunate. Because they were now clogging up his lungs, making every inhale a challenge, suffocating him from the inside—

"Isn't the music wonderful?" Irene exhaled, taking his hand and twining her fingers between his own.

That was when Wilfred blew out the remaining air in his lungs and realized that actually, if he never breathed again, he had probably lived a full life.

There was something truly magical, him sitting here with his hand and Irene's hand intertwined. Something deeply elating. Something that settled his heart rate yet at the same time made his pulse flutter.

"I would not change anything about this moment," came Irene's soft voice under the sound of the violin. "It's just perfect. Any change would ruin it."

That was when Wilfred realized that he could not do it.

His free hand had been halfway through pulling the ring box from his trousers. He had wanted to show her, with something tangible she could hold, and touch, and feel, just how desperately he loved her. And now he could not.

"Any change would ruin it."

"Just think, our friendship is perhaps unique," Irene continued, utterly oblivious to the fact that she was slowly slicing parts of Wilfred's spirits to shreds. "It's... It's precious. We have something precious, Wilfred, and I...I am sure neither of us would not wish to risk it by changing it."

The tightness across his chest would surely let up. Wouldn't it? Surely, Wilfred could not spend the rest of his life with this agony, this restrictive misery that threatened to suffocate him with every passing second?

"Wilfred?" Irene looked at him now, worry so evident on her face that it were as though she were screaming. "Nothing is going to change, is it? I...I wouldn't want to lose this."

And she squeezed his hand.

Wilfred tried to think, but his body was making demands of him he absolutely could not deliver.

Obviously, she didn't want things to change. The moment he opened his mouth and revealed his deep and abiding affection for her, Irene would have no choice but to pull away. He wasn't sure they could keep being friends, at least as they were right now. Irene might not even want to face him, knowing that she could never love him the way he so desperately wanted her to love him.

No, it was safest, best for all of them, if he just reminded himself that what he had already was...good. Was great, even. He was in the life of the most spectacular woman he had ever met, and she enjoyed his company.

Could that ever be enough?

"Wilfred?" Irene repeated, the concern now deep in her eyes. "Wilfred?"

Wilfred cleared his throat. It sounded like he had been eating gravel. "You're never going to lose me, Irene. Not... Not even if things change. You will always be my friend. My best friend."

There was relief in her expression now, but it was mingled with something he did not recognize.

Irene turned back to the musicians. "Good. Right. Good."

It did not seem that she expected a response, which was all to the good because Wilfred was not certain that he could give her one.

She did not want things to change. Well, he would have to be a gentleman and respect that. Goodness knew, the fear of losing her was one he fully understood. It was the primary reason it had taken him all these years to even conceive of speaking to her about his affections.

Wilfred placed his unencumbered hand upon the bulge in his trousers—of the ring box, naturally.

Well, he would simply have to take the ring back to the bank and resign himself to the fact that the Aynor line would die with him. It was not such a terrible thing, in the grand scheme of things. Worse things happened every day, he was sure.

And the idea that he could ever take a woman to his bed who was not Irene Chance was completely laughable.

If he was stricter about making sure she took with her a chaperone or companion, he could protect the Chance family reputation from scandal and honor her wishes to be nothing but a friend for life. If scandal broke out because Irene would just continue to insist on being wonderful, glorious Irene and he *had* to marry her, well, he could promise it would be only a marriage on the surface, that she need not give him heirs, if that was more than she could ever offer him. It was better than a life without her.

"Wilfred?"

"Yes?" he said, turning to her immediately and trying not to notice how his heart constricted painfully as he did so.

Irene smiled as she squeezed his hand. "You make me happy."

The cloud Wilfred was now sitting on was delightful. In a strange sort of fluffy haze, he listened to the rest of the Christmas concert, utterly unsure what they were playing and not paying attention closely enough to applaud at the relevant moments.

There was no point. He was sitting hand in hand with Irene Chance.

As the conductor bowed and Wilfred blinked, realizing that Irene had finally released his hand so she could applaud both the conductor and the musicians, he shook his head slightly as though ridding water from his ears and wondered where the evening had gone.

"Weren't they marvelous?" said Irene with shining eyes. "I'm so glad we got to hear them together."

She slipped her hand back into his immediately after finishing such a statement, which was when Wilfred realized he had to do three things.

Firstly, he had to protect the heart of Irene Chance with his life, and if that meant never breaking it by never marrying and changing the friendship that they so enjoyed, so be it. If that meant marrying her to protect her reputation and the marriage was not a real one, he'd accept that too.

Secondly, he would have to learn immense restraint to prevent himself from punching the lights out of any other gentleman who came within ten feet of her.

Thirdly, he would need to write a note to Miss Fletcher. He had only used her services once, but he would not need them again. This false courting nonsense… Precisely how Michael had managed to talk him into it, he did not know. The whole idea was preposterous—and worse, if the rumor started around Bath that the Duke of Aynor was engaged to be married, Irene would be undoubtedly crushed.

He would tell the truth. One day.

And Wilfred promised himself that as they rose, the sound of chairs squeaking across the wooden floor and the murmurs of the audience filling his ears, that he would propose marriage to Irene one day.

He had to help her fall in love with him. It was as easy as that. One day, hopefully someday soon, she would wake up and realize that the affection she held for him was far more than what friendship could encapsulate.

And then he would tell her.

"Look at them."

Wilfred looked at where his best friend was pointing, and

almost recoiled.

It was a pair, a lady and a gentleman. They were walking with eyes devoted on each other without a care in the world, almost not looking where they were going.

"The younger Miss Quintrell—or at least, that was what she had been before she wed," Irene said curiously. "How strange, to see someone so besotted. Don't you think?"

Wilfred tried not to look at his friend, certain his gaze would feature the exact same devotion. "Hmmm."

"I never thought marriage could look like that. At least, my parents are that devoted to each other," Irene mused aloud. "I just… Well, to think that *I* could ever meet someone with such a heart full of devotion. To feel drawn to their presence continuously, to be unable to look away from them."

"It's what I want," Wilfred found himself saying before he could stop himself. "It's surely what everyone wants."

To know that person and to be drawn to them, unable to look away—how well she'd put it. If only she could feel such a thing for him, but it could not be more clear that she did not.

"Goodness, you look pensive," remarked Irene as they walked arm in arm out of the concert room and into the lobby, where frantic-looking footmen were attempting to reunite the guests with their outerwear. "What on earth were you thinking of?"

Wilfred would have prevented his tongue from speaking if he'd had any control whatsoever. "How beautiful you are."

Irene's flush was such a dark pink as he had never seen before. Unfortunately for him, it only made her more alluring. "I— what… I beg your pardon?"

Well, no use in attempting to backtrack now. "You are beautiful," Wilfred said simply.

Perhaps she had expected more. Irene merely blinked as though dazed, even dazzled. It was no bright light shining in her eyes, but the brightness of his conviction.

"Oh," she said blankly. "Right."

"Your pelisse, miss," said a footman most inexcusably coming out of nowhere. "And your gloves, and your scarf, and your—"

"Yes, thank you," Wilfred said hastily.

It was starting to become a habit of his, using the excuse of helping Irene on with a pelisse to get close to her, and even though she had made it perfectly clear this evening that absolutely nothing was going to change between them, he could hardly resist.

The footman's eyes widened, but he obediently handed over the lady's accoutrements, and Irene smiled up at Wilfred as he carefully positioned her bonnet atop her head.

"There is no need for this, you know," she said quietly.

"Oh, I don't know," Wilfred murmured, his pulse quickening as he handed over her gloves. "I like helping you."

I like being close to you. I like the excuse to touch you, to step into your space and breathe you in.

Was what he did not say.

But it did not seem to matter. Somehow, Irene appeared to read his mind, her cheeks flushing as she carefully placed her hands into the arms of her pelisse.

Wilfred held his breath as he slowly moved the fabric up, up past her elbows, up to her shoulders, and of course he had to stand mere inches away to ensure that the pelisse sat correctly upon her frame, and it was a simple coincidence that he leaned closer and inhaled just at the same moment.

Oh, his questing fingers wanted to do so much more. Wanted to skate up to the nape of her neck and tangle themselves in her hair. Wanted to remove the pelisse, and the gloves, and feel the sensation of his fingers pressed up against hers. And while there, why stop? Why not take off the bonnet, the gown, the—

"Wilfred?"

Wilfred blinked. Irene turned slowly on the spot, maintaining the closeness between them and looking up with wide eyes.

He swallowed. They were in public. They were standing in the lobby of the Assembly Rooms where absolutely anyone could see them. If anyone noticed she did not have a companion with her, that would be gossip enough. But if he *kissed* her?

"Thank you," Irene said quietly, and she leaned up on her tiptoes and kissed—kissed his cheek.

Wilfred attempted not to feel disappointed, even as he looked around to be sure no one noticed. Luckily, it seemed as if no one had. "Thank me? For what?"

"For such a lovely evening. For... For understanding," Irene said, her eyes downcast now, as though she had done something scandalous. "I do hope... That is, I can't ask you not to seek the companionship of others. But I hope you won't forget me."

Wilfred found his tongue frozen. Forget her? Forget Irene, the light of his life?

But then, she must have still thought he was courting Miss Fletcher, even though he had appeared just once in public with the woman.

Blast. He really hadn't thought this through.

"Have a good evening, Wilfred. My father allowed the carriage to wait for me, so I must be off."

And she was gone, stepping out of his arm's reach, out of sight so swiftly, he rather wondered how she had done it.

Wilfred cleared his throat and wondered if he would ever gain equilibrium again.

One day, if he could overcome his cowardice and persuade Irene without using actual words to fall in love with him, he would ask this woman to be his wife.

Chapter Thirteen

December 23, 1840

DON'T THINK ABOUT *how much you love him.*

Don't stare at the curl falling down over his forehead.

Don't consider what those fingers would feel like if they traced the lines on your palm...

Irene choked.

"I have said it before and I will say it again," Wilfred said with a smile, handing her a napkin and shaking his head. "You drink your hot chocolate too quickly."

It was all she could do not to snort, not a particularly ladylike thing to do in public. Though in all truth, the thoughts that had been swirling around her mind were hardly very ladylike, and if anyone else at Don Saltero's Chelsea Coffee House had known them, Irene was certain she would be censored immediately by public opinion.

Especially since she had once again managed to evade her poor, overworked lady's maid. Then again, she was sure, had Wharton made it all the way to the coffee house with them and not been lost on the streets of Bath, she would have understood. The Pernrith Chance servants were used to Irene and Wilfred's unconventional friendship. But they had no idea that things had changed.

And things *had* changed. At least in Irene's mind.

As it was, no one—not even Wilfred—knew what she had been thinking. Which was all to the good.

"Y-Yes," she managed to splutter without too much difficulty, though she could still taste the burning-hot liquid in her nose. "Too fast. Too fast."

Not, Irene couldn't help but think, *that the same could be said of my revelation about my feelings for Wilfred.*

Too fast? Too slow. So slow that Wilfred had evidently no idea of her affections and so had found someone else to return his ardor. Someone else to laugh with. Someone else to caress…

Heat blossomed across Irene's entire body, but she trusted to the fact that she had just inhaled a large gulp of hot chocolate to cover that fact.

"You look a little warm," Wilfred said, voice dripping with concern. "Maybe you should slow down with your beverage."

Irene tried to smile. "'Slow down'?"

She had already been too slow, and now she feared no amount of speeding up would ever provide her with the goal she so desired.

Wilfred. Wilfred Matthew Kirk Chesterham Zouch. The Duke of Aynor.

It was only 'Wilf' who really mattered to her, the name he had given when they had first met all those years ago, and now there would be another woman who would call him that. Another woman who would enjoy that intimacy.

Or rather, Irene thought as her stomach twisted into a painful knot, this Miss Fletcher would be the *only* woman. For how could she, Irene, even contemplate calling this handsome, charming, kind gentleman by such an intimate name once he was…married?

The thought was so unpleasant that Irene purposefully took an unpleasantly deep swig of her hot chocolate. The liquid burned, but it could not completely burn away the dissatisfaction curdling within her.

"Wilfred," Irene said, not quite sure what she was going to say next, but knowing she had to say something. "Wilfred? Wilfred!"

Wilfred started. "I beg your pardon?"

His eyes had drifted off into the distance before being returned by Irene's… Well, yell.

Her gaze narrowed. He had been slightly distracted ever since they had met at Don Saltero's Chelsea Coffee House twenty minutes ago. It was one of their favorite places—had been a family favorite, according to her Aunt Alice, which was a strange thought. It was difficult to imagine her parents, uncles, and aunts as young people.

As it was, she and Wilfred had been coming here often. There was one in London, the original Don Saltero's Chelsea Coffee House, and there had been one in Bath the last few years. It was usually a place she and Wilfred—usually, unfortunately, with Wharton successfully accompanying her—came to laugh and gossip and observe people.

But Wilfred had perhaps been doing far too much of the latter. His attention was meandering, his answers unspecific, and when Irene took a closer look at him, it was to see a vagueness in his eyes she had not seen before.

"Wilfred," Irene prompted.

Wilfred did not appear to hear her.

Surreptitiously turning around to see what the dolt was looking at, Irene could see nothing that would particularly capture the man's attention. There was Miss Quintrell, a pretty, young woman to be sure, but Irene could recall Wilfred once saying how intimidated he was by her intellect. Surely, he could not have been staring at her.

"—never saw such a thing in all my life—"

"No, indeed. I was startled to see it—"

There was a pair of gossiping ladies that Irene vaguely recognized: a Mrs. Lymington and a Mrs. Howarth. Their voices modulated in volume, and precisely what they were speaking of—or who—disappeared from legibility.

She realized with a start that despite her earlier confidence no one in the place would recognize her, there were quite a few people she recognized now. A slight, sinking feeling inside her might have, on introspection, revealed a little bit of regret that she had managed to leave her lady's maid behind somewhere three blocks over.

But Wilfred was clearly looking at someone, and Irene had to wonder who. There was Lady Romeril, though Irene knew Wilfred well enough to know that he would not wish to seek an audience with her. There was Lord Dalton, a gentleman of some consequence, true, as he had a fortune and had recently acquired his marquess title after the passing of his father. He had been the Earl of Burnell before then. But he was not a gentleman with whom—as far as she was aware—Wilfred had any close connection. There was his daughter, who had gone abroad for the better part of a year now, if Irene remembered correctly, and had only just returned in the past few days.

The thought flashed through Irene's mind before she could capture it, and her stomach turned. Yes, but Lady Majorie had quite a sizable dowry… Wilfred had no need of sizable dowries. Surely, Wilfred had no interest in *her*?

No, she knew that he did not. Irene's mind realized the truth in that instant, and it was painful.

She knew Wilfred had no interest in Lady Marjorie because she had already met the woman he was in love with.

Miss Fletcher.

"Wilfred, you seem…distracted," Irene hazarded.

Wilfred nodded ambiguously, though as he made no verbal reply, it was impossible to know whether he had actually heeded her.

Irene bit her lip. Was he thinking of Miss Fletcher? It was rude of him, indeed, if so, but then…if he was in love with her…

"—absolutely outrageous—"

"—would never permit my daughter to do such a thing—"

"—utterly scandalous—"

The whispers of two ladies behind them had now grown to such a volume that Irene could no longer ignore them.

"If she were my daughter, I would take her in hand. In fact—"

"Mrs. Lymington, you cannot think to—"

The scraping of a chair was accompanied by the swishing of skirts, and Irene blinked in surprise to find both Mrs. Lymington and Mrs. Howarth standing by their table.

"Mrs. Lymington. Mrs. Howarth," Wilfred said, starting as his mind had so evidently been elsewhere. "Good afternoon."

"Is it, Your Grace?" said Mrs. Lymington curtly as she glared at the two of them—quite rudely, Irene could not help but think, and entirely unprovoked. "Is it, indeed, Miss Chance?"

Wilfred looked at Irene with blank confusion, and she shrugged, though a lump caught in her throat. It was not the most genteel of openings, to be sure, but she was starting to understand what was going on here, and she was not sure she could survive the chastising her mother would have in store for her once she found out.

"I would be mortified, I say, *mortified*," Mrs. Lymington was saying, "if my daughter should act in such a manner!"

Irene could not help the delicate flush—what she hoped was a delicate flush—rising to her cheeks.

"To gad about Town with a gentleman to whom you are neither married nor engaged, not a chaperone in sight!" Mrs. Lymington hissed, as though speaking the crime any louder would increase its potency. "Whispers have reached me about the two of you, but I was glad that I had never borne witness to it. And now… Well, I've never seen the like!"

Indignation burned on Irene's cheeks. "Mrs. Lymington, it is none of your business."

"If your father and mother cannot keep you in hand, then it is my duty as—"

"Please, Mrs. Lymington, do calm yourself," Wilfred said, his gaze flickering from Mrs. Lymington, fairly thrumming with outrage, to Irene, wondering if she could melt under the table and never be seen again. "You are making a scene. And I will have you know, I do not consider myself to have ever *gadded about* in all my life. I don't even own a gad."

Irene snorted with laughter and attempted to immediately

cover it up with a sip of hot chocolate.

Mrs. Lymington's eyebrows rose. "You can treat such perfidy with lightness, Your Grace!"

"I can treat it as my business, and not your own, Mrs. Lymington," Wilfred said calmly.

Irene swallowed. There was a resonance in his voice she had not heard before, a gravitas, a certainty, a comfort in the rightness of one's speech and a confidence that one was not to be shaken.

It was…devilishly attractive.

Mrs. Lymington was gaping. *Like a fish*, Irene thought silently. Like a pike that had been brought to dry land much against its will. "But—but—but—"

"Miss Chance and I are good friends, and her chaperone is not far behind," Wilfred continued in that calm, considered, and utterly unflappable voice. "We have just merely… lost her a moment. Regardless, her parents see no reason to object to the two of us spending time together. It is their opinions that matter in this. Not yours."

Irene's face did not know whether to laugh at Mrs. Lymington's wrath, smile at her friend Mrs. Howarth's clear embarrassment, sigh with happiness at the way Wilfred had taken charge of the situation, or wince inwardly at how…how brotherly he was being.

I don't want you to be my brother, she cried from the sanctity and privacy of her own mind. *I want you to be my—*

But she did not know what. As Mrs. Lymington hmphed and harrumphed her way out of Don Saltero's Chelsea Coffee House, accompanied by the scurrying Mrs. Howarth behind her, Irene tried to smile at the man she adored without letting him know, obviously, that she adored him.

It was mortifying enough to fall in love with a man whom you had previously considered your brother. It was even more shameful to do so mere weeks after discovering that he had fallen in love with another.

"I am sorry you had to endure that," Wilfred said quietly,

sipping his coffee with the unflustered mien of a gentleman who had encountered a small hillock in his path, and had merely stepped around it. "Society has a lot to answer for."

Irene tried to smile. "Yes. Yes, it does."

A great many things, she could have said. Such as, why is it only now that I realize how unusual it is that we spend so much time together without becoming the subject of gossip sooner? Mrs. Lymington may not have put her query in such polite terms, but the woman surely could not be the only one in London or Bath to have noticed about us without a chaperone in plain sight.

Lady Romeril seemed to allude to such gossip. So why hasn't it appeared in the papers?

It was odd to the extreme, how Irene had never realized just how unusual it was that Wilfred and herself were alone together so much. Alone! Without a chaperone! And yet she did not, at least before now, appear to be ruined in Society's eyes. Had she really been so clever until now not to be caught? What had changed? What had made her forget herself and boldly walk into this coffee house without Wharton trailing behind her?

And yet nothing Society might have *assumed* had happened had actually happened. Well, except that kiss. That kiss that kept her up at night. That kiss that had transfixed all her attentions and raised such confusion. That kiss that she had hoped at the time had been a mere accident, and now she cursed herself for not launching herself back into Wilfred's arms and accepting every kiss he had been willing to—mistakenly, and in his cups—bestow.

"Shall we have another?" Wilfred did not wait for her response but turned his eyes to one of the servers.

The serving man responded instantly. It was a common occurrence, Irene knew, when one was a duke. Her father was an illegitimate viscount and she bore no title; she did not receive this sort of service.

"Another hot chocolate, another coffee, and can we have a plate of those delicious-looking biscuits? I simply must try one. Or three," Wilfred was saying to the serving man. "But not strawberry. Nothing with strawberry. Or raspberry. Thank you."

Irene took the opportunity to stare at the man who had captured her heart and had not even realized it.

How was it that this man became more handsome every time she looked at him? It was most unfair. The lilt of his smile, that little nod as he thanked the serving man…had anyone ever been so alluring?

Then her mind caught up with her. "'No strawberry'?"

Wilfred leaned back in his seat with a smile. "No."

"But you love strawberry," Irene said, bewildered.

"And you hate it," Wilfred said softly, smile broadening. "You think I would forget?"

Do not, Irene told herself firmly, *declare your undying love for this man in the middle of Don Saltero's Chelsea Coffee House like a wild woman.*

But she had to admit that was sort of what she was. Always "losing" her chaperones or pretending one was out of sight.

Would it really be so bad to take it one step further, especially now that they had been, effectively, caught?

"Oh. Thank you," was all she squeaked out despite her growing boldness, which wasn't nearly enough, she knew. But it would have to do.

"Have you finished all your Christmas shopping?" her best friend asked. "You only have today and perhaps tomorrow to complete it, if not."

Irene swallowed. She had, in fact, though the gift she had purchased for Wilfred felt trite now that she sat opposite him. "Yes. Yes, I have. And you?"

Wilfred shrugged. "Mrs. Ansley, it appears, did not like the idea that she would have that responsibility taken from her, so I have left the gifts for the servants in her capable hands."

"But what about m—" Irene caught herself just in time. "There must be other people. Friends, I mean, for whom you wish to purchase presents."

His dark gaze caught hers and threatened to never let her go.

She didn't want to be let go. She wanted to be held by this man forever.

"I have bought all the presents that I wish to give," was all that he said, though Irene could see the additional unsaid words teasing across his lips.

His immensely kissable lips.

Get a hold of yourself, woman!

"I have wrapped all of mine, though some of them with great difficulty," Irene said in a rush, hoping to goodness that forcing herself to speak would distract her from how close Wilfred's hand was, resting on the table about six inches from her own. "I had to ask Dempster to help me, in the end."

"And was he much help?"

"Not at all." Irene smiled. "Despite that, considering all he does for us, and how long he's been with us, we really should offer him a promotion to butler, but we can't because…"

Her voice trailed off.

Wilfred's expression was caring, considerate, kind. "Because?"

She swallowed. It was not the sort of thing her father would want talked about, she knew, but with Wilfred… Well, that was different. Wilfred was family.

Parts of her ached for him to become her actual family.

But he wasn't. But he was.

Oh, goodness, this is far too confusing.

Irene inhaled deeply and plastered a smile across her face. "Because we are not rich, Wilfred. Not compared to most of the *ton*."

The little puckering frown between his brows was one she knew so well. "I do not see how that signifies. You can afford a housekeeper, can you not?"

"But we cannot afford the wages of a senior manservant. That is," Irene amended, "Mrs. Kinley does deserve her senior position. Her mother had it before her. Many households have both housekeeper and butler. Still, manservants are more expensive. My father's income, it… Well. We do not have a country estate, where we hire a second household of servants, as my uncles do. We can barely afford the ones we have…"

Her voice trailed away, as she became suddenly conscious again that they were in public. She probably should not have spoken so candidly about her father's business where anyone—another Mrs. Lymington, for example—could hear her.

But Wilfred smiled and nodded slowly, as though he truly understood her concerns. "I can see how that would be troublesome. But it is a fine coincidence. My steward wrote to me just a few weeks ago suggesting I find a butler for my country estate, as the one I employed there has recently enjoyed retirement. If… Well, if you ever could bring yourself to part with Dempster, I would be honored to employ him myself."

Irene's lips parted in astonishment. "You—You would… But you…you owe him no obligation, no great regard."

"And that is where you are wrong," Wilfred said steadily. "Ah, thank you," he said to the serving man who deposited a tray on their table. "Look," he continued as the serving man departed and the duke himself picked up her hot chocolate and pushed it toward her. "Your family footman has been kind to me for…oh, twenty years?"

It was impossible to do anything but stare, but Irene managed, just about, to nod.

"Twenty years of kindness, and excellent service to the people who matter most to me in the world… I would say that those actions garner not just obligation, but a great deal of regard," Wilfred said with a shrug as he placed a biscuit decorated with chocolate onto a small plate, which he placed before her. "Don't you think?"

Thinking was, at this time, entirely impossible. Irene had heeded every word the man had said and could not help but admit to herself that there were clearly new depths of Wilfred's character to love…but speak? She could not find the words.

"You make no remark," Wilfred said quietly. "You disapprove of my suggestion. I suppose, then, your own household would need a new footman, but with the money you save on Dempster, then…"

"No!" Irene spoke so hastily, she almost shouted. Her smile was awkward as she continued. "No, it's just… I had never thought of it in that manner."

"Your family is the closest thing to family I will ever have," her best friend and the man with whom she was irrevocably in love said, with more than a small amount of emotion. "I admit I shall miss you all until next week."

Miss us?

Evidently, her confusion was visible, for Wilfred chuckled and helped himself to a biscuit. "Christmas, Irene. You and your parents, your siblings, you have such wonderful Christmases— but we are past that age now. One Pernrith Chance sister is married, and I'm no longer an orphaned waif in need of company for the holiday season. It's… It is high past time I stop taking advantage of you all. I shall hold my own festivities, if only a modest celebration for my household servants, this year."

Christmas? Without Wilfred?

Or did he mean…he had plans with Miss Fletcher?

Irene was not sure what made her do it.

Well, fine, she knew. It was her love for him. Falling in love with a person, Irene was slowly discovering, was to devote every minute of your day, your life, to bettering their life. It may only be in a small way, but something that was small to you may be of great significance to them.

And it was precisely because it was small that she said it. "You can't! You absolutely must spend Christmas with us. Wilfred, how could you ever think otherwise? It simply isn't Christmas without you!"

Wilfred blinked. Irene blinked, astonished to hear the words that had come out of her own mouth.

"What do you… Do you mean that?" Wilfred said slowly.

"In fact, though I know the commute is a short one, and you usually excuse yourself at the end of each day, this year, you should stay. Spend the entire week—from Christmas to New Year's. Yes, yes, you'll have to. It's the best way to experience a Pernrith Chance Christmas." Irene cleared her throat. She was sure her parents would not object to him spending the week. It was true, with everyone growing older, Christmases had become more cramped. There was little room at the Pernrith Chance Bath townhouse, but with Jessica spending the holidays with her husband's family, Teddy and Gwen could share a room.

Instinct led her to reach out and take his hand. She could feel his pulse and a searing heat of something roared up her arm, and Irene flushed and saw the flush in his face and thought, *Is this it?* Was this the moment, perhaps, that Wilfred fell out of love with Miss Fletcher, and into love with her?

Surely, he could not go the entire week of Christmas without seeing Miss Fletcher if he was seriously considering marrying her.

"But wouldn't it be a great inconvenience to spend the night, particularly for an entire week?" Wilfred asked, squeezing her hand and further warming her—until his next words threw a chill over her. "Though I suppose I am almost already family."

It took a great deal of self-control not to withdraw her hand.

'Almost already family'? No, no, that was not who he was at all. He was not her brother. Wilfred could not have been less like her brother if he tried.

Irene swallowed. She wanted Wilfred as a man wanted a woman, craving his touch, needing his affection...and now, though he'd once, in his cups, said otherwise, he saw himself as only her brother.

She withdrew her hand. "It will not be an inconvenience. We are a large family, after all. One additional cousin, or person, it makes no difference."

Her intention had been to reflect back to him essentially what he had said to her, and yet for some reason Wilfred now looked crestfallen, a hitch suddenly catching his breath. He stretched his hand, the hand she had so recently been holding, as though it ached.

What did it mean?

The trouble with falling in love, Irene thought darkly, *is that it makes one look for signs and signals everywhere!*

The door to the coffee house opened and in stepped Wharton, her beady eyes narrowing in on Irene almost at once. At least no one would witness Irene and Wilfred leaving the coffee house alone together. Perhaps they could stave off gossip and ruin for another day. As if giving her blessing to save Irene from the worst of it, Lady Romeril nodded at the sight of the maid weaving her way through the tables.

"And as I said," Irene added, picking up a biscuit and trying to think calm and dull thoughts before Wharton reached them to give her an earful, "I want you there."

Wilfred's smile made her think the very opposite of calm and dull thoughts. "Good. In that case, I gratefully I accept and spend the week at your townhouse. I will spend Christmas with you."

Heat sparked down to Irene's thighs, heat that had nothing to do with the gingerbread in the biscuit.

"And your family," Wilfred added.

Irene tried to smile. *Hell's bells.* What had she let herself in for?

Chapter Fourteen

December 24, 1840

WILFRED WAS NOT sure what to expect when he rang the bell pull outside the Pernrith Chance townhouse.

What he had not expected was this.

"There you go! Now you are adorned like us." Irene grinned, pulling him into the hallway after she had attached a boutonniere to his jacket. "Ready for the onslaught?"

Wilfred wanted to say, *Absolutely not.* 'Onslaught' was not a word that he generally attached to the Christmas season. 'Festive,' perhaps, or 'merry.'

Not 'onslaught.'

Though when he considered the last few minutes—hugged warmly by Irene on the top step as she and not the family's housekeeper or footman had opened the door, his luggage whisked away by Dempster, and a sprig of holly attached to his lapel—Wilfred had to own that it was a kind of onslaught.

The trouble was, Irene was grinning and so Wilfred felt he could do absolutely nothing but grin inanely back.

"'Onslaught'?" he repeated, as the sound of a pianoforte being played beautifully tinkled through the house.

Irene nodded sagely, her smile undiminished. "I am sorry to remind you that there are a great number of traditions we indulge in over the Christmastide, and many of them start today. For example, I hope you are in fine voice."

"Oh, please don't ask me to sing, Reeny." Wilfred did not wish for his throat to dry up and sound so hoarse, but it was a natural response to the suggestion of singing. "You know I do not—"

"I am afraid you do not get a choice," Irene said lightly as she took his hand and started pulling him to the drawing room. "Time to select a Christmas carol, and swiftly. Here he is, Mama!"

A rush of warmth swept over Wilfred as they stepped into the drawing room, and it was not just the heat from the fire cracking merrily. Several voices cried out in delight at his arrival, and the Viscountess Pernrith stepped forward with her arms open, engulfing him in a hug.

"Wilfred! We were absolutely delighted when Irene told us you were coming for the full week. We're a child short with Jessica married so recently. It's a delight to have you."

Wilfred tried to smile at the welcoming embrace, and not wince at the insinuation—kindly meant—that he was a child of the family.

What he wanted from their second-eldest daughter was anything but brotherly.

"I cannot thank you enough for inviting me for the week—or at least, allowing Irene's invitation to stand," he said aloud as the older woman released him. "I hope I will prove a pleasant houseguest."

"Nonsense. We know that you are a good soul," said Irene's father, who was sitting by the pianoforte playing a duet with Theodora. "We would have you spend the night for the holiday week in years previously if we'd only had the space. Tea?"

"Why not whiskey?" called Michael from the sofa on the other side of the room, casting a wink in Wilfred's direction.

Irene tutted. "Michael Chance, it isn't even eleven!"

"But it's Christmas!" protested her brother.

The two of them fell into bickering as she stepped across the room to berate him and Wilfred smiled to watch them at it. He'd never had any siblings to bicker with.

He had thought himself alone, but the viscountess was still beside him and she sighed as she shook her head, though her face showed a brilliant smile.

"It is usually Gwen and Michael who have such rows," she said, her expression mirthful. "But I suppose there's always change in a family. Tell me, Wilfred, how are you? Sit beside me and tell me all your news."

Wilfred swallowed hard as the mother of the woman he loved guided him toward another sofa. "'News'? I have no news."

Except he had paid a woman to pretend to be courted by him, something he had immediately regretted and tried to put an end to, and he'd only done it because the viscountess's only son had recommended it, and he had only done that because Michael had seen instantly that he was in love with the viscountess's daughter…

Perhaps that was not the sort of thing that he should be speaking of, however.

"I was thinking of finding a new butler," he said instead. "For my countryside estate."

Irene's mother lowered her voice. "Yes, Irene mentioned it, and I think it's a marvelous idea. While you are here, perhaps you can speak with Pernrith about it."

"Wilfred's turn!"

There was mingled laughter and retorts of "Can the man even sing?" as Wilfred saw with sinking spirits that the viscount was rising from the pianoforte stool.

"I'm afraid it's tradition, young man," twinkled the father of the house. "You can't use the excuse that you are only 'dropping by' not to participate this time. Do you know 'The First Noel'?"

To Wilfred's great relief, he did—and Theodora played beautifully and thankfully did not continue with all six verses. As he sang, Wilfred attempted not to catch Irene's eye. She was smiling broadly, but he could not tell and did not wish to know, whether she was laughing at him or merely enjoying seeing him put on the spot.

Then, somehow, it was luncheon.

"As you know, we don't go in for anything special on Christmas Eve," Irene said, handing Wilfred a plate. "Just a cold sideboard for luncheon and dinner. It gives the servants a rest. Cold ham? Or would you prefer pheasant?"

Cold ham, cold pheasant, cold salmon, cold pies, cold potatoes, cold beef—for all that the Chances said they had nothing special, Wilfred's eyes bulged at the sheer amount of food laid out on the sideboard. It was more than he ever remembered there being.

"Disappointing after last year," said Irene placidly, as though this was a devastating blow but she would live through it. Did she not recall the size of previous feasts? "I suppose we shall have to hope that tomorrow will impress you. You've never been a proper houseguest before. I don't think we've ever fed you three times in one day."

"'Impress me'?" Wilfred said with a laugh as he settled back on the sofa with the plate on his knee, utterly unsure how he would be able to eat like this. "I am seriously impressed as it is!"

She smiled, and Wilfred's pulse skipped a beat, and he wondered whether this was a mistake.

Oh, he was enjoying himself no end. Being a part of the Chance family for Christmas was something he had looked forward to most as a child. He'd gone home every evening those days, wishing he could stay longer. Now he'd be here the entire week. As if he were one of the Pernrith children proper.

But he was no longer a child, and what he wanted from them was far different.

He wanted Irene.

When luncheon was over, Wilfred sat back with a groan—his eyes had been far larger than his stomach but he had been unable...fine, *unwilling* to put any of the delicious fare back. At least he could now spend the afternoon relaxing and doing nothing so taxing as—

"Charades," Irene said promptly, to calls of jubilation from her family.

Wilfred's smile faded. "'Charades'?"

"You knew to expect this. We've played before," his best friend and the woman he loved said smartly. "How shall we divide into teams?"

It's all very well, he could not help but think, *for Irene to say that I have played before.* Of course he had; charades was an annual Chance Christmas tradition, as well as a most popular after dinner game, and one the two of them had played together at the Duke of Axwick's dinner party just this past autumn.

But it was quite one thing playing with friends and acquaintances whose opinions do not matter to you while three glasses of wine were inside you. It was quite another to play entirely sober, in the cold light of day, with someone as competitive as Michael.

"I say, that's cheating!" the man protested.

"It is not cheating if I move my mouth but make no sound!" Gwen shot back in anger. "Mama, tell him!"

"I cannot possibly argue with someone on my own team, my child," the viscountess said serenely. "I say instead, *you* are a cheat!"

The family collapsed into laughter, even Gwen putting on a smile, and Wilfred looked around, feeling, in this chaos, somehow at peace.

It was all...all so much. The Chances were always so much. That a family could accuse each other of cheating and yet there be no true anger, no falling out? It was intoxicating.

Wilfred swallowed hard as he sat down after his go. He had been fortunate, indeed, to have Irene on his team—she thought like him, or knew how he thought so well that it took but a half a minute for her to guess 'The three Magi.'

And that meant he was momentarily left alone with his thoughts, and they were this: that they, the Pernrith Chances, were his family. Even if he'd never be so bold as to accuse any of them of being a cheat.

Perhaps his parents, had they lived, would have had more children. Perhaps he and his parents and those siblings would have played charades. Perhaps they would have bickered about whether 'magi' or 'kings' was the correct answer. Perhaps laughter would have filled the room, and there would have been shrieks of outrage as someone feigned something false, and perhaps he would have never known the Chances because he would have already had a family.

Wilfred's throat was dry. He would never know. For some reason, he couldn't find it within himself to long for what he had never had.

"It's snowing!"

He turned to the window at Irene's sudden statement—arguably a cheat, as Michael was currently stating, because she had spoken while it had been her turn.

It was snowing. Snowing hard. Flurries of white flakes were cascading down from the heavens and the garden upon which the drawing room overlooked was being swiftly covered in a sheet of white.

"Are you thinking what I'm thinking?" Irene said, and Wilfred's stomach twisted with a thrill as he nodded.

"Snowball fight?" he guessed, and her smile was reward enough.

As it turned out, it was not enough for everyone else.

"Only if we switch teams," Michael was saying, as the entire Chance family—minus Jessica, with the addition of Wilfred—attempted to put on scarves and gloves in the cramped hallway. "I will not have Teddy on my team."

Theodora stomped her foot. "Of all the low blows!"

"I'm just saying. You're a terrible shot and I want you failing to hit *me*!"

Irene giggled beside him and Wilfred's stomach turned over. "Are you having a good time, Wilfred?"

A good time? How else could he describe the joy he was experiencing, being a part of this family, if only, in technical terms, as a houseguest?

Her face fell, just for a moment, and Wilfred said hastily, "Not a good time. The best."

Her smile returned yet was transformed into a shriek as they stepped out into the freezing air and a snowball hit Irene in the chest.

"Michael!"

"That was me!" The Viscount Pernrith grinned, another snowball already held in his hands. "You took too long getting ready, you lot—prepare to be bombarded!"

The shrieks of laughter and giggles as backs were hit with snow, the snorts of mirth as Michael slipped and fell to the ground and the cackle of glee as Gwen threw a snowball that hit her brother full in the face—Wilfred could concentrate on none of them because he was too busy pulling Irene aside to avoid an errant shot from Theodora as his best friend slipped into his arms with a giggle.

"Careful!" Wilfred said before he could stop himself.

Irene looked up at him, her arms around his neck, her fingers somehow twisted in his hair. "I *am* being careful."

It was a moment—just a moment, that was all. A moment Wilfred wished he could freeze in time and look at, every day of his life, at his leisure.

Then Irene pulled away. "You are a terrible shot, Teddy. Have this!"

Perhaps it was an hour later, or perhaps two. Wilfred had been amazed that the Chances had stayed out playing with snowballs, the younger girls creating snow angels, until the sun kissed the horizon and their mother declared it was time to go inside for hot tea and cake.

"No exceptions," the viscountess said firmly as her son stomped inside and her husband walked in hand in hand with his youngest daughter. "Come on, Gwen, you know your nose goes a tremendous shade of red if you catch a cold!"

Wilfred was still chuckling as he and Irene, the last two to go in, dropped the snowballs they had been preparing to throw. "I do not think I had any idea just how violent Gwen was!"

"Oh, everyone is taken in by her," Irene said calmly as they stepped into the back hall.

Somehow, they were the only two still there. Several damp and dripping coats, scarves, and gloves were all the evidence that anyone else had been here, though Wilfred could hear the clink of china and the happy muffled chattering of the rest of the family coming from the drawing room door, which was closed.

It *had* been closed. The viscountess opened it and peered at them. "Tea and cake, you two!"

"I'm going to have to go upstairs to change, Mama. My gown is sodden," Irene said, spreading out her skirts. "I won't be long."

"I may have to change too," Wilfred said ruefully, thinking of the moment when Michael had grabbed him from behind and the two of them had fallen into a snow-covered bush. "But please, do not wait on our account."

"I'm afraid I was not going to." Irene's mother smiled, reminding Wilfred just how similar she and her daughter were with her expression. "Get dry, then come downstairs, you two. Don't be long!"

The door closed, and they were alone.

Wilfred tried to smile as he looked at the woman he loved. If he had been prescient enough to truly admit his feelings for Irene this year—truly admit them, without hiding behind the excuse he had given when he had kissed her all those weeks ago…why, then he could have been celebrating Christmas with the Chances as their future son-in-law.

As it was, he had not been brave enough, and now Irene had made it perfectly clear that she saw him as naught but a brother.

Being her brother would have to suffice.

That was, unless anything came of Mrs. Lymington's confrontation at the coffee house, and the two of them were forced to be married to protect Irene's honor and… No. He was grateful nothing seemed to have come of it. Grateful. Irene would not want to be forced into marriage, not even with him. Perhaps *especially* not with him.

"Here, let me help you," Wilfred said instinctively before he could stop himself.

He had moved before he could halt his fingers. Irene had been struggling with one of her hairpins, which had gotten tangled with her knitted scarf, and Wilfred was now mere inches away, his nose almost touching her own, as his fingers delicately untangled the metal from the wool.

Wilfred swallowed hard as his body stiffened at her proximity. *Do not think about how easily you could kiss her right now. Do not think about how you're breathing her air, and one day, should her reputation remain intact and she decide to marry, you might never be able to again. Do not think about how your fingers could trail down to her neck and lift up her chin...*

"Th-There," he said hoarsely, allowing the sodden scarf to fall to the ground.

When he met Irene's gaze, it was to see to his utter surprise that she had wet her lips. Or was that just a trick of the light, daylight fading and casting them in shadows, this private intimacy of their own?

"Wilfred," Irene said softly in barely a whisper.

Hot, urgent need sparked through him, but Wilfred forced it down. "Yes?"

She was going to ask him to step backward, he just knew it. Or suggest he help her with removing her pelisse. Or inquire about whether or not he had purchased her a present. Or—

"Kiss me," Irene whispered.

Wilfred did not need a second invitation. Spearing his fingers through her hair and dislodging so many pins that her light-golden curls cascaded damply down her back, Wilfred claimed the lips of the woman he loved and poured into that kiss all the passion and need he had been fighting for so long.

And she—she responded. Like a dream he had barely allowed himself to indulge in, Irene tilted her head, parting her lips to give him entrance as her hands found their way around his neck and pulled him closer.

Euphoria roared through Wilfred and his manhood stiffened

with aching ardor as the kiss deepened and somehow became more than a kiss; it became a promise, one that he wanted to make to them both.

That this would not be the last kiss they would ever share.

Eventually, Wilfred had to stop. The temptation to push Irene back two steps so that she was pinned up against the wall, unable to do anything save receive his pleasure, was too great.

He let go. He stepped back. And he hated that he had done so.

"I-I am sorry," he managed to breathe.

Irene's face had been unreadable but was now an open book. It was not a happy book. "Why?"

How could Wilfred explain it?

Because he had overstepped a boundary, once again, that he had promised himself he never would again? Because he had muddled the waters once again, confusing his own mind and body and making it impossible for her to understand what he truly meant? Because if one of her family, any of them, save, perhaps Michael, had stepped into the back hall at that moment, they would be forced into a marriage to save her reputation, trapping her into a marriage with a man who adored her but whom she clearly did not want like that?

Though... Though the thought finally struck him: *she* had asked *him* to kiss her.

Perhaps it was a shame no other Chance had discovered them. They'd escaped mention in the gossip rags, but surely, kisses in the hallway were not something even the trusting viscount and viscountess could ignore. Wilfred fought down the urge to kiss her again while knocking over an umbrella or something to gain their attention.

That would hardly be a very gentlemanly thing to do.

"You...asked me," Wilfred said in a wonder.

Precisely why he had said that aloud he did not know, but it caused a deep-red flush to stain Irene's cheeks. "I did."

"You... You asked me to kiss you," he said, his mind unable

to take in the fact that nonetheless was undeniable. "Why?"

It was his turn to ask and Irene's turn to stand there, unable to explain. And his mind whirled with desperate hopes and expectations that he knew could never be realized as he waited for her to speak.

"Because... Because..." Irene stammered, color still heightened and fingers now twisting together before her. "Because I... You kissed me before."

Wilfred cleared his throat, snow still dripping from his greatcoat. "I did."

"And you said that you loved me," she continued in a low voice.

Much against his will, Wilfred dragged his eyes away from the woman whom he did indeed love to check that the door to the drawing room was still completely closed.

It was. That did not assist him in formulating a response, but at least it meant they would not be overheard.

"I... I did. I did say that," he said, his voice slightly hoarse.

This is the moment. If he did not reveal, for a third time, his true affections now... Well, then, he would not deserve her. He just had to make sure she truly understood.

Wilfred inhaled deeply. "I told you then that it had been too much whiskey, and in a way it had been. I had intended to tell you of my affections, of my...my devotion to you in a much more coherent manner and the whiskey—"

"'Devotion'?" Irene's eyes were wide.

But she had not moved.

"Devotion," Wilfred said slowly, taking a step closer to her until he was but an inch from her. "I cannot lie to you any longer, Irene, nor myself. I am devoted to you in a way I shall never be to another. My love for you, the love not for a friend nor for a sister but as a woman, as a woman whom I hope to make my wife, it is strong and true and has been present for...for too long to go unspoken."

Her eyes were wide, her lips parted, and perhaps it was his

imagination, but it appeared that Irene's breathing was irregular.

And she had not moved.

"And I know you cannot love me as I do, that your feelings for me are warm but not ardent in the way I adore you, Reeny," Wilfred said, his words almost stumbling over each other in his desperation to get them said, once and for all. "But you needed to know. You should know how adored you are. You should know how I would kiss the very stones you walk on. And you should know I would do anything—anything—for you, even though you do not return such feelings."

There. He had said it.

Wilfred rather felt as though he had run a thousand leagues. His lungs were tight, every inch of him ached—though that could of course be due to repressing the need to kiss Irene senseless—but he had said it.

Everything, almost, that he felt. Everything he wanted her to know. Everything Irene needed to know about his affection.

Irene swallowed. "Don't call me 'Reeny.' And I am in love with you, too."

Wilfred winced. "I am sorry, I know. I keep trying not to fall into the habit of calling you that, but it was your name for so…so…"

Only then did his mind catch up with him.

Wilfred blinked. "I-I beg your pardon?"

"I didn't realize how much, how I loved you, until—it was all too late and I knew, or I thought I knew you loved another," and somehow Irene was babbling and he could not catch hold of her meaning. "So I thought I would retreat. I would make it clear that I did not mind that you did not return—"

"Wait, 'return'?"

"—thought I was doing the right thing, for I knew I wanted you, but the sensations, these desires, they were so new and I did not know how to tell you—"

"Reeny." Wilfred clasped her hands with one hand and placed a finger from his second on her lips.

Irene looked up at him, a flash of annoyance mingled with the embarrassment. "You know I don't like that nickname." She swallowed. "What about Miss Fletcher?"

"Forget about Miss Fletcher. *I've* already forgotten about Miss Fletcher. You love me," Wilfred said, half-bewildered, half-ecstatic.

She flushed, glancing down at their intertwined hands as she murmured, "Yes."

"But not as a brother," he insisted, using that same finger to lift up her chin, claiming her gaze with his own.

Irene's smile was nervous, but her boldness saw it through. "No. I want to take you to my bed, Wilfred. That sort of love."

That sort of love.

There was only one adequate response to such a thing. Slowly, almost reverentially, Wilfred lowered his lips to hers. Irene lifted her face up, clearly eager for his touch, and he groaned low and dark as his tongue met hers, their kiss a passionate embrace full of understanding.

It could not have been true. Yet it was true: she loved him. *She loves me and wants me clearly as much as I want her.*

That thought, which flashed through Wilfred's mind, was enough to spark a greater heat through the kiss. Somehow, her pelisse was unbuttoned and Wilfred's hands were around her waist, pulling her closer, needing to be tighter, but it was impossible and her hands were removing his scarf and unbuttoning his cravat and—

"Wilfred," Irene said, breaking the kiss.

Wilfred was breathing so hard, he could see stars. "Yes?"

"We should go upstairs."

It was not disappointment exactly that filled him at her remark. She was right; their clothes were absolutely soaked with snow. They would catch their deaths if they did not get into dry clothing.

Still. It was a shame to halt such a passionate moment of kissing with such a statement of banal reality.

"I suppose so," he said with a sigh.

Irene arched an eyebrow and flushed as she said, "Well, that's not quite the response I was expecting after I invited you upstairs to ravish me and ruin me for all other men. But fine. We don't have to."

Chapter Fifteen

THERE WAS NO sound but the dripping of melting snow onto the floor and the thudding of Irene's heart.

Ravish me? Ruin me? Had… Had she truly said that? Out loud? With her mouth?

Wilfred was staring as though he were considering the same question. Perhaps she had intended to say such a bold and outrageous thing, but had the words actually exited her mouth? Was it truly possible to speak such shameful things?

Irene swallowed. She was standing so close to Wilfred, she could almost breathe his air, yet she wanted to be closer still. She wanted her skin on his, no clothes obscuring their touch.

And he wanted that too…did he not?

"Irene," Wilfred managed to say through a strangled voice.

Heat blossomed in her cheeks as she waited for him to say more. It appeared, however, that no additional words would be forthcoming.

"Wilfred," she said softly.

His groan sounded like one of pain.

"I am sorry," she whispered, embarrassed now. "I should never have said that."

"You do not know what you are saying. You cannot understand the temptation to—"

"I am not trying to—to tempt you," Irene interrupted, a spark of irritation flaring. *Did the man truly not wish to understand?* "I am offering myself to you."

"I am not going to accept you on a plate as though you were a thing." There was an anger in Wilfred's eyes she had never noticed before. "Irene, you are—you are precious, yes, but a man should not possess you. You are far too brilliant, too important to be owned."

There was, it appeared, genuine anger in his tones, but Irene could not understand why.

Her head drooped. Well, it was never nice to receive rejection in any quarter, but this was particularly excruciating. She would just have to pretend she had never said anything.

"Irene."

She examined the floor as she spoke. "I just… I don't want to lose you again."

"Irene—"

"It feels ridiculous, doesn't it, the two of us loving each other and not knowing? Or at least, I did not even know my own mind." Irene laughed bitterly. "All that lost time, I did not even know what I was missing, and now I know and I am about to lose you all over again—"

Soft fingers gently lifted her chin and she was looking up again, up into the brilliant, shining eyes of a man who clearly adored her.

It did not make any sense. She loved him. He loved her. So why would he not take her?

"This is not a *no*," Wilfred said gently. "It is a *not yet*."

"But why?" Irene could not help but ask, her hand reaching out to splay against his chest. His pulse beat fast there, belied by his calm manner. "We love each other. I still can't quite believe—"

"You cannot believe that I would love you?" His incredulous tone made her smile. "You, Irene? God, you have no idea, do you?"

It was not a question, so Irene was not sure how she should answer. It would sound big headed, after all, to declare that yes, she knew she was lovable. Besides, precisely why someone like Wilfred—someone who knew all her faults, even, especially the ones she kept hidden from the world—would love her was quite beyond her.

Her breathing quickened as Wilfred continued to stare deep into her eyes.

"The issue," he murmured quietly as the sounds of her family chattering in the drawing room increased slightly in volume, "is not that I do not want to kiss you. It is that I do not think, once I begin again, I will know how to stop."

Irene swallowed, tasting the desire in her throat. *If he feels half the need I do...*

"Then don't," she said softly.

At once, she realized she had not explained herself well, for Wilfred dropped his hand as his expression hardened.

"Yes, you are right. We have both gotten carried away."

"I meant, don't stop," Irene interjected, keeping her voice low as an aching need for his touch thrummed through her. "Why should we, now that we finally know how deeply we care for each other?"

Wilfred's eyes had widened. "You... You truly mean it? You would...give yourself to me?"

A smile parted her lips as she entwined her hands around his neck. "Oh, Wilfred. You already have me."

The kiss was swift and sharp and Irene lost herself in Wilfred's touch. His strong arms encircled her and she leaned against him, secure in the knowledge that he would hold her tight.

This, this love between them... Irene still did not completely understand it. The idea that Wilfred could love her, knowing her as he did, was incredible.

But she did not have to understand it as Wilfred moaned in her mouth and twisted his jaw, allowing the kiss to deepen. She just had to accept it, grasp at the opportunity with both hands. Take advantage of this moment, this connection between them that surely no one could break.

"Irene," Wilfred groaned against her neck, his hands somehow removing the final few hairpins so her hair feathered out across her back and his fingers sank into it.

Somehow, she did not know how, Irene had pulled at his cravat and undone the blasted thing, and their breathing was heavy and she needed more, though precisely what, she could not tell.

"Wilfred," she whispered, pulling back.

When she caught his eye, it was to see reflected in his gaze the same desire she felt. Irene could not help but glorify in it. There was something intoxicating about wanting a man and being wanted in return.

She glanced at the staircase. "Upstairs?"

Wilfred did not reply—at least, not in words. Without a syllable being uttered, he took her hand and started to lead her up the stairs.

Started, being the operative word.

"Wilfred!" Irene hissed, delighted at his indecent act.

They could be found at any time; her family could come out of the drawing room, or a servant could step into the back hall, and what they would see would scandalize them all.

Irene, pressed up against the wall as Wilfred's body covered hers, his hands on her waist.

Or at least, they *had* been on her waist. Now one of them had slowly meandered down, caressing her hip, now cupping her buttocks and lifting her up. Irene had never felt more alive.

Wilfred lowered his lips and pressed reverential kisses on her neck. "You have no idea how long I've been waiting to do this."

Excitement thrilled through Irene's body. "Y-You have?"

The idea was extraordinary. The very thought that Wilfred, her best friend, had considered her worthy of being pressed up against the wall like this—just a few weeks ago, she would have laughed at such a thing.

She wasn't laughing now. Tendrils of sparking bliss were wending their way through her body, beginning at every point where Wilfred's hands touched her, and Irene was grateful that he had pressed her against the wall, for she was not certain she would be able to stand without it.

"Come on," she murmured, managing to extricate herself from his grasp and feeling immediately less joyful, less warm without his touch. "My bedchamber. No one will look for us there."

It was fortunate indeed that the sleeping arrangements had been so easily organized. Jessica's bedchamber had been offered to Wilfred, who had gladly accepted it, so Irene was not sharing with either of her younger sisters. That meant that when they finally managed to reach the upstairs landing, it was her bedchamber at the very end of the corridor, and Jessica's beside it meant that no one was likely to hear—

What?

Irene swallowed hard as she reached her bedchamber door. She was hardly ignorant; some of the Chance gentlemen, her cousins more than her brother, were rather boisterous when it came to discussing such things, if they thought the ladies were not around. Several years ago, she had been bold enough to ask her flushing mother what they had meant. Irene had been astonished to hear of more of it, and a tad incredulous, but she had accepted it as a part of a woman's duty in a marriage.

Beyond that, she had not given the act of lying together much thought.

She was now. How, precisely, was he… That was, his…his *member* supposed to enter her?

It all seemed rather complicated.

"Reeny?"

Irene blinked. Evidently, she had grown lost in her thoughts and had halted for too long, for Wilfred was staring with a confusion so familiar, it jolted her stomach.

"Just… Just thinking," she said firmly, her hand still on the door handle.

She did not move forward.

Wilfred lifted his hands and cradled her face with his palms.

Palms she knew well. There was the little moon-shaped scar, a remnant of his first penknife. There was the finger that stuck out a little. He had broken it when he had been about twelve. How had he done that? Was that the time they had climbed the old oak tree at Stanphrey Lacey and the bough had cracked—or was it the riding accident he'd suffered, and she had been the one to run and get a grown up to help with—

"Reeny," came a gentle voice from a long way away. "You don't have to do this."

Irene blinked again, and Wilfred's concerned and adoring face swam into view.

Her secret place between her thighs ached, watering as though it hungered for him, and Irene knew she would always regret this day if she did not step forward in confidence and claim what she knew was hers.

Him.

"I *want* to do this," she said aloud, and she tried not to smile as she opened the door. "And don't call me 'Reeny.'"

Wilfred's gentle chuckle seemed to renew her afresh as they stepped into her bedchamber. "Goodness, the place hasn't changed a bit."

"I'd forgotten that you used to be permitted in here," Irene said quietly, shutting the door behind them and watching as her best friend, and now lover, stepped into her bedchamber. "How old were you when my papa took you aside and said it was no longer appropriate?"

"Oh, twelve, I think," said Wilfred with a shrug. He trailed his hand along her bookcase, smiling at the volumes, before turning to her bed. "But this… This is different."

Irene's throat went dry. "Oh, well… Papa said I was an adult now and needed an adult bed."

It was very different from the one Wilfred, as a child, would have seen. Why, she could hardly remember that old trundle thing. It was still poor Gweny's bed, but when Irene had come out into Society, her father had treated her to a new bed.

A large four-poster sat in the middle of the room. Its oak corners stretched up to the heavens, and the fabric that covered the top was a dark, rich green, as were the coverlets on top of the mattress.

Wilfred reached out and stroked the embroidered coverlet, and Irene found herself inexplicably envious of the fabric.

Envious! Of a blanket!

"It's perfect," he said quietly, seating himself on the bed and turning to look at her with a serious expression. "And so are you."

Irene did her best not to roll her eyes as she stepped toward him. "You don't have to say that sort of mushy stuff, you know."

"And what if I mean it?" Wilfred challenged with a raised eyebrow. "Irene, you are perfect. You... You don't know how long I have waited for you to open your eyes and see me. It might be your only failing."

Heat blossomed across Irene's cheeks. "I cannot understand why I didn't realize what I felt for you was different."

"It doesn't matter how long it took us to get here. The point," Wilfred said, holding out his hands as Irene took them, "is that we got here."

Irene could not help but smile as she leaned down, her legs nestled between his knees, and kissed him lightly on the mouth.

And then not so lightly.

Oh, this man, he made her want to take all her clothes off and allow him to kiss every inch of her. Even now, the pair of them fully clothed and herself standing before him, not even sitting by Wilfred on the bed, Irene could feel the sparks of sensual bliss he created with that wicked tongue of his.

"Reeny," he exhaled.

Irene did not quite know what possessed her to do it. All she knew was that one moment she was standing before Wilfred, her Wilfred, her hands in his, kissing him chastely—well, mostly chastely—and the next, she had mounted him, straddling him on the bed and kissing him furiously.

Wilfred moaned, but it sounded like a pleased moan, so Irene did not bother to move. Why should she, now that she was pressed up against the man with his tongue teasing a decadent route of pleasure in her mouth, one of his hands tangled in her hair and one cupping her buttocks?

His strong body, the hard planes of his chest, were perfect to melt against. Irene could barely think, only feel, knowing that the aching need within her was somehow growing even as she attempted to sate it.

"Wilfred," Irene whimpered, her fingers scrabbling at his shirt buttons as something in her begged for more.

What, precisely, she did not know.

His answer was naught but a groan, his hands moving to the hems of her skirts and pushing up the fabric until her knees were exposed to the air.

Irene halted her kiss. "I want—I want you. I want everything. I want—"

"Then let me love you," Wilfred replied, gazing up with such adoration that she was quite overcome by it. "If you trust me, Reeny, if you want to give yourself to me, let me accept."

All thoughts, all sense had completely disappeared from Irene's mind. Yes, these were the sorts of things one should say and share with one's husband alone—but surely, that was what Wilfred would soon be? How could he not be, considering how much they cared for each other?

She nodded, shyness unexpectedly preventing her from speaking.

His grin was half-teasing, half-serious. "No, I think after all these years of waiting—"

"*Wilfred!*"

"I need to hear it," he murmured, his eyes never leaving hers. "I need to hear how much you want me."

He was the most irritating, rascal of a man! Irene was in half a mind to dismount from the cad and march out of the room, even if it was *her* room...but then his thumb brushed innocently—

perhaps not-so-innocently—over the budded nipple struggling to free itself from her stays and a shot of pleasure made Irene moan.

She could never leave him.

"I want you to ravish me," she whispered, her voice only getting stronger as she laughed at his imperiously curious expression. "Damn it, Wilfred, I love you, and I want to share this with you. N-Not just tonight. Every night."

Unsure as she had been as to precisely what he was looking for, it appeared that she had found it. Wilfred's ravenous mouth had returned to hers and Irene whimpered as the pleasure returned, fizzing and soaring through her body like lightning. His mouth seemed to be everywhere, on her lips, at her throat, nestled into the swells of her décolletage, and his hands, his hands were everywhere too, cupping her cheeks, tugging the last pin from her hair, pushing her skirts past her thighs and undoing his—

Irene caught her breath as her fingertips suddenly reached warm skin and wiry hair. Goodness, had she been the one to undo all these shirt buttons?

"God, I love you," murmured Wilfred against her neck as his frantic hands undid the buttons of his trousers and—

It was not quite a cry, and it was not quite a gasp. It was probably something in the middle.

Irene looked down, wide-eyed, at…at…

"What did you expect?" asked Wilfred in a slightly worried tone, glancing up at her face then down at his large, jutting manhood, then back to her face.

Well. *Expected.* Expected wasn't quite the word. Irene had never… She had not thought…

"You went to that art exhibition with your cousin Evelyn," Wilfred was saying, his voice somehow distant and his cheeks definitely red. "Reeny, I thought you knew—"

"You're magnificent," Irene whispered.

And he was. He was just so much…so much *more* than she had expected.

Reaching down and brushing a thumb over its glistening head, Irene reveled unexpectedly in the sudden yelp and spasm that came over the man seated beneath her.

A strange flicker of joy, of power, of delight in the power she had over him, sparked through Irene. Dear God, so she could give just as much sensuality as he could. It was... It was marvelous.

Just like in their friendship, she could please him and he could please her and dear God, it was a wonder anyone did anything else other than this!

"You'll have to tell me what to do," were the words that slipped from Irene's lips, the vulnerability suddenly easy, natural.

After all, this was Wilfred. If she could not admit her ignorance and ask for guidance from Wilfred, from whom could she?

But for some reason, the redness in his cheeks was deepening. As though he were embarrassed. As though he...

Understanding, or at least a hint of understanding, dawned. Irene's jaw dropped. "You haven't done this before!"

"Well, with whom would I have done this?" hissed Wilfred, as though they could be overheard. "I've been waiting for you, you dolt!"

Irene could have laughed, though she was prescient enough to recognize that her best friend, now her lover, would perhaps not react well to such a movement. But it was difficult not to.

Of course, Wilfred would never have shared this with anyone else—the thought was abhorrent! But... *Well.* She had always presumed a gentleman was experienced in such a matter.

Wilfred looked up, adoration shining through his eyes. "I may not have practiced with anyone else, but that doesn't mean I don't know what to... What we need to... Do you trust me, Reeny?"

And she looked down at him, her thighs straddling his own and her whole body pulsing with need for him, and smiled. "Completely."

His deep and passionate kiss almost twisted her mind completely, and perhaps that was his intention, for Irene hardly noticed the strong, unhesitant hands that grasped her hips, lifting her up several inches, then moving her forward, then slowly, slowly, moving her down—

Irene's eyes shot open and she gasped into their kiss, "Wilfred!"

Oh, it was intoxicating, and it was invading, and the feeling of his manhood pressing against her folds was bewildering and yet the bliss was already soaring through her as he pushed deeper, deeper, and Irene could not understand how she could accommodate so much, but her body welcomed him and oh, it was everything. Everything.

He was everything.

And the gasping, panting Wilfred beneath her, gazing up not just with adoration now but with possession, a keen determination that she was his and he was hers, was the man she wanted. For the rest of her life.

"Now ride me," Wilfred whispered, kissing her neck, her lips. "I've seen how well you can ride. How many times have we gone out together, just the two of us?"

Irene could barely think, barely breathe. "'R-Ride'?"

The man she loved nodded. "Ride."

Hardly sure if the man had a good grasp of his own wits, Irene decided to appease him. After all, what harm could a little movement—

"Oh!" she gasped.

A little movement, it appeared, could do very little harm but could do much, much good. Just a few inches up on her knees, pulling herself free but not entirely from Wilfred's manhood, that had felt good—but thrusting down and spearing herself on him had felt *very* good.

Wilfred's eyes gleamed. "Ride me, Reeny."

And so she did. Panting heavily, hands clutching his shoulders and her head eventually falling back with the overwhelming carnality, Irene rocked and rode on her lover, her voice slowly growing, unable to hold back. "Yes—yes, oh, God, yes, that's—Wilfred, you feel so—"

"And you feel so damned good," gritted out Wilfred through his teeth, and for some reason, the poor man looked just as pained as he did pleasured. "Take it, Reeny, take all the satisfaction you want."

She did not need such an instruction. Irene's body seemed to know what it wanted, plunging harder and harder onto Wilfred's thick manhood, which sparked teasing, aching joy through every inch of her body, and yet there appeared to be something more, something just out of reach, and she could weep for the frustration.

And somehow, he knew.

Naturally, he knows. Wilfred is my best friend, Irene thought wildly as one of his hands reached out and caressed her breast, his thumb and forefinger capturing her nipple and twisting in a way that made her whole body buckle.

"I need—I need," Irene panted.

She was unable to say more, for Wilfred had covered her mouth with hers, his tongue twisting with agonizing ecstasy, and God, it was infuriating. She was so close—

Irene's eyes widened and her squirming shout of surprise was swallowed by his kiss as Wilfred's other hand moved to beneath her skirts, to where they joined, and his thumb reached into her folds and circled slowly around a part of her that...that...that...

Irene exploded.

She had not meant to. She had not known it was coming, this undulating blast of bliss, this decadent detonation of ecstasy throughout every pore of her body, but it was here and she could do nothing but let go, losing herself to the peak, and beneath her, Wilfred was bucking and crying her name and all it did was push her higher, higher, until she reached a peak that wrenched a cry from her lips.

"Wilfred!"

How, precisely, Irene had collapsed onto her best friend, the two of them tangled in skirts and shirts and sheets on the bed, she did not know.

What she did know was that she was lying in the arms of Wilfred, having shared the most inexplicable pleasure, and she would never, never be the same again.

Chapter Sixteen

December 25, 1840

WHEN WILFRED OPENED his eyes, his lips were curled into a grin.

How could they not have been? Somehow, he had managed what he had considered to be impossible: he had forced Irene to declare that she loved him.

Well. 'Forced' was a strong word.

"Don't call me 'Reeny.' And I am in love with you, too."

She loved him. *She loves me.*

Wilfred wriggled underneath the bedclothes with unbridled delight. Even just thinking those three words filled his heart with heat, a heat he had never known before.

And speaking of sensations he had never felt before…

Wilfred's eyes widened as he sat up hurriedly and looked in the bed beside him. There was no one there.

Perhaps he should have expected the pained sense of emptiness that the sight gave him. Irene had evidently slipped out in the middle of the night, undoubtedly to retreat to her own bedchamber.

No, not retreat. Wilfred felt as light as a feather as he settled back down in the welcoming bed against the soft mattress. She never had to retreat from him again—but they would have to pretend, at least to her family, that their love had not entirely been consummated.

Not that he could think of a way that their love could be consummated to a greater extent…

It was perhaps ten minutes later, or maybe an hour, when a clanging from a large clock interrupted Wilfred's attempts to think of a way that their love could have been even more consummated.

That damned clock. It *would* keep going on and on.

And on. Wilfred groaned as he turned onto his side to look at the longcase clock. *Why did it keep going on like that?*

Because it was ten o'clock.

No. It couldn't be.

Perhaps it could be. Wilfred's feet winced away from the cold floorboards as he swiftly rose, pulling aside the curtains to reveal windowpanes seared with frost, but a frost melting against the brilliant Christmas Day sunshine.

Christmas Day. And it was near ten o'clock. Goodness, what must his hosts have been thinking!

"Arghh!" muttered Wilfred unhelpfully as he rushed to his trunk and stared at his clothes.

This was ridiculous. He was the Duke of Aynor. He was a grown man. He had a degree, and a fortune, and the love of a good woman, and he would be blowed if he was going to struggle to dress himself.

After all, he had taken the blessed things off himself at times before, hadn't he? How hard would it be to put the blasted things on?

As it turned out, very hard. Giving his valet the week off had felt generous at the time, but now he couldn't understand what he had been thinking. Wilfred could not understand it, but there was clearly some sort of secret skill to understanding precisely how a cravat was supposed to be tied, and his waistcoat buttons appeared to dislike him. It was all he could do to pull his boots on, then tug them off and put his slippers on, then agonize over what would be most appropriate as a guest, then put his boots on and then his slippers on—

"Aren't you up yet?" called a very recognizable voice through the door. "Goodness, come on, you dunderhead!"

"I'll be there in a moment, Michael!" Wilfred called out.

Michael. *Irene's brother—his future brother-in-law.*

The thought was an unbalancing one. As soon as Wilfred had thought it, he tipped over from attempting to put a slipper on one foot and tug a boot off the other. The resounding *thump* would surely be heard downstairs and the whole Chance family would think him a—

But no.

Wilfred hummed as he settled himself on the side of the bed, inhaled deeply, and put his slippers on. The Chance family had never thought him a fool, even when—especially when—he had been one. They had always trusted him, always known him to be a good man.

There was no reason to suppose that they would take against him, now that he wanted to be one of their number forever.

Fears settled, slippers on, waistcoat buttons rebuttoned the moment Wilfred had realized that he had missed one, he opened the door and froze at the landing.

No one was there. Evidently, the family must have been downstairs—perhaps had even breakfasted.

Wilfred tried not to puff out his chest as he slowly descended the wide, sweeping staircase, but it was a challenge. He was engaged to be married to Miss Irene Chance. At least, as good as engaged. Within moments, the whole thing would be announced to her family and there would be champagne and congratulations—

"Do you mean to tell me that Aynor never told you?" came Michael's voice through the drawing room door.

It was ajar. As Wilfred crept up to it, thanking his good fortune that he had plumped for the slippers and not the boots, he could continue to hear the conversation.

The conversation, he swiftly realized, that was clearly about his affections for Irene. What else could it have been about?

"He never told me. Not a word."

Wilfred blinked. Irene's voice was a mite... Well, dare he

think it, a mite upset. It was only natural, he supposed. It had been a rather large secret to keep for such a long time.

"And to think, we thought we knew him!" That was the viscountess's voice.

Strange. She sounded offended.

Wilfred swallowed. *Ah.* Yes, perhaps he should have spoken to Irene's parents before giving way to his feelings. It was only right and natural that her mother and father be offended that he had not sought their permission first.

He leaned closer to the door, pulse thumping.

There was a corresponding *thump* inside the room, as though someone had...dropped a book?

"I would have thought the man would have had the decency to talk to me about it!"

Wilfred's stomach dropped. That was the viscount—and there was a terseness to his tone he had never heard before. The man never angered...though Wilfred had never witnessed anyone disrespecting his daughters, as the man clearly thought had occurred.

Bother. Suddenly, staying for Christmas did not seem to be the cleverest thing he had ever done.

"I just don't understand it," came Theodora's voice. "Wilfred?"

It was difficult not to be mortified by the sound of her voice. Wilfred was not a proud man—at least, he did not consider himself to be so—but surely, he was not that bad.

But what did not make sense, and what crinkled his brow, was Irene's response. He had expected... Well, not perhaps a passionate defense, but *some* defense.

"What can I tell you?" she said, her voice listless as it crept through the ajar door. "I could never have believed it of him."

Wilfred swallowed. She did not have to sound so...so despondent, did she? Was it possible—surely, it could not have been possible that she regretted what had happened last night?

Worse: she hadn't told them, had she?

His worst fears appeared confirmed as Irene's mother's voice spoke again. "I know it is very disappointing, Irene, but you have to face it. It's happened now, and it can't be taken back."

Can't be taken back?

Wild thoughts whirled through Wilfred's mind. What could he have possibly done to merit such a statement?

Had he not pleasured her sufficiently? It had always been his worry that he would not know how to—but then he had read that book, and it had been most informative, and she had sounded like…like…

Wilfred's cheeks reddened as he stood alone in the hall. Irene had certainly sounded as though she had enjoyed herself. So why the despondency? Why tell her whole family?

"I suppose the whole of Society will know now," came Michael's voice, quiet and clearly upset.

Wilfred almost fell over. *The whole—why on earth would anyone know?* Dear God, this had gotten out of hand. Though he had plainly offended Irene in some way, he had hoped—presumed, perhaps—that if that were ever the case, she would come to him about it.

Not tell her whole family. Dear God.

Well, there was nothing for it. He could not hide out here any longer.

Inhaling deeply and wishing to goodness he wasn't wearing his slippers, Wilfred opened the door and stepped in.

The entire Chance family froze.

The Viscountess Pernrith was standing by the blazing fire, a hand on the mantelpiece and distress in her eyes. Her husband was seated in the armchair, presumably that morning's newspaper dropped to the floor beside him and anger on his brows. Michael appeared to have been pacing—that would explain the modulation of his voice—but had frozen with his hand protectively on the shoulder of Irene, who was not looking at him, while Theodora and Gwen were seated side by side on the sofa, both of them glaring. Most surprisingly, they were not glaring at each other…but at him.

For some strange reason, Wilfred's mouth was dry, and when he came to speak, it was in an odd sort of croak. "Good… Good morning."

"Is it?" snapped Michael, charging toward him like a bull. "Is it, indeed?"

Wilfred did not flinch—the man did not scare him—but it was most unpleasant. "Yes," he said firmly, his gaze shifting to Irene. "It is. The best sort of morning. A morning full of good news."

He had hoped she would meet his eyes, smile nervously, perhaps even with a hint of embarrassment. After all, the whole family appeared to know what they had shared the previous evening.

That did not occur.

"Good news," breathed Irene's mother faintly.

"I cannot believe it," Gwen muttered.

Michael, most inexplicably, curled his fist. "How dare you?"

"Look, the wedding will be as soon as I can possibly arrange it," Wilfred said hastily, lifting up his hands in an attempt to calm the situation. Honestly, did they really believe he would bed Irene and then not marry her? Did they not know how he felt about her? "I will be doing everything in my power to make the wedding as beautiful as—"

He wasn't sure what he was going to say—he was hardly a wedding connoisseur—but that did not matter. The Viscountess Pernrith burst into tears, as did Theodora, and the two of them along with Gwen were swiftly and inexplicably marched out of the room by a stone-faced Michael.

"What—but—it will be a lovely wedding," Wilfred said helplessly, utterly lost.

He turned, as he always did when the ground underneath him was shifting and the world was most confusing, to his true north. Irene.

Her face was white and there was anger in her expression.

Actual anger. Wilfred could not recall the time he had ever seen such a countenance in Irene's face.

Panic, something he had dampened down and ignored for the last few minutes, rose up in force. What on earth had happened? He loved this woman, he had told this woman he loved her—multiple times—and last night, she had seemed to welcome his affection. Surely, she had understood that he meant to marry her? Had he not been clear, just now, that he would organize the wedding as soon as possible?

"Irene," Wilfred began.

He halted as Viscount Pernrith slowly rose from his seat. The man's presence was uncanny; he was not a large man, nor a violent one. No hands were bunched into fists and there was no suggestion of vehemence.

Yet Wilfred took a step back. It did not matter whether or not Viscount Pernrith was a violent man. He clearly believed his daughter had been wronged in some way, and there was no telling what a man in that position would do.

"I think," the Viscount Pernrith said quietly, "you have a serious conversation to have with my daughter. I will be just outside, and if she calls for me, I tell you, by God, even after seeing you grow from a boy to a man—"

"Papa," Irene said softly.

A bullet, a bull, a raging beast could not have slowed the Viscount Pernrith in his path, yet two softly spoken syllables from his daughter did.

Wilfred swallowed, throat dry, as father and daughter exchanged a silent look before the elder departed the room. The door closed. They were, to all intents and purposes, alone.

Right.

"What in blazes is going on?" Wilfred hissed as he strode toward Irene, not angry with her, merely desperate to be near her.

She shied away. His Irene. She stepped back.

Wilfred halted, his feet unable to continue. Desperation filled his lungs. Something had gone wrong here, but it was something small, something simple, surely? Something they would sort out swiftly and explain to her family easily and laugh about, in years to come?

It had to be. He couldn't face the alternative.

"I don't understand why your family had to know," he said quietly.

There was no petulance in his voice, but Irene glared as though he had no right to say such a thing.

"That's a strange position to take," she said coldly. "I don't see you keeping it to yourself."

Wilfred swallowed. He hadn't exactly told many people about his feelings for Irene, but perhaps telling her own brother had her nettled. Yes, perhaps that was it—she was miffed Michael had known before her.

Was that it?

"The wedding will take place soon," he said soothingly. Surely, that would calm her nerves? She was worried that she was ruined, yes? "Whom else do you think we should invite? Besides your entire family—Irene. You're crying."

His beloved was crying. Just a few tears, but they were sufficient to tear his heart out.

Wilfred swallowed. "We don't have to invite the rest of the *ton*. We don't have to invite anyone."

"I cannot believe you are asking me about whom to invite to your wedding!" Irene choked out, striding to the window. "After—After everything! After all we shared!"

Something was wrong here. Wilfred was not the brightest button in the box, he knew that, but he knew they were talking at cross purposes, weren't they?

"Why wouldn't I ask your opinion about whom to invite to the wedding?" he asked, his head tilted.

Irene strode past him, picked up the newspaper, and thrust it against his chest with enough force to leave a mark. "Because I never thought I would be helping you organize your wedding to another woman!"

Wilfred stared. The words rang in his ears as though a large elephant had attempted to whisper a secret.

"I don't understand," he said quietly.

Another few tears had escaped Irene's beautiful eyes. "Neither do I! And y-yesterday, you said—"

"I know what I said and I meant it—what is this talk of another woman?" Wilfred asked, bewildered.

For some reason, the question appeared only to aggrieve. "You cannot seriously think I would not see it! That I would not *notice* when it happened, whether I'm *invited* or not!"

"See what?" Wilfred had not intended to raise his voice, but dear God, he was being pushed to it. "Make sense, woman!"

"Oh, you are a fine one to tell me to make sense!" Irene shot back, cheeks pink and eyes sparkling. "After all the talk of *love* last night, you had placed the notice in the newspaper already, you absolute cad!"

Silence fell in the Chances' drawing room.

Wilfred tried to speak. Tried to move his mouth, move his mind, but nothing was working.

Notice? Newspaper? Other woman?

'Flabbergasted' was insufficient. 'Utterly daggled' was insufficient. There was no word that could sufficiently describe his whirling thoughts.

"I... I don't—"

"Page forty-six," Irene said, blinking rapidly as though to force her tears back. "You cad."

'Cad' was perhaps a tad strong. There was evidently some mistake, Wilfred reassured himself as his scrabbling fingers attempted to rush through the newspaper. Perhaps the gossip rags had finally mentioned him and Irene, not naming her and only calling her 'a lady,' and they had presumed—

Oh. Oh, dear God.

"We have discovered that there will soon be an engagement announced between Wilfred Zouch, Duke of Aynor, and a Miss Fletcher,

daughter of a Mr. Thomas Fletcher."

Well, that was him. And that was…

Wilfred's stomach surged, its nausea growing, and it was a damned good thing he hadn't come down in time for breakfast, for it would certainly have been making a return visit.

"Ah," he said weakly.

"So, you admit it, you *are* engaged!" Irene shot at him, pacing away and turning from the window to glare, presumably from a safe distance.

It was such a shame her position made her perfectly outlined by the Christmas Day sunshine. She positively *glowed*.

Damn it, man, this is not the time to—

Holding the newspaper carefully before his thickening manhood, Wilfred attempted to gather his thoughts. "There is a very simple explanation to all of this."

"Yes, you have been courting this woman—and I saw you with her, I cannot believe I have been so stupid!" Irene snapped, glaring. "I don't know *when* you've been courting her, seeing as how I see you so often, but you certainly have been busy! And now you are engaged and clearly not satisfied with one woman, you—"

Her eyes darted to the door, which Wilfred only now realized had been pushed ajar. *Ah, yes. Her father.*

"Well," continued Irene, and her cheeks were flushed when he looked back at her. "My point is, you are engaged to another woman! And all this time, I thought—"

"Not *all this time*. You didn't seem to love me like that until recently. And you only realized that I loved you yesterday," pointed out Wilfred fairly—or what he thought was fairly. "It hasn't even been four and twenty hours!"

It was completely the wrong thing to say.

"Oh!" said Irene, markedly nettled. "So there is a time limit, is there, from you announcing your affections—which were clearly false—and me securing you before you wander off with another woman, is that it?"

Wilfred groaned, though he was careful not to move the newspaper.

How could this have gone so wrong?

Well, the whole misadventure had been a mistake from the start. He should have realized, right from the beginning, that asking Miss Fletcher to pretend to be a woman he was courting would only lead to trouble—but he had wanted to pique Irene's interest!

And wait a minute, didn't Michael know all this? And he had gotten angry alongside Irene, as if entirely ignorant of the affair? He didn't... He didn't honestly think Wilfred had fallen in love with the woman he'd suggested Wilfred use to make Irene jealous, did he?

He risked a glance and winced. And he *had* made her jealous. Even so, he had been out with Miss Fletcher *once*. He hadn't even introduced her to anyone during the walk. Who could have run this piece of gossip, naming her and her supposed father, and why *this*, so soon after he and Irene had been called out, instead of a piece about him and Irene instead? He had not checked that Miss Fletcher had received his note, calling off the whole pretense, but he could not imagine the woman would go this far without his permission or further payment. Unless...she hoped to blackmail him into additional payment. He hardly knew the woman to judge if that was possible.

There had never been a more embarrassing moment in his life—but Wilfred was not going to lose the only woman he had ever loved merely because he was a dolt. He had always been a dolt. He had not always had the affections of Miss Irene Chance.

"Look, it's quite simple," Wilfred began cheerfully. "I paid Miss Fletcher—"

"You paid a—I do not want to know about your nighttime harlots!" hissed Irene, scarlet blotches now appearing in her cheeks.

Wilfred almost fell over his own feet in his haste to rush toward her. "No, I meant—"

"And you said, last night," Irene whispered, then she lowered her voice even further, her gaze darting to the door to the hall, "you said you had never—with anyone before!"

Oh, hell. "I hadn't," Wilfred said in a whisper. "Miss Fletcher was only paid to—"

"I do not want to know the sordid details of your connection!" Irene snapped. "And now you're engaged to her! Well, I suppose I should be grateful that you are acting honorably to at least one woman, though how you expect Society not to gossip about the low origins of your new bride, I cannot say!"

"Irene, you've completely misunderstood. This is gossip. Mere gossip. Miss Fletcher and I are not like that."

"Gossip has its origins in *something*! It reads like a proper engagement announcement! And to think you have manipulated me into—well, you know!"

Wilfred tried to grasp her hands, but Irene pulled away as though scalded. "Reeny, it's not—"

"Don't you dare."

He stopped, his lungs tight. He had never heard Irene speak like that before.

She was panting heavily, scowling as though…as though she did not know him. "You have manipulated me and you have lied to me, telling me you have been in love with me for years and yet never saying anything, and all this time—and what if, because you were not free, I had wanted to marry another?" She whispered again. "And he found out you had *ruined* me?"

And now Wilfred had never heard himself speak like this before. "I would not have let that happen, Irene. You are mine."

"No, I'm not." And she was crying again now, angrily and fiercely, dashing away the tears with the back of her hand as she maintained a direct stare. "I cannot be yours, not now. Wilfred, you fool, this engagement, you cannot just back out of it! It's been announced, it's in the newspapers, I can never—we can never—"

"It's not an official announcement!" Panic stifled every

breath. "She's just a—it's not real. It's not serious. It's all a misunderstanding—"

"You are a duke. You think you can just break an engagement now that it has been alluded to in the papers, whatever her origins?" Irene's tears only made her more beautiful as she stood erect, calm and yet raging at him, and Wilfred had never wanted to hold her, comfort her, more than he did now, when she would recoil at his touch. "You lied to me. You betrayed me. You took everything from me and now I can never have you?"

Wilfred tried to think, but the sight of Irene before him in such distress was untangling his thoughts swifter than he could catch hold of them. "I love you—"

"Well, you have a very strange way of showing it," snapped Irene, crossing her arms. "I want you to leave, Your Grace."

He inhaled deeply. *Yes, perhaps it would be best if we calmed down separately and—*

His mind finally caught up with him. "'Your—Your Grace'?"

"I think you should leave this house, Your Grace," Irene repeated, a strange sort of detachment in her tone that Wilfred did not like. "You are not welcome here, and I presume you will have much preparations to do. After all, you will soon be welcoming Miss Fletcher to your home as your bride."

No. No, this could not be happening.

"Irene—Irene, it's *you* I want to welcome as my bride!"

"Well, then, perhaps you shouldn't have led the world to believe that you will soon be announcing your engagement to another woman," Irene said coldly, stepping past him to the door, which she opened.

The Viscount Pernrith and his son were waiting outside. The elder had a face of stone. The younger had his arms crossed. How could Michael, the instigator of all of this, not even take his side? Did not one Chance trust him, after all?

He suddenly felt a cold, stabbing sensation inside him. He'd thought they were family, but this was all it had taken for them to turn their backs on him. The mere printed gossip of an unknown source—when Michael, at least, knew the circumstances of its origins and could help him make his case. And still, even Irene's brother believed that nonsense over Wilfred's account of the matter.

"Goodbye, Your Grace," Irene said coolly, as though…as though she had never known him, let alone loved him.

Wilfred did not know what to do. He could not think, could not breathe. All he could do under the triad of glares from the Chances was traipse past them, through the hall, out of the front door that a glaring Dempster had opened, and into the freezing Christmas Day sunshine.

He turned on his heels. "Irene—"

The door slammed in his face.

Chapter Seventeen

December 26, 1840

THE UNWRAPPING WAS over. The ribbon had been tidied away. Gwen had already broken one of her Christmas presents, and she and Teddy had squabbled over who was able to play the new pianoforte music first. The servants had been sent home for their day with their boxes. Michael had wandered off, much to their mother's chagrin, and Irene…

Irene stared out of the window at the frost-covered lawn. The garden had received no sunshine today, Boxing Day, and its tendrils of icy art traced over every leaf.

If she had been her artist cousin Evelyn, perhaps she would have been able to find some beauty in the sight. As it was…

"I think you should leave this house, Your Grace. You are not welcome here."

Irene clenched her fists, sitting all alone curled up in the armchair near the fire by the library, but unclenched them just as quickly.

What was the point in getting angry? What was the point in attempting to rationalize the fool's actions?

He had done it. She believed him when he'd said he hadn't officially announced any such thing, but he had evidently acted so indecorously with this woman—whatever her origins, if the gossiper knew her father's name, perhaps she was not too low to be a duchess, after all—at some point that the whole world considered him engaged to another, and now…now Irene and Wilfred were forever separated.

Irene brushed an errant tear away. With every moment that she promised herself she would not cry over Wilfred Matthew Kirk Chesterham Zouch, Duke of Aynor, another tear seemed to come. Apparently, she was just as unable to control her idiotic eyes as she was her idiotic best friend.

Her former best friend.

Footfalls in the hall, and chattering, laughing voices. A ghost of a smile brushed across Irene's lips. It appeared her two sisters had made it up, from the sound of it. She had always thought she and Wilfred would never fall out, not properly. Not for long. And yet…

How could she ever forgive him for this?

Her head fell listlessly back against the wing-backed armchair. There appeared to be no energy in her limbs, no drive within her to sample the baking, the smell of which had wafted up from the kitchens since daybreak. Her parents had gone out for a Boxing Day stroll, as had presumably many of their acquaintance, but Irene had pleaded a headache and no one had been brave enough to argue with her.

And so here she was. Alone. *As I always will be.*

Irene almost laughed, her own thoughts were so ridiculous. But they were true. How was she supposed to love, and be loved by, another man after what she and Wilfred had shared? That intimacy, that complete abandon…no. No, she would never feel that again.

Shifting her slippers off so she could slip her feet under her knees, Irene sighed. The garden remained unchanging. Just like she had thought her friendship with Wilfred would be.

Another tear slipped down her cheek.

"Your headache still giving you trouble?"

Irene started but did not look around. She knew that voice. "No, Mama."

The door closed—in truth, she had not noticed it open—and gentle footfalls meant her mother's face soon appeared before her. The Viscountess Pernrith slowly lowered herself onto the sofa opposite her daughter and examined her.

Irene looked away. She did not want to be looked at, even by her own mother. She did not want to be beheld by anyone ever again. What had that gained her? There was nothing, nothing to be gained by such connection.

Her truest friend, her better half—and now that Wilfred had made his confession, she could not but see him as the man she loved, even as she hated him—had gone from her forever.

She would be alone. Forever.

"You know," her mother said quietly, "I do not think I have ever seen you look so miserable."

Irene let out a pitiful laugh as she brushed aside the treacherous tears. "Thank you, Mama."

"Still very pretty, as always," her mother continued with a lilting smile. "But still. Not happy."

'Not happy.' Well, it was not an inaccurate description.

"No," she said quietly, not quite able to face her mother's gaze. "I am not happy."

Happy, that the best man she had ever known had lied to her? Happy, that the man she had always thought would be by her side was gone—and not just gone, but gone to stand by the side of another? Happy, that the best and the brightest of Society would soon be attending the wedding of the Season: the wedding of the Duke of Aynor?

"You know," her mother said delicately, "you might want to talk about it. It might help."

Irene tried not to laugh as she shifted her feet, pulling the blanket she'd tucked around herself over as she moved. "Thank you, Mama, but I don't think talking about it with you will help."

There was just a hint of a pause. "Oh. Talking about it *with me* won't help?"

Bother. She caught that, did she?

Irene forced herself to look up. Her mother was still incredibly beautiful—that was, she could not recall a time when her mother was not one of the most beautiful women she had ever known. Oh, age had added a line or two here and there, and her hair could not be described as dark auburn any longer, but these marks of age had merely accentuated her beauty, not marred it.

She was so beautiful. *And Father is so besotted with her*, Irene could not help but think wistfully. Theirs was a love that was so pure, so easy, she half-wondered whether her mother would understand anything about courting in today's modern world.

After all, theirs was a love match. All the way back in 1812!

"I mean no disrespect," Irene said quietly. "It's just... Well. You cannot possibly understand. You and Papa, you were made for each other. Everything has always been so easy for you."

Laughter was not the response Irene had expected, but it was the one she received. In fact, there was a great deal of laughter. So much, it started to aggrieve her.

"Well, I don't see what's so funny," she snapped, against her better judgment.

Her mother did not appear offended, despite Irene's rudeness. "Oh, Reeny—"

"Don't call me that."

How could anyone ever call her that again, after what she had shared with Wilfred, whose soft lips had called her that name during the act again and again?

The Viscountess Pernrith still did not appear offended, another mark of her good nature. "I am sorry, Irene. I am not laughing at you, more... Well, what you said. I am sure I have told you part of the story of your father and me before, but I wonder... Yes, I wonder whether hearing the full tale might aid you in this moment."

It was all Irene could do not to roll her eyes. How would hearing her parents' perfect love story help her get over the worst heartbreak anyone had ever known?

"I am always happy to hear the story, Mama," she said politely, "but I am certain I could tell it to you. You met, Father was besotted with you—"

"He was rather," said the Viscountess Pernrith with a charming smile.

"You fell in love, you got engaged, and Grandpapa—"

"Threatened your father with a duel, you know," her mother said lightly, adjusting her skirt as though grandparents frequently menaced their sons-in-law.

Irene knew it was not precisely ladylike, but she could not help it.

Her jaw dropped.

"Yes, you know part of the story," her mother said, her voice low and unburdened with shame. "The story we told everyone, the story the *ton* heard and my father, your grandfather, was determined to keep to. But I wonder... I wonder whether hearing the full tale might assist you."

Irene was still attempting to lift her jaw from the floor. "Grandpapa threatened Papa with a duel?"

"Well, he *had* found him compromising me heartily only the second or third time we met," her mother said, small pink dots appearing in her cheeks even as she spoke.

It was a good thing Irene was seated, for those words would have surely made her fall to the ground if she had been standing. To hear such things about anyone was scandalous enough, but one's own parents!

Then she shot out a pointed finger. "I always knew Michael was born only seven months after—"

"Yes, well, timings cannot always be completely accurate," interrupted her mother hastily, a glance at the door. "That is not something I have ever shared. But the story of how your father and I fell in love, well...That may be a story you could enjoy."

Irene could hardly believe what she was hearing. Her father, threatened by her grandfather? A fake engagement?

Her mother, compromised!

"I am not sure I want to hear the details of such a tale," she said warily, attempting not to think the unthinkable.

To be sure, she had always known her parents had—that was, that her mother and father, in order to have five children, had—

but... *Well!*

"Your father was, and is, a very handsome man," her mother said dreamily, lifting a hand to her hair and adjusting a pin with a faraway look. "And when I saw him—and then we were alone, and the opportunity to know just how he tasted was too good to—"

"*Mama!*"

To Irene's great relief, her mother cleared her throat and sat up straighter.

"What I mean to say," the Viscountess Pernrith said, her voice stronger, "is that love can start in all sorts of ways. Your father and I... I liked him—"

"*Mama!*"

"I was going to keep the details to myself this time!" her mother said with a laugh, though there was just a tinge of shyness in it.

Irene did not know whether to bury herself underneath her blanket and put her fingers in her ears or launch herself from the armchair and make a break for the door. No daughter in the world should have to suffer through this!

"We were discovered. By my father." Her mother sighed with a wistful smile. "I do miss him, and it's memories like this that I think about most often. He insisted your father marry me, but... Well, he was considered beneath me. You know why."

Irene nodded, her curiosity overcoming her distaste. She knew why. It was not something she thought about often, naturally, but she was no fool. Her father had been born illegitimate.

Her mother was continuing the story. "None of us wanted scandal, and I thought at first that the easiest thing would be to falsify an engagement. I could break it, after a while, and then no one would have their reputations ruined."

It was difficult not to gasp. "But, Mama—a broken engagement!"

"Better than no engagement at all," her mother quipped

wryly. "Besides, both your father and I knew precisely what we were getting into. There was to be no romance, no feelings, just…an arrangement."

Though they both knew how that had ended. "How long did that last?"

"Not long at all." The Viscountess Pernrith grinned, twisting her wedding band on her hand as she laughed. "The trouble with your father is that he is such an excellent man. Such a kind gentleman. Such an impressive kisser—"

"*Mama!*"

"Before we knew it, the false engagement had become all too real for each of us, but neither of us wished to entrap the other. It all got considerably complicated at the end," her mother said with a wistful sigh. "It's a miracle that it ended well—but my point is, it did not start as a love match. It was an arrangement—not an arranged marriage, a false engagement. Entirely a construct. And yet here we are."

"Well!" Irene sat back in the armchair and tried to make sense of all she had heard.

It was…puzzling. Strange, indeed, to have one's presumptions about one's parents completely retold when one was an adult. *You think you know a person…*

Her stomach curdled. She had thought she had known Wilfred, had she not? And look at how wrong she had been in that case.

As though her mother was able to read her very thoughts, the Viscountess Pernrith leaned forward slowly. "Irene, you do not know what sort of agreement Wilfred and this woman—"

"Miss Fletcher," snapped Irene, her anger instantly baited. "I cannot believe he would—"

"My point is, false engagements—false courtships—are rare, but not impossible. After all, you are the product of one," her mother said quietly.

It were as though her mother had stabbed her with a red-hot knife. "You—You think Miss Fletcher is already with child?"

"No!" The Viscountess Pernrith paled as she uttered the syllable. "No—oh, bother, I'm getting this all wrong. Your Aunt Dodo was always so much better at these sorts of conversations."

Irene tried not to laugh. "Well, that flies in the face of absolutely everything I know about her, but if you say so."

"No, I mean…odds. Probability. What is the probability that this is just a huge misunderstanding between the two of you?" her mother persisted. "I know Wilfred. I've known him from a boy. Not the brightest man—"

"*Mama!*"

"—but you have always defended him," her mother continued with a wry smile. "Your affection for him has been something I have watched grow with interest. I always wondered when you would see sense. See that you needed him."

Irene swallowed. It was most disconcerting to discover that one's secrets—a secret, indeed, from herself—had been so blatant to others.

"I know I was as upset about this as you were at first, but the more I've thought over it… Wilfred strikes me as the sort of man, like your father, to get himself tangled in something accidentally," the Viscountess Pernrith said with a modicum of pride. "The difference is, your father fell in love with the person he entered into a false engagement with. Your Wilfred—"

"He's not *my* Wilfred," Irene said automatically.

Her mother gave her a look. "Your Wilfred," she continued without missing a beat, "has been in love with you since before I think he was even aware of such an emotion."

Irene wriggled in her seat. "That's not possible."

A myriad of memories were flickering through her mind as she said those few words. It wasn't possible—yet had it not been Wilfred who had always played with her as a child, when Jessica had been off at pianoforte lessons being finished, and Michael had been at school, and Gwen and Teddy had had each other? Had it not been Wilfred who had brought her those oranges when she had cried that all the other Chance families had had them but her father was too poor? Was it not Wilfred who had always defended her, lied for her, even, years after they had left childhood?

Even when it had not mattered?

A strange, hot aching sensation in her was making it most difficult to think.

"And I am not the only one who knows, either," added the Viscountess Pernrith, and this time she did look uncomfortable. "A certain person came to see me this morning, early. They had a confession to make."

Irene glared. "I don't want to hear what Wilfred had to—"

"It was not Wilfred, though I had to say I am saddened that you and your father threw him from the house. Honestly, Irene," her mother tutted. "That is no way to behave."

Her temper flared again. "And Wilfred should never have—"

"You truly think Wilfred is the sort of man to come up with such a foolhardy scheme?" Her mother shook her head. "I thought you were more observant than that. Come, now. What person close to you would wish for your best but undoubtedly achieve it in the most idiotic—"

"Michael," groaned Irene, dropping her head into her hands. "What did he say to Wilfred?"

"I believe he should tell you," their mother said gently, her expression kind, though tired. "And I do not say such a thing to absolve Wilfred. He acted most foolishly, but he acted, Reeny, out of love."

Love. Irene had thought she had known what love was, and then Wilfred had had to go and say all sorts of declarations, and she had felt…hot, and joyful, and free, and chained to him in a way she could never have predicted.

But now it hurt. How could love hurt so much?

"He cannot love me," she said aloud, her voice hoarse. "He would not have done this to me if he loved me, whatever Michael's involvement."

"You know," her mother said, almost as an aside, "I have

always been a little envious of the two of you."

That was sufficient to gain her attention. "'Envious'? Of me and Michael?"

"You and Wilfred," the Viscountess Pernrith said wistfully. "Your father is truly a wonderful man and he makes me very happy. I like my sisters-in-law greatly, and my brothers-in-law…are an acquired taste to which I have been happy to grow accustomed. But I never had a friend, not like you did. Not as a child. Not throughout life."

Irene stared. She had never expected anything of the sort to come from her mother. *Friendship?* It was not much to envy.

And yet…perhaps it was. Wilfred had always been there, like a rock. No, like a tree. Like sunshine, sometimes fading in the winter when he had to go to school, but still there, writing to her, teasing her, encouraging her. He hadn't gone on his Grand Tour, had he? The longest amount of time he'd spent on the Continent had been four months. Oh, he'd said at the time that he had no great interest in mountains or temples, so…so he had stayed with her.

Irene swallowed. "I feel like I've found a great treasure and it's been snatched away from me."

Her mother leaned forward, took her hands in her own, and looked up into Irene's eyes with love, but also a tired exhaustion. "Well, Irene," she said quietly. "I would say you've let it slip through your fingers. Are you going to grasp it again?"

"But it's over—"

"It doesn't have to be."

Chapter Eighteen

WILFRED INHALED DEEPLY, then put the book down. "I said, I am not at home."

His stiff-backed butler coughed politely—at least, Wilfred presumed it was a polite cough. "I know, Your Grace, but—"

"And when I said I am not at home, I am not at home," Wilfred continued doggedly.

He hated doing it; he had never been one of those men who could shout at their servants. They had been his family, far more than his parents ever had. To shout at the man would be like shouting at his father. Except worse.

"I am aware, Your Grace." His butler cleared his throat again. "But in this circumstance, I thought—"

"Well, it is what I think that matters in this house. Thank you. That will be all."

Wilfred cringed as he looked away from the man and resolutely opened his book, a book whose words were stubbornly refusing to stick in his mind, but he couldn't bear to see a single person. Not after what had happened. Not after losing everything he loved.

The sound of the door closing echoed through the library, and Wilfred put the book aside.

How could he read? How could he lose himself in the joy and excitement of an adventure story when the adventure he himself was on had already turned out to be such a disaster?

"I cannot be yours, not now."

It was his own fault. Oh, Wilfred knew that; he had been the one to contract Miss Fletcher to this silly ruse. He still did not know if she was responsible for the piece in the paper—and if not, who else would have gone so far as to name her supposed father—but he could not bear to even confront the woman. It was possible it had not been she behind the accursed bit of gossip, but rather someone who had observed them together and somehow knew her name. *Blast.* If he had only continued to pursue Irene as he had... Well. Not that his approach there had been working in any capacity.

But still, it had been his actions and his actions alone that had precipitated this—and there was nothing to be done. Irene would not see him. He had tried returning to the Chance house twice today already and the servants had been most cold toward him. Distant.

It had been most alarming. The Chance servants had been... Well, Wilfred did not like to think of it like this, but like his servants.

His, in that they had played a part in raising him. It had been their hands that had bandaged scrapes, and their kindness that had led them to feed him treats from the kitchen, and now—now they looked at him as though...

Wilfred swallowed. *As though I have done them a great harm.*

Perhaps he had.

"Now, then, Master Wilfred," came the storm that was Mrs. Ansley, "what's all this about refusing to see your nice guest?"

Something deep within Wilfred cringed. "Mrs. Ansley, really—"

"I have never known you to turn away a friend at your door," his housekeeper said brusquely, brandishing a finger at him like a professor with a pointer rod. "A friend who has come special to comfort you."

"Mrs. Ansley," said Wilfred weakly. What was he supposed to do against such an onslaught?

"And you've always liked those Chances so well," she continued, unabated. "I don't see why you wouldn't see—"

"'Chances'?" repeated Wilfred, treacherous hope rising like hot honey.

Chances—special friend?

It has to be Irene. It just has to be. Joy fluttered through him, a pulse irregular yet welcome, and he rose so swiftly to his feet that this book, whatever it was, fell to the floor.

"Yes, yes, show her in!"

For a moment, just a moment, Mrs. Ansley's brows furrowed and there was a flicker of confusion in the woman's face. "But—"

"Come now, Mrs. Ansley, half a breath ago, you were chastising me for not welcoming my guest!" Wilfred said jovially, trying to tighten his cravat and straighten his waistcoat at the same time. "Show her in!"

How was his hair? He hadn't even looked at his hair in the looking glass that morning—there had been no point—and now Irene was here, and he hadn't matched his buttonhole flower to his cravat, but that did not matter. She had come. Everything was going to be—

Michael Chance walked into the library.

Wilfred deflated; first his torso, then his head drooped, and finally his voice said dully, "Oh. It's you."

His housekeeper cleared her throat. "I did try to say—"

"Yes, thank you, Mrs. Ansley," Wilfred interrupted curtly.

Well, it was his own fault. He had presumed. How many times was he going to presume with this family and turn out to be completely wrong?

"No tea, thank you, Mrs. Ansley," Michael was saying cheerfully to his host's housekeeper. "I know where the master keeps the whiskey, and we'll need it. Both of us."

"Right you are, Mr. Chance," bustled the housekeeper, gently brushing off their guest's shoulders with her palms like a valet smoothing out his master's wrinkles before seeming to come to herself and striding out of the room. "And play nicely, the pair of you!" she admonished them both over her shoulder as though they were still eleven years old.

The door closed and Wilfred dropped onto his chair.

He should have expected it. Michael clearly had forgotten his own role in how this whole mess had started, or he somehow seemed to believe that Wilfred had, at some point, not been pretending at all. Irene's father perhaps was too important, too angry even to come here himself, but it made sense that Irene's only brother would come here and—

Not challenge him to a duel. There hadn't been a duel fought over a lady in… Well, not officially. Not for ages.

What was it to be, then—a demand of money? A stricture never to darken their doorway again?

Wilfred glanced up at his childhood friend's brother and saw him swallowing, a strange war of emotions in the man's face. *Was that…regret? Surely not.*

"I had planned to come here," Michael said slowly, walking over to the secret compartment in the second-left bookcase and pressing down on the Bible, "to congratulate you."

The hidden spring pushed open what had appeared to be five books on agriculture. A bottle of whiskey became visible.

"I knew you had found out about that," Wilfred said dully. "Since we were eighteen."

"Well, it didn't seem fair that only you and Reeny got to have the whiskey," Michael said cheerfully.

Wilfred snorted. "I thought it was disappearing rather quickly."

And yet what did it matter? It was only whiskey. Whiskey could be replaced.

Irene could not.

"Yet here we are, commiserating over your expulsion from my parents' home," Michael said in that same cheerful voice, now reaching behind the whiskey for two glasses. "The newspaper announcement was a damned unfortunate thing to happen, you know."

"'Unfortunate'? You were the one who suggested the whole

damned ruse in the first place!" Wilfred exploded.

It were as though a dam had finally burst, as though he was finally being given permission to be angry—and by God, he was angry.

Mostly at himself, true. But also at this man: this man who had attempted to help him and then had had the gall not to stand up for him when he'd discovered how far the ruse *he* had suggested Wilfred undertake had gone.

"It's all your fault!" he shouted at the man who was helping himself to Wilfred's own whiskey.

And anger, pure anger the like he had never known before, roared through him. Yes, this was it, this was something he could blame—it wasn't his own fault, it was Michael's! Michael, who had wheedled out of him that he was in love with Irene; Michael, who had suggested making his sister jealous; Michael, who had suggested Miss Fletcher herself; Michael, who had stood there, indignant alongside the rest of the family, not saying a word about his role in the whole affair!

Perhaps—and at this point, Wilfred was hardly sure whether he was in control of his thoughts, or his thoughts were in control of him—perhaps Michael had sabotaged the whole thing! Had he perhaps gone to Miss Fletcher, asked her to put the gossip in the newspaper? Had he placed the piece himself? That would make sense. Who else would even have known the name of the lady, and her supposed father as well?

"Are you quite finished?" asked Michael calmly, sipping from one of the whiskey glasses and wrinkling his nose. "Goodness, this is fine stuff. From the Highlands, I take it?"

"*Michael!*" exploded Wilfred.

His guest winced. "You know, if you really want to berate me, you could not have picked a better way. That is precisely the way my mother shouts at me when she is disappointed with me. Well done."

Wilfred stood there, lungs tight, anger still nice and hot in his veins...but the utter lack of reaction from his friend was startling.

"Why… Why aren't you fighting back?"

Michael slowly swilled the whiskey glass, staring at the amber liquid. The silence between them stretched out in a most alarming way, until finally, the gentleman looked up and met Wilfred's gaze with a steady one of his own.

"Because," Michael said quietly, "you are absolutely right. This is my fault."

Opening his mouth to retort against the absolute slander that the blaggard had surely said, it took a moment for Wilfred's mind to catch up with him. He hesitated, mouth agape, then he slowly closed it.

"Your fault," he repeated, all the wind taken from his sails.

"Yes, my fault," said Michael simply, stepping forward. He gestured to a chair. "May I?"

Wilfred hardly knew what to do with himself. Irene had loved him, and now she hated him. The Chances, the only family he had ever truly known, had thrown him out. Michael was drinking his whiskey and saying the whole damned situation was his own fault.

He wanted to sit down.

Grasping with relief to the final thought, Wilfred nodded brusquely and sat down himself. Before his guest took his seat, he poured a healthy dollop of Wilfred's own whiskey into a fresh glass and handed it to his host.

"Drink up," Michael said quietly. "You're going to need it."

It was hardly a logical argument, but Wilfred was not in a position to argue. He drank the whiskey. In one.

"Steady on, man. I need you conscious to hear my apology."

"Your ap-apolgy?" spluttered Wilfred, blinking through the fiery burn of the liquor.

Michael's smile was fleeting. "You sound like my Aunt Florence. Yes, my apology. It's my fault you're in this mess, you know."

"I do know!" Wilfred said hotly, temper flaring. "And—"

"And yours, of course," interrupted his guest, his voice level.

"But I thought it was only fair that you shared the blame."

Wilfred gaped at the impertinence of the man. He dared to blame him, Wilfred, for hurting Irene—when all he wanted to do in the world was give her pleasure?

Probably not the best thing to say to the woman's brother, now that he came to think about it…

"Look," Michael said darkly, "you and my sister—you were made for each other."

It was difficult not to snort derisively at that. "'Were.' Past tense."

"You *are* made for each other, then—damn it, man, are you going to be this difficult about everything?"

Wilfred glared at his friend. "Yes."

For a moment, Michael just stared. Then he laughed. "Good. You know, I always worried that Irene would walk all over you. That you would simply acquiesce to every demand she ever made, and you'd end up kissing the ground she walked on."

It was a fair comment, and Wilfred was loath to admit that it was still completely true. Probably best not to demean himself too much.

"And then I thought…good," said Michael softly.

Wilfred was starting to get dizzy from all the different twists and turns this conversation was taking. Pushing the book off his seat and taking another sip of his whiskey—a smaller one, this time—he tried to respond in a way that was charming, and refined, and befitting of a gentleman.

"What the hell are you talking about?" he said wearily.

Well. He had made an attempt.

"I thought, good," repeated Michael, his smile faint. "My sister, all my sisters, deserve to be loved by men who are going to adore them. Who will do anything, everything for them. Who will believe them and fight for them and love them no matter what occurs. And I thought that was the sort of man you were."

Wilfred did not know whether to be aggrieved or pleased. "I am that man."

"But you're here, stewing," pointed out his friend.

"I am here, drinking whiskey with you," countered Wilfred sharply. "And I came by your house—your parents' house—twice today, and each time—"

"Yes, I am afraid you are being treated with the cut direct at la Casa de Pernrith," said Michael with a twisted smile. "And that was even after I went to my mother and confessed everything."

'Confessed'... 'Confessed everything'?

Not for the first time, Wilfred wondered why it had not been himself and Michael who had become close friends all those years ago. The boy had always been on the periphery, to be sure, but it had been Irene who had caught his attention. Oh, they had gone up to university together, as two young men only a year apart, and a gaggle of them had done the Grand Tour...but it had always been Irene.

Perhaps he had missed out on having two close friends, rather than one.

"Look, I am sorry," Michael said suddenly, his expression one of contrition as he downed the last of his whiskey. "I feel responsible."

"Good," muttered Wilfred.

"It was my fault for pushing you toward Miss Fletcher in the first place," continued Michael, whose voice was filled with regret. "And... Well... I paid the paper to print that gossip."

Wilfred swallowed. "You... You *what*?"

He'd suspected Michael, briefly—it would have made his outrage at Christmas, his inability to step forward and help Wilfred, make sense, considering he must have been hiding his involvement—but he hadn't suspected the man to come out and admit it.

"Made up the name of her dad and everything—found a man of business with the name Fletcher in Yorkshire who might suit, to make it seem as if she were from a family better fit for a duke. Albeit still a merchant's family, but that had to be better than a harlot's, you know?"

No, Wilfred did not *know*.

"I was an idiot, I know. Miss Fletcher said she hadn't seen you in weeks, that you'd sent a letter that you were done with her services. But it had only been that *one* time, which clearly hadn't been enough. You spent so much time with Irene, but the two of you never seemed to make any progress—"

"We'd *made progress* Christmas Eve!"

Michael gaped.

"Never-Never mind that," he said. "The point is, Irene confessed her feelings to me, and we understood each other. At last. Until I came downstairs and found a wall of infuriated Chances formed against me. Yourself included, I might add!"

The solitary Chance in the room swallowed, then winced. "I feel... Well, as though I have destroyed things for you."

It was on the tip of Wilfred's tongue to say that he had; that it had been Michael who had ruined everything, that it had been Michael who had ended his opportunity to not only marry Irene, but to become a Chance, to join the family he so admired and revered.

But even as the words formed themselves in his mouth, Wilfred found—to his great annoyance—that he couldn't say them.

"You were part of the tale," he said quietly. "A *large* part, it seems. But you cannot take all responsibility."

"My mother wishes me to," Michael said darkly. "She said a great many things, some of which were far sharper than I could have believed of her. And she was right. Mostly."

He did look mostly penitent, Wilfred had to admit. The picture would have looked complete if the man hadn't been downing a glass of his own whiskey at the time, but Michael did in fact look a tad morose.

As though he...regretted what he had done. A new experience for Michael Chance.

"If I had never suggested Miss Fletcher or gone to the papers with that tale of lies," Michael said dully, "this whole thing wouldn't have happened, and you and I would be supping champagne in my father's house about now."

Wilfred's stomach tightened. *I can hardly deny it.* "And yet you did, and I did—there, we are both to blame."

"No, no, it is time I started taking responsibility for my actions. Or at least"—his guest grinned—"that is what my mother said, and I was not in the mood to disagree with her. She was wielding a knife at the time."

Wilfred blinked. The image of the Viscountess Pernrith threatening her only son with a knife was a most incongruent one. "I am sorry. 'She was wielding—'"

"Well, a needle, same difference," Michael said with a wave of his hand. "She was doing some embroidery at the time of my confession and you know, she looked most upset and I would not have put it past her to stab me in the eye with it, considering her fondness for—"

"Irene," Wilfred breathed. It was almost a blessing, to be able to say the name aloud.

Michael frowned. "Well, yes, but I was going to say 'you.'"

Me?

"My parents have a great deal of affection for you, you know," his friend said quietly, as though he did not comprehend just what a gift he was giving his host. "I think that is why the whole debacle has rankled so much. It's not just their daughter they are upset about. It's their second son."

Was it Wilfred's imagination, or was there a hint of pain in his friend's voice?

"And it is all my fault," said Michael heavily.

Perhaps if he had opened with that, Wilfred would have agreed with him. It would have been pleasant, to blame someone else, to feel the relief of absolution across his shoulders.

But he was no cad, no matter what Irene had thrown at him.

"I accept your apology. But it doesn't matter."

Michael raised an unbelieving eyebrow as he settled back in his chair. "It doesn't?"

Wilfred shook his head. "No. No, I am really the one to blame. I claim credit for pretending even just once to woo the woman. I have to accept the blame when it does not go to plan. When it goes completely disastrously, as it happens, but yes. This is on my shoulders, and now...now it is over."

Over.

That was the first time, he realized, he had said that aloud—but it had been true for many hours now.

Over. Any chance of his happiness—for he would never love another, Wilfred was certain about that—had ended. Perhaps the newspaper gossip would put an end to all chance of there ever being a piece about him and Irene, thereby protecting her reputation. Perhaps that was for the best, as much as he hated to think it. Irene would go off and marry someone else, someone better, someone more suave and charming, and he...he would have to look into the family tree and find an heir somewhere. There had to be a distant cousin, did there not? Surely, he could not be the very last Aynor?

And if he was, indeed, the last, well... So he would be.

"Oh, well, that's all right, then."

Wilfred blinked. So lost had he become in his thoughts, he had almost forgotten that Michael was still there. "'All right'? What the devil do you mean, 'all right'?"

His companion shrugged. "Well, if you can say that it is over so easily and without any real fight, perhaps you did not love her at all."

And Wilfred was on his feet again—how, he did not know, but he was and there was rage pouring through his heart and words he had not even known he'd possessed were spilling from his lips.

"'Not love her'—not love Irene? Not love the only woman who makes me feel—who knows me and sees me and—and everything she does is sunlight!" Wilfred knew what he was saying simply did not make sense. He did not care. He had to say it. "'Not love her'? I have loved Irene for as long as I have breathed—there are no memories within me when I did not love her! Loving her has been the greatest privilege of my life and I will never love again like—Irene is... And if she asked me to cut my own heart out, then I would tear it out with my bare hands!" Wilfred was shouting, but the shouting could not stop until all the words were out. "I love her, Michael, and I-I may not deserve her, but I do not deserve slander like that! It's an outrage!"

He was panting heavily, his hands clenched to fists at his sides, and there was boiling rage coating the insides of his lungs and Michael—

Michael just sat there...laughing.

Wilfred shifted his feet as though to check that the library floor was still level. Yes, it was—so why did it feel as though he had just been tipped sideways?

Michael was still laughing.

"Why—Why are you—" he began defensively.

"Oh, please, I mean no offense by it." His guest grinned. "I just did not expect to get a rise out of you so easily."

Wilfred groaned, dropping back onto his seat and putting his head into his hands. "You shouldn't be allowed to do that."

"It comes from growing up with four sisters." Michael chuckled. "It becomes all too easy to see the ways one can prod at another. You really think I did not believe your affection for Irene was real?"

Embarrassment flooded through Wilfred as he groaned into his hands.

The voice of his guest came from before him. "Oh, come now, it's not that bad. You hardly humiliated yourself, though I have to admit, I will remind you of that 'ripping your heart out of your chest' comment when Irene wants to paint your library a nice lilac and you disagree."

The thought of Irene here, redecorating his home—making it their home—crackled in Wilfred's mind.

He looked up. "You seriously think there is any future in which Irene and I are—"

"It's the only future I can see," Michael said lightly. "Here you are, miserable because you are not with her, and there she is, miserable because she is not with you. It's all mightily obvious."

Wilfred could not help but glare. "Fine, magical miracle worker. How would you fix this damned mess?"

His friend's eyes twinkled. "Ah, far be it from me to take the pleasure of solving the whole thing away from you. Besides, would you trust me to be the one to fix it, when it looks as if I've made the whole thing worse?"

Wilfred glared at him before shaking his head.

"No, you will have to seek help from another Chance. *I* will stick to what brothers-in-law are really for: teasing the newcomer to the family."

Wilfred snorted.

"Not that you are much of a newcomer," continued Michael, his voice calmer now. "I mean, you've been part of the family for so long, it'd be odd if you didn't marry one of my sisters."

'One' of them? Oh, it had only ever been Irene. She had been like a sister to him, Wilfred knew, until…until she had not. Until the very last thing he'd wanted from her was sisterly affection.

Until he had realized his life would be utterly incomplete unless he had Irene by his side at all times.

"So," Michael said lazily, reaching forward to pick up the whiskey bottle—Wilfred's whiskey bottle—and pouring himself another large measure. "Tell me."

Wilfred blinked. "Tell you…what?"

His friend lifted his now-full glass in a toast. "How are you going to win back my sister?"

Chapter Nineteen

December 28, 1840

“ AND I SAID that I never wanted to come in the first place,” muttered Irene, smiling brilliantly at the crowds of people who were clearly staring. *Aren't they? How do they know?* “So why don't I return to the carriage with Michael and—”

“Firstly, because Michael has clearly decided he has somewhere else better to be,” said her father stiffly. “Of course.”

Irene turned around wildly, surveying the growing crowd in the concert hall then sighing heavily. “Of course.”

Honestly, they were going to have to do something about Michael. He had always been—well, not necessarily the best brother in the world, but he hadn't been in the habit of summarily dropping his family and wandering off.

As he had clearly done now.

“It doesn't matter. I invited a friend in the certain knowledge that Michael would not wish to sit through a full concert of Mozart,” said Irene's mother with a sigh. “Though honestly, he could do with the musical education. That school of his—”

“They were very good to me, dear,” said Irene's father as the trio pushed through the crowd toward their allotted seats. “I never suffered there.”

“My point is, music is a balm to the soul, as I was telling my friend whom I invited to join us,” the Viscountess Pernrith said tartly. “Something Michael could do with.”

Perhaps that's why my parents have dragged me out this evening, Irene could not help but think as she picked at the lace at her collar and wished to goodness she was home, carefully tucked away in bed. A balm for the soul.

Her soul hadn't been much balmed recently. The last few days had passed in a haze of tears—mostly hers—and anger...also mostly hers. Her parents had attempted their best, and Michael had put his hands up and said he wasn't going to get involved any longer, which confirmed all her suspicions about her brother's meddling, and her sisters... Well, Jessica had sent a lovely letter, but she hadn't heard when she had written it, so it had been all about Reginald, her husband, and how wonderful he was...which had been a tad galling.

And as for Teddy and Gwen...they had kept themselves to themselves.

Which was precisely what Irene wished to do. She tugged her father's arm. "Papa—"

"No, your mother is most insistent that we attend this concert," her father said with a twinkling smile, somehow able to guess precisely what she had been about to ask. "And I am not the sort of man who can say *no* to your mother."

Irene could not help but smile at that. "I suppose not."

The trouble was, the whole place was stifling. Far too many people—she would be surprised if those gathered would find enough seats—and someone near her was wearing far too much scent. It was hot, and muggy, and her stays were somehow too tight.

The music had better be good—though whether it would be a sufficient balm for her wracked soul, she did not know.

"Now, there was a bit of trouble with the tickets," came a voice near her.

Irene glanced at her mother, whose cheeks were pink. "'Trouble'?"

"Was it anything to do with...?" began her father.

The Viscountess Pernrith tapped her husband in a very intimate manner and smiled even as her cheeks flushed a darker pink. "Now don't be silly, dear. No one cares about *that* anymore."

Irene did not need further explanation. She knew her father. He was concerned his parentage was the reason—and she could not understand why. Indeed, her father had been legitimized long before she had even been born. Why would anyone in Society have an issue with him now?

Her father was scowling. "You know what people say."

"Well, they don't say it to us, dear, so I wouldn't worry about it," said the Viscountess Pernrith smoothly. "No, I meant to say that I booked four tickets, but it appears that they are in two pairs, across the aisle."

Irene groaned.

She knew precisely what her mother was going to say. She had undoubtedly invited some old biddy, some crone of her mother's friendship circle who had no one else to attend concerts with, and Irene had been brought along to sit with her.

Well, she would make the best of it. Hopefully, the other woman wouldn't bore her to tears with a running commentary through the music.

"Now, Irene," said the Viscountess Pernrith brightly. "I wondered if you could do me a small favor."

"Yes, Mama," Irene said dully, opening her fan and fluttering some stale air toward herself. "I will sit with your friend."

"Throughout the whole concert?" For some reason, her mother was looking at her most pointedly with a sharpness in her gaze that Irene did not like. "I can't have you wandering off like Michael. My friend would be most aggrieved."

Irene sighed. *Naturally, she would.* The woman would probably pick holes at Irene's gown, too, and complain that the seats were insufficiently near the front. "Yes, Mama."

Her mother did not appear mollified. "You promise?"

"My love," intervened the Viscount Pernrith quietly. "Surely, you don't—"

"I asked for your word, Irene Chance," said the Viscountess Pernrith, raising an eyebrow.

For goodness's sake—it was bad enough to be treated like a child at the best of times, but now, after she had experienced… Well, what it was to be an adult, it was most galling.

"Yes, yes, I promise," she said with a false, bright smile. "I will sit beside your friend for the entirety of the concert and put up with anything she says. Are you happy now?"

"Very," said her mother sweetly. "Here *he* is—good evening, Wilfred."

Irene's stomach did not drop out of her torso; it fled, taking with it all her strength and poise.

Her mouth fell open.

There, in a moderately dashing evening suit that she had never seen the man wear before, was Wilfred.

Wilfred.

Here. At the concert that she and her parents were…

Irene groaned. "This—*This* is your friend?"

"I am sorry. Is a lady not permitted to have friends?" asked her mother innocently, fluttering her eyelashes. "Thank you, by the way, for *promising*"—and there was just a hint of emphasis on that last word—"to sit all evening and converse with my friend."

Irene groaned again. *This was an ambush!* A trap, that was what it was. Her parents were clearly in cahoots with Wilfred, and—

And he looked most astonished in turn, his breath hitching, his jaw slackened, his eyes darting wildly to Irene and her mother and back.

"My lady?" Wilfred was saying in a hurried tone. "You said I was to sit with Michael."

"Yes, well, Michael seems unable to attend the concert to-night and I thought there was no point in missing out on such a wonderful evening," said the Viscountess Pernrith blithely, as though she frequently orchestrated matters in such a way.

Irene almost laughed. For all she knew, perhaps her mother did.

Her father was looking at his wife with admiration. "I never stood a chance against you, did I?"

"Not a whit," said the Viscountess Pernrith with a smile. "Shall we take our seats?"

Irene was in half a mind to storm out of the place entirely. Surely, she could not be kept to a promise she had made without fully understanding the consequences? Why, she could march out of here right now and...

Her wandering attention fell upon Wilfred.

He looked uncomfortable. More than that, he looked mortified. Evidently, the man had no idea what cleverness her mother would wreak, and he was most unhappy about it.

A strange sort of delight filled her. Well—good. He deserved to feel unhappy. *Now he knows a modicum of what I felt when he—*

Irene pushed the thought away. No, she did not want to return to that way of thinking. She might have had her heart broken, but she was not cruel.

She didn't *think* she was.

"Fine!" she snapped with very bad grace. "Where are the seats?"

After being directed mutely by an only slightly abashed Viscountess Pernrith, Irene stormed over to the seats on the end of the row, sat on the very end—perfect for an escape, should the need arise—and glared at the man who had followed her.

Wilfred shuffled from one foot to the other. "Erm. I need to get past... My seat."

Irene glared. Then she rose, stepped into the aisle, continued to glare as the man stepped awkwardly past her, making a great deal of effort not to touch her in any way, then sat down in her seat once that man had done the same.

That man. Was she truly unable to think the name 'Wilfred'?

It was most disconcerting, being so close to a person at whom you had been shouting the last time you'd been together, and the time before that, his fingers had been... *Well.*

The trouble was, the seats were not wide. Her hips pressed up against his, try as she could to avoid the sensation. His elbow bumped against hers.

"I am sorry," Wilfred muttered as the conductor stepped out and accepted the rapturous applause.

Irene folded her arms—anything to keep her away from him. "It's fine."

"It—It is?"

Why the man sounded so astonished, she could not tell.

Which was odd in and of itself. Why, she knew Wilfred better than…better than herself. She could predict the man's movements, speech, decisions in a way that felt almost like an extension of herself. How had she never noticed that?

And yet now Irene sat beside a stranger.

"Yes," she said curtly, tightening her arms across her chest as the conductor tapped on his music stand. "It's fine."

It had only been an elbow bump, after all.

Wilfred, however, looked amazed, his shoulders softening, his small smile widening. *Not that I am looking at him,* Irene told herself firmly as she forced her attention back to the musicians, who had just started to play a beautiful concerto. Not looking at him at all.

"I…I did not think you would accept my apology," whispered Wilfred, gaining him the ireful glare of a woman who turned to frown at them. "I've been agonizing over the—the right words, and so I have been slow, slower than I would have liked to approach you with them. If not for your mother's assistance this evening, I can't say when I would have felt…felt ready."

What on earth is the man talking about? "It's just a touch of your elbow," Irene muttered, trying to focus her attention on the music.

That was what she had come here for, after all. Not being forced to sit beside the man she loved and had then been betrayed by. Goodness, she was going to have a talk with her mother after this.

"Ah," came Wilfred's awkward whisper. "I was… Well. I was apologizing for, well…the other thing."

Irene stiffened. *Oh.* Well, that made far more sense. "I don't want to talk about it."

"But—"

"I don't want to talk to you," she said steadfastly in a low voice. "I'm listening to the music."

She expected him to argue. A part of her wanted him to, Irene knew, wanted him to protest and make a declaration. It wasn't that she would accept such a thing, obviously, but it would be nice to receive it.

Instead, Wilfred nodded sagely and turned to the musicians. "Very well."

And then he sat there. Just sat there! *The nerve of the man!*

Irene quietly stewed in growing anger for at least a full minute before she snapped, "Why are you even here?"

"Shhh!"

Whoever it was who had hushed them, she did not know, but it certainly did nothing to dampen the feelings of irritation within her. The nerve of them! Did they not see that she was attempting to reconcile—

Not 'reconcile.' *Blast it all to hell and back, but this is infuriating!*

It was impossible. She had to talk to him.

Conscious of her parents' gazes literally across the aisle of the concert, Irene turned completely in her chair to scowl at Wilfred, who had the good grace to turn red. Especially about the ears.

"Why are you refusing to talk to me?" Irene hissed irritably.

"Did you not say we ought to enjoy the music?" whispered Wilfred, not even looking at her.

Oh, the man is infuriating!

"Is that *all* you intend to do this evening?"

"Does there have to be anything else?"

Irene gaped at the imbecile. This wasn't like Wilfred; Wilfred always did what she wanted. He always obeyed, always accompanied, always helped. He was the one who had helped her smoke her first cigar—a disgusting experience, as it happened. He was the one who had covered for her when she had been late home that warm summer day three years ago. He was always there, always obliging, always…Wilfred.

She narrowed her eyes. "And you did not know my mother was up to one of her schemes?"

"Not in the slightest," came his calm reply.

And there was no hesitation. Irene paused, just for a moment, and surveyed his face, looking for falsehood, and saw…

Wilfred. Handsome, and silent, with that strong jaw and those blue eyes. Wilfred, a man whom she could paint by heart if she had any skill with the brush at all. Wilfred, her better self. Wilfred, a man who had captured her soul and she had not even known it.

A desperate need to be close to him overpowered Irene, just for a moment. She managed to hold it at bay, but the sudden thrum of need had rocked her, moving her closer to him.

"I promise you," Wilfred said quietly, as though utterly unaware of the most inconvenient emotions pulsing through her, "I had no idea your mother planned to seat us together."

The two of them, in perfect synchronized motion, looked to their right. There were Irene's parents, and she saw with a roll of her eyes that they had both been staring at them. The Viscount and Viscountess Pernrith hurriedly turned their attention to the musicians.

Irene sighed. "Honestly."

When she turned back to Wilfred, there was a tweak of a smile in the corner of his lips. It disappeared immediately.

She drew her hands together in her lap and fiddled with her fan as the beautiful music of Mozart flowed over them.

This was intolerable, being this close to him and unable to speak. Not that she had anything to say!

"There really is nothing between Miss Fletcher and myself, you know," Wilfred said in a low voice. "And there never will be. I will tell you the truth finally: I paid her to accompany me on that walk, solely to make you jealous. It was just the one time. If you want to know why that resulted in some gossip in the paper, well, speak to your brother about it."

"Hush there!"

"There is only one person for me," he continued, utterly ignoring the shushing man, "and that is you. And you don't have to do anything about it. I just thought…you should know."

Irene swallowed, filing the remark about her brother away for later.

There was such heart in his tones, such affection. It was the Wilfred she knew, and yet in a way, she was still acclimatizing herself to this new Wilfred: a Wilfred who loved her and whom she loved. It was disorientating. He was the ground upon which she stood and now he had moved, and she was shaken.

But she was still standing.

Irene chanced a glance at his hands. Wilfred had carefully placed them upon his knees. Why, his right hand and her left were only inches apart. If she just moved…

But she couldn't. Not after getting so angry. Not after shouting such things. Not after—

Wilfred moved his right hand and interlaced his fingers with her left.

And love, passionate and affectionate love, poured through her.

Oh, this man. He did not need words. He did not need to say anything. Oh, his apology had been pleasant enough, and it was a relief, indeed, to hear that there was nothing between Miss Fletcher and himself.

But it was the action that mattered. Wilfred had known, somehow, that she needed to feel him, hold him, know his touch. And Irene had not been brave enough to instigate it.

She didn't need to be. She had Wilfred for that.

"I'm sorry—" she started.

"I apologize for—"

"Will you two be quiet!"

Irene could not help but laugh, the nervousness and irritation melting away through the motion, at the sight of the fuming woman with piles of gray hair balancing awkwardly atop her head who had once again turned around to berate them. "I do apologize, I—"

"If you would rather chatter on," declared the woman loudly, causing heads to turn all across the concert hall, "than listen to this wonderful music, I suggest you leave!"

"Ahem! Madam!" This was the conductor as the music went quiet, a few straggling instruments fading off into nothing. He had apparently not heard a peep from Irene and Wilfred...but had certainly been interrupted by the hushing woman.

Irene tried not to giggle as the woman, flushing furiously, settled down in her seat and whispers flowed through the room.

"Well," said Wilfred lightly, squeezing her hand. "Shall we go?"

The pair of them rose together, Irene attempting to ignore the beaming smiles from both her parents as they did so.

There was nothing so infuriating as pleasing one's parents.

Their footfalls echoed in the concert hall, but Irene could think of nothing but the gentleman currently holding her hand. There was nothing shameful in it, and Wilfred clearly was proud to stride out of the place with his fingers interlocked with her own.

Irene could have burst to see it. She may not have been perfect—maybe—but Wilfred adored her regardless.

As they stepped out into the atrium, she found she was breathless. Had they really walked, almost *run* out of there? She checked over her shoulder. Her parents ought to have followed them, she knew, but everyone was so distracted by the commotion at the concert, she wondered if anyone had even noticed. Not that she actually thought her cheekily meddlesome mother would interrupt this moment. Not after what she'd learned about her parents' own history. She shivered.

They halted, and Wilfred looked instinctively at Irene. "Do you wish to return home?"

'Home'? Return home—how could she return home when he

was standing right before her?

Reaching forward, she splayed her free hand against him. His pulse was racing. "I am home."

Wilfred emitted some sort of growl that was certainly not a sound Irene had ever heard from him before, and she yelped as he yanked her suddenly toward a door.

"Wilfred?"

He ignored her unspoken question and pulled her through the door, into a corridor. They were definitely not supposed to be there.

"Wilfred, what are you—"

"In here," Wilfred said in a gruff voice, opening a door with his free hand.

Irene blinked about them, bewildered, as Wilfred shut the door behind them. They were standing in… Well, it could only be a practice room, or a storeroom, or some sort. There was a large grand pianoforte there, though it was covered with a large cloth, plenty of music stands, some chairs, what might have been a broken violin—

"Reeny," said Wilfred in a jagged voice.

She turned her attention back to him and found, for the rest time in her life, that she really did not mind the name from his lips. Her own curled into a smile. "Wilfred."

"I do hope you can forgive me for—"

Irene did not permit him to repeat the same apology—not after she had already forgiven him. Besides, she had missed kissing him, missed his touch, his taste, the way his hands seemed to know precisely what it was she wanted, needed from him.

And just as he had almost never done in their entire lives, Wilfred did not disappoint. He groaned, curling a fist into her hair to bring her closer, his other hand making straight for her buttocks.

"Wilfred!"

"Tell me to stop if you want," he growled, pressing kisses down her neck. "I dare you."

Irene did not dare. Not while such dark and delicious sensations were cascading through her. "I—I never thought you had it in you!"

Wilfred pulled back, just for a moment, and there was a hint of worry in his eyes. "I've—I've held back for so long. Only you make me feel like this, Irene, but if you want me to stop, I can—"

"Go back to growling," Irene ordered with a thrill of delight as Wilfred gave her a wicked grin. "And keep on kissing me."

Chapter Twenty

December 30, 1840

WILFRED INHALED DEEPLY. No need to think about it too much. Just walk forward.

Walk forward into the rest of your life.

Wilfred stepped into the drawing room to the sound of loud cheers—but it was not the cheers that he cared about. It was the warmth, not of the fire, but of the welcome. The smiles, and the outreached hands from two gentlemen and the cries of delight from three women…and the quiet, certain silence of the woman he loved.

"Oh, here he is, the man of the moment."

"Give the man room, Edie. He can barely move."

"I'll hug my future son-in-law if I want to, Frederick, and there's an end to it!"

Wilfred would not have described it as a hug, so much as a gentle garroting. The Viscountess Pernrith was clutching him so tightly around the neck, if her husband had not rescued him, he may have expired.

Which would have been a terrible shame, just a few days before his engagement party to be followed the next day by special-license wedding.

"Well, you got here in the end." Michael grinned as he clapped Wilfred on the back. "With no small help from myself, may I add—"

"Yes, thanks to our enlightening discussion the other day, dear brother, I now have quite a clear idea of how much *help* you have been." Irene smiled with daggers in her eyes as she stepped forward. "You've been an age."

She leaned forward and kissed Wilfred on the lips, and he was forced not to sweep her completely into his arms and take her right there, right now on the carpet of the Chances' drawing room. There were no blankets, for a start. And a plethora of family.

"Please, not in front of us!" chorused the two younger Chances.

Wilfred grinned bashfully at Gwen and Teddy. "Sorry, Gwen and Teddy."

"Don't you apologize," Irene said firmly, tapping him on the arm.

"Sorry, Reeny."

The room was filled with laughter and Wilfred's smile became a spot sheepish. But it was his family's laughter—*his family*. Strange, to think that he had believed marrying Irene would have made a difference to how included he felt.

Unbeknownst to him, he had been a part of the Chance family for many years.

"Come, I pulled out a rather splendid case of champagne I have been saving for my second daughter's engagement," said the Viscount Pernrith with a wink to his wife. "I had to buy them by the dogcart, for I was certain I would marry them all off—"

"And now it's our turn!" said Gwen with a shiver. "Now that both Jess and Reeny—"

Irene stomped her foot. "Don't call me that!"

"—will be married, Teddy and I are officially *out*," finished his future sister-in-law.

Was it Wilfred's imagination, or did neither of the two youngest Chances seem pleased by the prospect? He had always presumed the tension between the sisters had been that Jessica's and Irene's lack of husbands—former lack of husbands—had prevented Gwen and Teddy from attending the many balls, concerts, recitals, picnics, and dinners that the elder two had.

And yet—

"Baron and Baroness Llyne, my lord," intoned Mrs. Kinley by the doorway.

Wilfred was torn from his thoughts by the rush of Chances toward the door.

"Jessica!"

"Oh, Reginald, we did not expect you for hours!"

"Tell me, is the moat really deep enough to swim in?"

Wilfred chuckled as he stepped back—mostly to protect his feet—and found his arm taken by the most beautiful woman he had ever seen.

"It's all a bit of a fuss, I know," Irene said quietly with a wry smile. "But I wanted it. A...A welcome for you, to the family. Officially."

Wilfred's spirits stirred as he looked around the drawing room. Michael had just nudged Reginald's shoulder and offered him a glass of champagne, while the Viscountess Pernrith was carefully examining Jessica for tiredness, though goodness knew why. Teddy had disappeared—oh, he realized, he hadn't noticed her go—and Gwen was scowling over at the sofa as her father appeared to be persuading her to go and talk to her eldest sister.

He sighed happily. This was what he had always loved about the Chances—the Pernrith Chances, anyway. The ones he knew best.

They weren't perfect. The family had its own set of scrapes and alliances, there were arguments and there were disagreements, and they loved each other. Nothing came before that.

And they had loved him, as a child then as a man, without question. Without needing anything in return.

Wilfred blinked away tears. *I am not going to cry.*

"I hear congratulations are in order," Llyne said with a grin, stepping around his brother-in-law and grasping Wilfred's hand in a strong handshake. "I have to say, I wasn't surprised."

"'Wasn't surprised'?" said Gwen from the sofa, her eyes wide as she looked around. "I couldn't have seen it coming from a mile off!"

"Did you not? Oh, I had these two down for future happiness a long time ago." Irene's mother smiled, making Wilfred flush.

Was I truly that obvious?

"Are we late?"

The voice by the doorway was a new one, though not new to Wilfred.

"Lilianna—and Evelyn, and the husbands!" said the Viscount Pernrith with a smile. "I hope your parents accompany you?"

"Do we only get described as 'the husbands' now?" Lilianna's husband, a man with mischief always dancing in his eyes, said with a grin.

"Yes, I think so," Evelyn's husband said, matching his smile yet standing a little less loosely, his shoulders tight as he kept a careful eye on his wife. "I say, is that champagne?"

The room grew more and more crowded as more and more of the extended Chance family arrived. Cousin Thomas sent his apologies, as his wife and their newborn were not travelling from Stanphrey Lacey, Frank had them all in stitches by arriving in trousers—"Francesca Dorothy Chance!"—and Wilfred found his hand shaken and his shoulder clapped so often, he was a little surprised bruises had not appeared.

It was... Well, overwhelming. To be amongst such a family was one thing. To *join* it, officially, was quite another.

And throughout the onslaught of affection and welcome, Irene stood by his side, her hand either in his own or slipped into the crook of his arm, and Wilfred knew he could face down armies if he needed to with her support.

Not that the gigantic Chance family was quite as large as an army.

"I must say, I am delighted to be able to officially welcome you to the family as a member, not as one of our dearest friends," the Viscount Pernrith was saying to him.

Wilfred blinked. *When had the man stepped there?* "Oh. Oh, thank you, my lord."

"I think at the very least you can call me 'Pernrith,'" Irene's father said with a laugh. "Unlike my unconventional eldest brother, I am unlikely to be handing my title to my son anytime soon."

It was not impossible to miss the wince from Irene beside him, and Wilfred was so attuned to her, he almost felt it.

"Ah, Lindow," said Pernrith with a smile that was perhaps slightly tight. "My favorite brother. Come on in. Warm yourself by the fire. Champagne?"

"I had not realized absolutely everyone was going to be invited to this engagement party," Wilfred hissed to his betrothed.

Irene frowned. "What do you mean, everyone? It's just family here."

Just family. That was the odd thing about the Chances. They were divided into their branches, Wilfred knew, and yet still they were all one family.

"So, half the family seems to have known this forever," said a grinning Samuel, the eldest son of the Marquess of Aylesbury, after everyone had arrived and settled across the room on chairs, window seats, and sofas, all with champagne goblets in their hands. "And half the family seems to be surprised. Which camp is everyone in?"

There was a chorus of answers as heat rushed up Wilfred's spine.

"Wasn't it obvious?"

"Never saw it coming!"

"I thought I saw something last year—"

"I always knew," said Samuel over the hubbub.

"Nonsense," shot back his brother, Benjamin, painfully handsome and well aware of it, with a lazy smile. "You just want to seem clever."

"Better than seeming foolish, as you so easily manage," returned the elder brother.

The squabble managed to encompass half the room, and the other half were chatting amongst themselves about the upcoming wedding, the recent birth of Thomas's little one, the state of the weather…

"So. When did you know?" came a quiet voice by his side.

Wilfred turned to see Irene offering him a glass of champagne. "'Know'?"

"That you loved me," she said easily, with no hint of embarrassment whatsoever. "When did you know?"

When did I know?

When had the stars been born? When had the oceans not been deep? When had the deserts bloomed? When had time itself had only just begun?

The answer Wilfred wished to give sounded foolish in his throat. He couldn't say that. She would laugh at—

No. No, she wouldn't. Oh, Irene often laughed with him, but she never laughed *at* him.

"From the very beginning," he said simply, conscious of the tenderness of his fingers against the cool of the glass. "From the first moment I saw you."

Irene rolled her eyes. "We were children!"

"Even then, I knew there was something special about you. Something special between us," Wilfred said with a wry smile. Somehow, they had managed to step away from the rest of the family toward the wall, and in a way, it was as though they were all alone. "Something different."

Though Irene was clearly attempting to prevent it, her lips were curling into a smile. "You did?"

He nodded, gazing down into those spectacular eyes. "I did."

Her laughter was nervous. "I didn't."

Wilfred squeezed her hand, knowing she would need his reassuring touch. "I know."

And he would never hold it against her. How could he? There were no rules on how love should grow. Would he have preferred it if she had loved him earlier? Perhaps. But that would not have been their story.

"Things might have been different, had you wanted us to stay friends," Wilfred said in a low voice, and he ached to see her face fall. "But then, things would have been different." He squeezed her hand again. "And I rather like things the way they are."

Irene gave a shaky laugh. "Good."

"And what about you?"

"What about me?"

There it was, that little line that always appeared between Irene's brows when she was quizzical about something.

Fighting down the urge to lean forward and kiss it, Wilfred asked the question that had been dwelling on his mind ever since she had first admitted her affections for him. "When did you first fall in love with me?"

Irene did not miss a beat. "Oh, about a fortnight ago."

The jaw that dropped was entirely out of Wilfred's control. So was the spluttering as Irene laughed. "B-But—But—"

"You look so crestfallen!"

"I *feel* so crestfallen," he admitted with a wry smile, his stomach twisting.

Had he truly been so invisible to this wonderful woman for that long? How could he possibly hope to deserve her if she had essentially never noticed him?

And in that moment, despite the gladness in the room and the laughter around him and the welcome he had received and the woman standing beside him—

In that moment, Wilfred was filled with doubt. He could never deserve such a woman—he had always known that—but to hear so plainly that she had not considered him anything more than a friend for so many years, when he had been right there, pining after her, desperate to gain her affection…

It was disheartening, to say the least.

And then there was the scent of honey and lavender, and a kiss was being pressed into his cheek by the softest lips.

Wilfred turned, sadly not in time to capture a kiss, but to see the love and devotion in Irene's eyes.

"I was already in love with you," Irene said quietly, her

cheeks pinking at the intimacy of the admission. "I just did not know it."

Glancing around the room, Wilfred saw the family chattering away without much need for them. No need for them at all, actually. Which meant...

He turned to Irene, and evidently what he wished—what he desired—was so evident upon his face that she immediately replied to the unasked question.

"*Wilfred!*"

"Well, no one would miss us," he protested in an undertone, doing his best not to grin and failing miserably. "And I have missed you, Reeny."

In times past, she would have glared most furiously, perhaps elbowed him hard, and opined that the next person to call her 'Reeny' would be shot out of a cannon the next time they visited Stanphrey Lacey.

As it was, her breath hitched. "And I have missed you, but we can't—"

"Isn't it a little late for carols?" someone was saying across the room.

"Nonsense! Is Lilianna here? She can play the pianoforte and we can—"

"I've told you before, Frank, I am never again playing that damned instrument—"

"*Lilianna!*"

"We could literally march out of here with a band," Wilfred said in a murmur, allowing his hand by Irene's waist to slowly drift down to her delectable behind. "And no one would notice."

He glorified in the way that Irene stiffened, then softened into his hand, her welcoming buttocks resting perfectly in his palm. As though they had been made for him.

And hadn't they?

"Fine," Irene said imperiously, as though she were deigning to give him a most great favor. Which, in a way, she was. "But if anyone stops us—"

"No one is going to stop us," Wilfred reassured her.

In truth, he half-expected her mother, or one of her sisters, or at the very least Michael to interrupt them on their way to the door and ask why they were leaving their own engagement party. As it was, they were almost completely ignored. The family appeared to be debating whether Frank should be made to change into one of Gwen's gowns, what the newest dragon in the family should be called, whether Thomas and family would be in Bath for the spring—

"And poor Great-Aunt Tessie, she'll be off soon," said Benjamin blithely as Wilfred and Irene passed him.

"Benjamin!"

In fact, as Wilfred closed the door behind the raucous bunch and stepped into the thankfully silent hall with Irene by his side, he wondered whether they would all have a better time without the pair they were supposed to be celebrating.

And he had something else he would much rather be doing.

This time, when he and Irene rushed upstairs to enjoy each other's bodies, Wilfred did so in the perfect knowledge that in just one day, they would be man and wife. Not that there had been any shame in what they had shared before—he had known it even then, innately.

But now she was his, and the wedding date set, and Irene—

"In here," she whispered, pulling him into her bedchamber.

Wilfred could do nothing but obey. In many ways, nothing had really changed in the last two decades.

The door closed behind them with a firm snap, and this time, Irene turned the key in the lock.

"No interruptions," she said darkly. "But you'll have to be quiet."

Quiet? How on earth was a man supposed to remain quiet with a woman like Irene beneath him?

Well, he could think of one way.

"Reeny," Wilfred groaned, stepping toward her and pulling her into an embrace before his lips crushed hers.

Oh, it was wonderful, holding her and knowing that nothing and no one could ever take her away. The pleasure she so swiftly wrought upon him was almost overpowering, and Wilfred could only hope that as his tongue trailed a devoted line across her lips, teasing them open before it delved into her mouth to eke out pleasure for her, that she was enjoying just as much.

She certainly appeared to be. Irene whimpered in his mouth, her fingers scrabbling at the many layers of fabric that were separating them. Her impatience only heightened his need, Wilfred's manhood throbbing and aching in his trousers.

How had he ever managed to keep from proposing in years gone by?

"I love you," Irene murmured as she broke the kiss—but seemingly only so she could get a better view of his waistcoat. "What the devil is going on with these buttons?"

"Who cares?" Wilfred said with a grin, all the crushed-down need that he had attempted to ignore for years bursting forth.

Rather like his waistcoat buttons. Irene gasped as he wrenched the garment from his body and stepped toward her.

"You—You wouldn't," she whispered, eyes wide and clearly begging for the same.

A sense of power, of domination and yet devotion, swept through Wilfred. "I would."

He seared hot kisses down Irene's neck and brushed the tops of her heaving breasts with more as his hands found the delicate buttons that trailed down the back of Irene's gown—and ripped the fabric apart. Buttons flew in all directions, bouncing off the bed and covering the floor, and Irene moaned, her legs quivering as her head fell back and her hands grasped his shoulders.

Swiftly moving an arm around her waist to support her, Wilfred tried not to think about the pressing need to plunge himself into her and focused instead on doing what he had wanted to do a week ago: strip the woman he loved to the skin.

It did not take long. For all that Victorian ladies now wore more layers than were sensible, Wilfred's fingers were swift and before long, stays and ribbons and stockings and more were lying on the floor. Standing in the center…

Wilfred swallowed. "Dear God, you're even more beautiful than I thought."

And she was. There Irene stood, utterly nude, her hands pressed together before her and her nipples nubbing in the cold—and he hoped, from desire. Their precious pink-shell color exactly matched the lips that she wetted as she stood, allowing his gaze to meander over every inch of her.

"Damn it, woman," Wilfred growled, wrenching at his shirt. "And I had promised myself our next time would be slow and seductive."

"Wilfred Matthew Kirk Chesterham Zouch, Duke of Aynor," Irene said lightly, "if you don't ravish me right now, I shall have to take matters into my own hands."

He did not think; he only moved. Picking her up by the waist and throwing her onto the bed, amongst her yelps of surprise, Wilfred allowed his shirt to drop to the floor and swiftly pulled off his boots. Before Irene could even sit up, his trouser buttons were undone and the fabric dropped to the floor.

He had worried that she would be afraid. What Wilfred had not expected to see in Irene's eyes…was hunger.

"Yes," she breathed. "Now."

Wilfred had never disobeyed an order from Miss Irene Chance in his life, and he certainly wasn't going to start now.

Covering her body with his own on the bed, he groaned to feel the warmth of her, the wetness between her folds as he slid an exploratory finger down her slit.

"So ready," he murmured, pressing a kiss on her nipple. "So ready for me…"

He took her other nipple into his mouth and nibbled at it with his teeth as he slipped two fingers within her and Irene arched against him, her back curved as she invited him in deeper. Wilfred could have wept at the welcome.

This was where he was meant to be.

"Ready?" he managed to say.

Irene looked up with lust in her hooded eyes, mingled with love. "Ready. Do it now, before—"

He silenced her with a kiss, almost certain he would explode right there if he heard much more, then slowly nudged her knees apart and nestled himself between her.

Slowly, lip-bitingly slowly, Wilfred sheathed his throbbing manhood into her secret place. Her whimpers of hedonism and twisting hips only made it more difficult to retain control. His jaw gritted, not with pain but with patience as he plunged himself deeper.

Finally, he rested, balls-deep in the woman he had made completely his own.

Irene stared, all confusion. "Why—Why have you stopped?"

Wilfred grinned, leaning on his elbow and kissing her deeply before replying, "Now you have to *ask* me."

"'A-Ask' you?" She kept staring, then laughed as she teased, "Is ordering you not enough?"

"No," he returned, hoping to goodness he could maintain his composure and not pour himself into her at the first opportunity. "I would have you ask. *Beg.* I've longed after you, Reeny, pined after you for longer than you can know, and for much of that time, I have dreamed of you begging me to please you. To pleasure you. Will... Will you do that for me?"

For a heartbeat, Wilfred thought he had gone too far. It was a huge ask for any woman, he had to presume, but for Irene—

"Please," she said quietly.

Wilfred slowly lifted his hips, pulling his erect manhood almost completely out of her—and then stilled.

Irene whimpered. "*Wilfred!*"

"Beg me," he whispered, taking one of her nipples into his mouth and sucking hard. "Beg me."

"Do it—do me—I want you, Wilfred. Please, please, there's such an ache in me—"

"Christ," Wilfred moaned, thrusting forward and picking up

the pace almost immediately, her words going straight to his loins. "More, Reeny. More."

"All I've wanted is you," gasped Irene, her hips now thrusting up against him, matching his pace. "I'll do anything, anything for you, Wilfred, just make me feel, please—"

It was all he could do to hang on. With Irene's begging words whispered into his ear and Wilfred's whole body desperate to climax, he somehow managed to pound himself into her, eking out his own pleasure as he slowly built up hers, until Irene's fingers were digging into his shoulders and her head had fallen back and—

"Oh, yes, yes—yes, Wilfred!"

He did not need her to shout his name to know that she was climaxing—he could feel the ripples within her, feel her body taking every inch of bliss it could—but it was damned gratifying, to say the least.

Now. Now I can let go.

"Reeny!" Wilfred cried into her hair, allowing his body's instincts to take over as he reached his peak and soared over it, ploughing into her and pouring himself into her depths.

When it was over, and it seemed to take far longer than he had ever expected, Wilfred fell into his lover's waiting arms and knew—knew—he had not come home.

No, he had made one, with his best friend.

Epilogue

January 1, 1841

IRENE COULD NOT help but snort with laughter as another piece of toast slipped off the long toasting fork and into the fire.

"Blast it!"

"I told you, you're leaning too far forward," she said through her giggles. "You'll never get a single piece of toast that way!"

Her best friend and husband leaned back ever so slightly but made sure to nudge her on the shoulder as he did so. "Who made you the Queen of Toast?"

"I have always been the Queen of Toast," Irene declared haughtily before collapsing into giggles.

Their laughter filled the large drawing room. Wilfred had offered to invite her entire family, even all her aunts and uncles and cousins, to see the New Year in after the wedding. Irene had considered it, for a short moment, but decided against it.

After so long not quite understanding each other, with Irene herself not realizing the incredible man she had right before her eyes, she was going to take some time to enjoy him on her own.

They had abandoned the thought of sitting politely on a sofa. The pile of cushions and blankets near the fireplace was where they had found themselves, creating a sort of nest of love and affection as the fire blazed. Wilfred's cook—*their* cook now, Irene had to remind herself in the privacy of her own thoughts—had offered to make them something to eat, but Wilfred had given all of the staff the night off.

As midnight had chimed through the Aynor townhouse—*my*

new home, Irene reminded herself with a thrill—she had kissed her husband and very soon the comfortable cushions on the drawing room floor had gained quite another use.

After they had enjoyed amorous congress, twice, they had pulled on a semblance of clothing and Wilfred had tugged a blanket around their shoulders, and they had sat, quietly talking about nothing while her husband failed utterly to make toast.

"Ouch!"

"Don't touch the metal too close to the bread, you dolt," Irene said lazily, all warm and full of previous attempts at toast that had been smeared with honey from the pot they had found in the kitchen.

Wilfred grinned, kissing her shoulder. "I should have listened to you, O Queen of Toast."

She smiled back, wondering how on earth she had managed to find such a perfect man.

In a way, she hadn't found him. *He* had found *her*—as Wilfred was eagerly reminding her of every single day, it seemed.

"Just because I didn't realize how I felt about you didn't mean that I didn't feel it," she had shot back to him last night.

And he had smiled, and kissed her, and Irene had felt more alive in that moment than all the moments preceding it.

Combined.

"So," Wilfred said quietly, bringing her back to the present, "it's a new year."

"1841," Irene tried out, not particularly liking it. "Strange to think just how much has happened this year."

"Many of your cousins have found spouses," he said quietly. "And so has your sister."

"And I've found you."

Wilfred snorted. "I was always here. You didn't have to find me. I was never lost."

No, but I was, Irene thought as she slipped her hand into his. *So lost, and I did not even know it.*

Now that she was here, her heart fully open both to Wilfred

and to herself, Irene marveled at the fact that she had not known the precious value of the man beside her. Oh, she had always appreciated him. As she had told him, inexpertly, at the opera—she had always loved him.

But realizing that what she felt for Wilfred was so unlike anything she had ever felt for any other man, for any other *friend*, that had taken time. Time she had not realized was... Well, not exactly *wasted*.

She would spend it better now.

"So, what is it to be?" Wilfred slipped the half-burned, half-hardly-cooked bread from the toasting fork. "Is that better?"

"No," said Irene happily, nonetheless taking a bite while in awe that he could be so inept. "It's a good thing you have a cook."

"*We* have a cook," he corrected with a shy smile.

Irene's stomach jolted, and not because of the inexpertly made toast. She had never thought much about her home in the future, but now she was here, within it, and she was already finding there was a great amount of joy to be found in organizing one's own life. Now that she was duchess, she wholeheartedly agreed with her husband to offer Dempster that promotion to butler at the Aynor country estate. That was among the first tasks they'd complete in the new year.

Being a mistress of her own home, however, was nothing compared to being the mistress of this man's heart.

"As I said, what is it to be?" Wilfred asked as he carefully placed the second-to-last slice of bread on the end of the toasting fork.

Irene frowned as she munched. "What is *what* to be?"

"What are your New Year's resolutions to be?" he clarified with a smile. "It's the first of the year."

"Barely."

Her husband glanced at the clock and shrugged. "Still, it is the first of January of a brand-new year. Everything is fresh. What are you resolved to do this year?"

"I don't know why you are asking me. You never manage to keep to New Year's resolutions!" Irene teased.

And it was true—he never had. Wilfred was a great man for ideas, but he rarely followed them through.

Except this time, when it had really mattered.

Wilfred snorted. "This year is going to be different."

Irene giggled. "Oh, yes? Are you suddenly fueled with a sense of willpower you have never had before?"

"*Reeny!*"

And she smiled and did not correct him because if there was one person in the world who was permitted to use that version of her name, it was him. Her Wilfred. "Yes?"

"I have excellent willpower, if you don't mind me saying," he said in a mock-haughty voice.

Irene giggled. "Oh, you do, do you?"

His eyes glittered. "I managed to hold back on declaring my undying love for you for years, didn't I?"

She leaned forward and stole a kiss, and though she had only intended it to be a quick one, the sensual bliss that flowed through her the moment her lips touched Wilfred's meant that Irene kissed him most heartily for several minutes instead.

When they broke apart, both were breathless.

"You were saying something," Wilfred exhaled. "Or I was. Damn it, woman, you always make me forget what I was thinking."

"That's because I didn't marry you for your thinking," Irene teased. "I married you for your skills in bed."

"That must be it." He chuckled, turning back to the fireplace. "Oh, damn!"

Irene collapsed into giggles. "It certainly isn't your toast-making abilities!"

Wilfred waved the toasting fork wildly in an attempt to dampen the flames now completely consuming the bread on its end. Eventually, he allowed the bread to drop into the flames with a wry smile.

"Well, one last piece," he said. "Hopefully, this time I'll manage."

"Why don't you give that to me," Irene said firmly, phrasing it not so much as a question, but as a statement.

Her hands moved, taking the toasting fork from the bungling husband of hers, and angling it perfectly over the flames so that the bread started to brown. Brown, not burn.

Wilfred leaned back on his haunches and examined her. Irene tried not to notice just how intense his gaze was, but it was his attention and not the fire warming her face.

"What is it?" she asked eventually.

"You," Wilfred said simply. "Where did you learn to make toast like that?"

Irene grinned, though the memory had tinges of sadness as well as merriment. "When I was…oh, about nine? Nine or ten? My father hit a bit of a tricky spot with money and we had to let our cook go for a time."

Wilfred sat up smartly. "I didn't know that."

"No one did," Irene said lightly, as though it did not matter. And it didn't, not anymore. But it had then. "My father was very careful to keep it just between us. Between us Chances, I mean. I know you visited at the time, but we didn't let you see us in the kitchen or anything like that."

"But surely, your uncles would have—"

"Between us Pernrith Chances, I suppose I should have said," Irene clarified with a smile. "My father is proud, you know that. He wasn't about to go to his half-brothers with a begging bowl. No, we had no cook for…oh, about three months? In that time, Mrs. Kinley did her best, and my sisters and my mother and I helped. However we could. I learned how to boil an egg, make toast, roast a vegetable stew that required no actual skills, and brew tea. We couldn't afford much meat, so it didn't matter that I never learned how to roast."

She spoke calmly, without a need for sympathy because that time was past and it wouldn't have put food on the table back then at any case. But she was not surprised to feel Wilfred's hands on her shoulders and a delicate kiss on the side of her head.

"There is still so much I have to learn about you," Wilfred said in a voice of almost wonder. "How is it that I can know you best of anyone in the whole world, and there is still so much that I don't know?"

Irene smiled as she turned to the man she loved.

Oh, Wilfred. How she had ever thought she could go through life without him, she did not know—but now she would never have to wonder.

The bread slipped into the flames.

"Oh, blast!" Irene cried as Wilfred descended into desperate laughter. "It's not funny!"

"All hail the Queen of Toast," he said solemnly but with a wicked grin on his face. "Who's the best at toast now?"

"Well, it's certainly not *you*, you idiot," Irene said with a laugh, carefully putting the toasting fork down with a rueful expression. "Ah, well. I hope you weren't too hungry."

"Oh, I've had my fill," said Wilfred, the wicked look only increasing.

Irene flushed. *He certainly had.*

"Now, New Year's resolutions," he began.

"Not *that* again." Irene groaned. "What makes you think that you are going to keep them this time?"

"Because I will be making them to you. And any promise I make to you will be one that I always keep. Because you are precious," Wilfred said quietly. "You are precious and I will never let you down again."

Irene's heart tugged and she kissed him briefly before saying, "Chance is, indeed, a fine thing."

He smiled. "So. What is it to be?"

She sighed, leaning against his chest and enjoying how his arms so easily moved around her. As though they had been married for years. As though this were their normal—and always had been. "I suppose I should take more of an interest in my family. Help them more."

That was, evidently, not what her husband had been expecting. "I'm sorry—*more* of an interest? You Chances are one of the most insular families on the planet!"

Irene could not help but laugh at that. "I suppose that is true, but I think this year is going to be a challenging one for us all. Some of us more than others."

She had not intended to sound so mysterious, so she was not surprised to see Wilfred lift an eyebrow.

"Which ones in particular? Not any of your siblings, surely?"

"No, it's my cousin Samuel. He's... Well. Our great-aunt died."

Wilfred nodded, his arms warm around her. "My condolences."

"Oh, we hardly knew her. She married into the family then had a falling out with our grandfather, apparently, and none of my uncles nor my father have ever met her. She sounded, in truth," Irene said with a smile, "rather like Lady Romeril."

She felt his shiver. "She must have been terrifying to behold."

"She was probably a lonely old lady who regretted ostracizing herself from the family," Irene guessed, without much evidence. "I've heard from my cousin Samuel that her will is to be read in Brighton, and my father believes it might contain a most fascinating clause in it. It's going to be complicated for my cousin Samuel."

She had felt sorry for him when she'd heard the whispers. It was all very well for the old lady to attempt to be generous, but honestly, she should have thought about the wording a little better.

Precisely what Samuel was going to do, Irene could hardly think...

"Well, enough about them. I want to talk about us," Wilfred said, pressing a kiss against her neck.

Irene smiled. "All we've done since we got married is talk about us."

"Isn't it marvelous? You're my favorite topic," said her husband, his smile warming. "So, how many children shall we have?"

"*Wilfred!*"

"What?" he protested.

"You say that so calmly because you are not the one who is going to carry and birth them!" Irene laughed, slightly irritated but mostly devastatingly in love with him. "And we don't even know if we *can* have children yet!"

"Oh, we'll have children," said Wilfred happily. "Lots of them. Several."

"Let's attempt to have one and then take it from there," Irene said warily, but with joy burgeoning up within her. "You never know, I may not… I mean, there is no guarantee that—"

"If we, because I would never blame *you*, if *we* cannot have children the… Well, the normal way," Wilfred said, a hint of ferocity entering his tone that she adored him for, "then why, we'll adopt. There are plenty of children out there who need a home. After all…your family gave me a home when I needed one."

Irene swallowed as affection for this man welled up in her. "We did."

"And now I get to give you a home," Wilfred continued, his eyes bright, but his voice firm. "Whether or not we have children of our bodies, I'd like to adopt. I'd like to show a child that there are good people in the world, people who want to open their homes and hearts to another. I'll work to make sure an adopted son can inherit, if we don't have a son the traditional way. Hang the traditions! The Chances and their titled brothers and dowager dukes have shown me we're not bound by traditions entirely."

How could I have ever teased this man about loving another woman?

Pressing a kiss on his lips and almost wishing they never had to leave this nest of blankets and cushions and love by the fire, Irene looked into the eyes of the man she adored and knew that this was, in turn, a New Year's resolution that she could keep.

One she would keep forever.

"Then here is my resolution for 1841," she said fiercely, smiling at the way Wilfred looked at her with such adoration. "We will have a child. Whether it's one I carry or one we find, we will have a child this year and we will love them like we love each other. Completely."

"Completely," echoed Wilfred as he leaned in for another kiss. "And forever."

A Short Letter From the Author

Hello! Thank you so much for reading *Chance Would Be a Fine Thing*, the tenth novel in my The Chances series. I truly hoped you enjoyed it and fell in love with Wilfred and Irene just as much as I did.

If you've read the first nine books of this series (which I strongly recommend!), then you'll have seen the four uncles fall in love, and five of the cousins. I had always wanted to write a series of brothers, but I could never 'meet' the characters who were quite right. After waiting years to meet them myself, I have had a lot of fun writing the four Chance brothers—and now we're diving into their children. Make sure you go back and read them!

If you're desperate to read the happily ever afters of Irene's siblings, then you'll want to look out for Book 9, *Any Chance You Can Take* (Jessica's story); Book 14, *A Chance of a Lifetime* (Michael's story); Book 15, *In With a Chance* (Gwendoline's story); and Book 20, *Leave it All to Chance* (Theodora's story). Our next Chance adventure is going to jump to a different branch of the Chance family, and you'll meet Samuel's (complicated!) happily ever after...

Being an author can be a lonely business, but knowing that there are readers from all over the world who are going to adore my stories makes it all worthwhile. Thank you for your support, and I hope you love reading more of my books!

Happy reading,
Emily

About Emily E K Murdoch

If you love falling in love, then you've come to the right place.

I am a historian and writer and have a varied career to date: from examining medieval manuscripts to designing museum exhibitions, to working as a researcher for the BBC to working for the National Trust.

My books range from England 1050 to Texas 1848, and I can't wait for you to fall in love with my heroes and heroines!

Follow me on twitter and instagram @emilyekmurdoch, find me on facebook at facebook.com/theemilyekmurdoch, and read my blog at www.emilyekmurdoch.com.